Archibald C. Gunter

A Lost American

A tale of Cuba

Archibald C. Gunter

A Lost American
A tale of Cuba

ISBN/EAN: 9783337386825

Printed in Europe, USA, Canada, Australia, Japan

Cover: Foto ©Andreas Hilbeck / pixelio.de

More available books at **www.hansebooks.com**

AMERICAN

A TALE OF CUBA

BY

ARCHIBALD CLAVERING GUNTER

AUTHOR OF " MR. BARNES OF NEW YORK '

COPYRIGHT

LONDON
GEORGE ROUTLEDGE & SONS, Limited
BROADWAY HOUSE, LUDGATE HILL
1898

CONTENTS.

BOOK I.

BEAUTY IN NEW YORK.

BOOK II.

THE BURNING PLANTATION.

BOOK III.

THE FORT ON CAYO TORO.

BOOK IV.

THE MOONLIGHT SURPRISE.

BOOK V.

THE FAIR HAND OF JUSTICE.

A LOST AMERICAN.

BOOK I.

BEAUTY IN NEW YORK.

CHAPTER I.

A NIGHT AT THE OPERA.

It is the evening of Wednesday, the fourth of November, in the year of our Lord 1873.

Capoul has been singing his sweetest and tenderest notes.

The wonderful dramatic *timbre* of Nilsson's voice joining his in the *finale* of that soft love song which always goes to the hearts of man and woman, "The Last Rose of Summer," has rippled through the Academy, its closing melody drowned by the enthusiastic plaudits of an over-packed house, when Miss Blanche Grayson, in her parterre box, clapping her hands languidly, as most Americans do, turns suddenly to her half-sister and whispers: "My goodness! You are crying, Laura?"

"Why should not I give tears to a love song, as well as laughter?" whispers Señorita Morales, turning a pair of deep, black, romantic eyes on to the bright, vivid blue ones of her half-sister, and adding falteringly: "You know——"

"Yes; I can guess. But, goodness gracious! Don't let *him* see. Señor Luis Vidal may guess also!" interjects Miss Blanche nervously, as she glances significantly over her white shoulder at a handsome young gentleman of slightly foreign appearance who is standing, mingled with the usual crowd of dilettanti at the entrance of the parterre circle, his dark eyes directed, not upon the stage, but upon the two young ladies who are whispering together.

And Señor Luis Vidal has good reason for turning his glance where he does, for there are no prettier girls than Miss Blanche Grayson, aged nineteen, and her half-sister, Señorita Laura Morales, *ætatis* twenty-two, in the galaxy of beauty that used to make the parterre boxes of the old Academy look like bouquets of gorgeous American flowers in the brave days of old when, under Max Strakosch, Campanini, Capoul and Maurel, made feminine New York utter ecstatic sighs, and Nilsson, Lucca and Duval caused the Italian colony in the gallery overhead to shriek, "Brava! Bravissima!" with all the force of Latin lungs and with all the power and vivacity of Continental expression.

Apparently Señor Vidal would join the ladies in their box—which, curiously, for the moment is bereft of gentlemen, though generally filled to repletion and much clustered about by the male biped -- did he not see signs of polite dispute between the two fair ones.

For the elder has whispered: "How dare you mention his name!"

"Pooh! you think of it often enough, Miss Romantic," laughs the other. "When not occupied in freeing Cuba, Luis Vidal is engaged in besieging your susceptible heart," the last playfully. Then Blanche goes on in earnest inquiry: "Laura, has he ever spoken?"

"Of course not; he is too noble," whispers the dark-eyed one. "An exile, cut off from family and fortune, with death staring him in the face should he visit his native isle, Luis is too generous——"

"Ah, yes. To ask an heiress to join her life to his uncertain lot," interjects the younger, a little sentiment coming into her voice. Then she goes on, with American common sense : "Generous and romantic ! But a generosity and a romance which *I* should not appreciate. If Miss Blanche Grayson were her half-sister, Miss Laura Morales, she would help Señor Luis Vidal on a bit." This is emphasized by a little playful sisterly pinch of white-gloved fingers on the delicate arm that is next to her, as she gets the *riposte* quick as lightning :

"Then why does not Miss Blanche Grayson help Mr. Howard Temple on a bit ? "

" Miss Blanche Grayson is proud enough to like to be asked. Mr. Temple is no Cuban exile, and his fortune is assured him. No false delicacy need prevent *his* asking," murmurs the American beauty quite haughtily, though her face flushes delightfully and her exquisite lips tremble.

" He has asked," says the elder, pointedly.

" For me ? Oh no, he has not !" And Blanche conceals agitation by languidly burying her nose in a magnificent bouquet of red roses that lies in front of her on the velvet rail of the loge.

" But he has. I accidentally overheard Howard Temple speaking to your father," replies Laura, earnestly, hoping to do the young New York broker and banker, whose devotion to business has not destroyed his romance in life,—a good turn, but doing him a very bad one.

" Asking my father for *me ?* " whispers Blanche, indignantly, as she drops the flowers with a start. Then drawing herself up, she mutters : " I am an American girl, not a French one, and propose to be consulted on that point myself. Where is papa? I must speak to him," and, looking eagerly about, adds disappointedly, "Oh! gone out of the box *again*. At the buffet, I suppose. He prefers drinks, business and politics to music!"

"Don't lose your temper and make a mistake," implores Laura hurriedly. "Mr. Temple will probably come to-night for his answer."

"And I will give him *my* answer."

"Blanche, I am your older sister."

"Yes; venerable twenty-two is well able to guide adolescent nineteen," sneers the younger beauty.

"Sit down; people will notice you. Capoul is commencing to sing again?"

"Oh, is he? Well, I could listen to Capoul during an earthquake," says the other, and sinks into her chair with a languid sigh. Then she whispers: "I am sorry you told me, Laura."

But she isn't; for the girl's heart is bounding joyously yet haughtily. and in her mind she is voicing: "Howard! Howard!" Though with the foolishness of youth she soliloquizes: "But he shan't win me too easily!"

So, the curtain falling on the act, Miss Blanche Grayson simulates the opera craze, and astonishes her sister by applauding with all the force of her pretty little hands, and excitedly throwing her gorgeous bouquet of red roses to Monsieur Capoul, who, with Nilsson, is recalled and is bowing before the footlights.

"Mercy, Blanche! I never saw you so excited before," laughs the elder sister, "and you have thrown away those magnificent flowers on a tenor."

"Pooh! they were only Señor Ortiz' flowers, and I had no particular use for them," returns the young lady, playfully.

"But Ortiz, in his foreign way, will be distracted if he knows you slighted his gift," says Miss Morales, adding very seriously : "He is beginning to love you too much."

"Fiddle-de-dee ! No man can love me too much."

At this, an anxious look coming into Laura's eyes, she murmurs : "Blanche, you never think of *him* as a—as a lover ?

"I think of all men as lovers," laughs the girl, "but don't love all men," adding : "Why did you ask ?"

"Because," remarks the elder sister, earnestly, "were not Señor Ignacio Ortiz such an intimate friend and trusted companion of Luis Vidal, there is something behind his extremely white teeth that would almost make me fear him."

"Pshaw ! Your Spanish blood makes you an impressionist, my sister !" laughs the younger ; then goes on with a pretty little pout as the applause has died away : "Where can papa be ? I wish he would not always enjoy an opera from the bar."

But Papa Grayson is not enjoying the opera from the bar. That gentleman is in the foyer just outside the box, speaking eagerly and earnestly to a fine-looking young American, who has that peculiar New York knack of mixing the manners of a club lounger and society exquisite with the directness of speech of a Wall Street business man.

"Howard, you will have to go to Cuba again to look after Laura's estates," remarks Mr. Grayson, who has clean-cut Yankee features, and bears his sixty years well and sturdily.

"But how can I leave ?" answers his junior partner, Mr. Howard Temple. "Stocks going to smash ; panic everywhere ; thousands of workmen out of a place ; New York Central dropped within the week

from 95 to 80 ; Western Union from 73 to 45, and Lake
Shore down to 60——"

"Don't go on with the catalogue of our financial
misfortunes," laughs the elder. "That is the very
reason I can spare you, my boy. Stocks have gone as
low as they can go, and, as we are on the right side
of bankruptcy by a million or two, that need not bother
us. But this other matter is pressing. The estates
willed Laura by her father, I have guarded even more
carefully than my own fortune, ever since her mother
left the little girl to my care, when she died. You,
Howard, know better than any one, how I, in my capa-
city of step-father and guardian, have kept very much
in touch with Cuban affairs."

"Yes, the whole Cuban colony is intimate at your
house. Ortiz, Vidal, Quesada, Marti, and every other
patriot of the Ever-faithful Isle."

"I don't mean that. I mean with regard to all news
from the island ; and I have just heard from Mr. Dennison, a young newspaper man, who keeps me posted
on such matters—" here the elder gentleman sinks
his voice to a whisper—"that information has certainly come that on October 31st, the fillibuster
steamer *Virginius*, flying the American flag, was captured off the Island of Jamaica by a Spanish war
ship. That is the reason I want you to go to Cuba
quick."

"I hope not," says the other impressively. "I hope
your news is not true."

"For your friend Luis Vidal's sake ? I believe he
has a brother on board."

"For the sake of every Cuban on board. The
Spaniards will probably butcher them."

"*What ?* Taken under the American flag ? " says
the older man. "They daren't do it."

"There is no telling what a Spaniard will do,"

mutters the younger.   " He acts first and thinks afterward.   You are sure the news is true ? "

"Yes ; it will be in the *Herald* to-morrow morning.   But be careful you say nothing of it to Luis Vidal.
Let his friend Señor Ortiz break the matter to him after
our supper-party this evening.   Don't make the young
Cuban's champagne bitter to him.   But this increases
my anxiety for my step-daughter's estate.   Laura's
interests on the island are so enormous, I don't dare
to trust them to a clerk.   Howard, will you go ? "

" I will give you my answer this evening.   I don't
care particularly to leave New York if—"

" If everything is right with you in there with
Blanche," chuckles the father, looking toward the closed
doors of his parterre box, and giving the young man
a playful nudge in the ribs.

"Yes !   I will tell you after supper."

"Then you are sure *not* to go, my boy," answers
Grayson, confidently.   "You know you have my
good wishes in the matter."   I shall have to get
Martin to take your place in Cuba—though in any
event you need not stay there more than a month
or two."

" I pray God you are right," remarks Mr. Howard
Temple.   " I hope I shall not go.   I will tell you after
supper."

And with an anxious face, which does not come
from the panic in Wall Street, the young American
business man goes in to meet the young lady to whom
he has given his whole heart, and thinks Miss Blanche
Grayson rather cold and slightly haughty to him.
Though perhaps she may not be really cold to him,
she may be only elusive, for the girl glances fur-
tively once or twice with almost the pride of possession
at the earnest face and manly figure that is beside her.
She has good cause for self-congratulation, as the

strong features show character and truth, and the hazel Saxon eyes display *love* and tenderness to the fair girl whose beauty the light evening dress makes ethereal and fairylike.

So it may be only that inherent diffidence in all maids' minds that causes them to play on the edge of the precipice before they jump into the chasm of matrimony, even where they love, even where they know they are loved, that makes Howard Temple think that Miss Blanche Grayson wilfully misunderstands some rather pointed sentences he whispers into her ear, as he sits behind her shining shoulders.

The opera gives her every opportunity for playful badinage, and it is not pleasant for that gentleman to have his whispered "You received my bouquet this afternoon?" greeted with "Oh, yes—certainly. It was too pretty to bring with me ; I was afraid I might throw it to Capoul when he sang '*M'appari*.' You know he is perfectly divine when he gets crazy. Do you love crazy men? I do."

"Not absolute maniacs," mutters Temple, surlily.

"All tenors, I think, have something of the lunatic in them. Perhaps all men have," says the young lady, lightly. "Capoul, I presume, is a maniac on high notes and the *ut de poitrine*, and you, I suppose, on stocks, bonds, New York Central, Lake Shore and Michigan Southern, eh? Papa said the market had busted all to flinders this afternoon—but seemed in a good humor. Short, isn't he?"

"No, *long!* No man of sense goes short at the bottom of a panic," replies Howard savagely.

"Oh, well, then I judged right. I bought three new dresses this afternoon, *after* papa came home ; one of them bright red. Señor Ortiz, you know, likes crimson ; nearly all Spaniards do—it reminds them of bullfights !" remarks the young lady laughingly. "And here he is.　Isn't it awful, I'm dressed in white this evening !"

This last is uttered as a gentleman of dark eyes, and that beautiful pink and white complexion peculiar to pure Castilian blood, enters the box.　He is apparently about thirty years of age and has a well-knit frame, covered by an irreproachable dress-suit, embellished at the buttonhole by a bunch of bright red carnations. This, with the extremely low cut collar of his immaculate white shirt, gives Señor Ortiz a foreign tone, to which his vivid gesticulations and excitable intense Spanish manner add color.

Bowing with Iberian suaveness before the young ladies, he murmurs : "Ah, delighted ! Señorita Laura and Miss Blanche.　Was not that last *morceau* exquisite ? Did you hear Capoul's high C?　Between ourselves, it is B ; but Capoul insists it is high C.　And no bouquets ? "

"We threw them both to Capoul when he finished his aria," cries Laura excitedly.

"Did you throw mine ? " whispers Temple sternly, into Miss Blanche's ear.

"Certainly.　I was so excited, I couldn't help it," laughs the girl.　Then she murmurs pathetically : " Come back," and, half repenting her fib, almost starts after him, as the gentleman with a muttered anathema leaves the box.

But she is cut off from any further words by the entrance of Señor Luis Vidal.　This young Cuban, who has lingered about, outside of the box, talking to Mr. Grayson, now comes in, and after greeting both ladies, seats himself behind Miss Morales' white shoulders and admires the brunette beauty of the girl in front of him ; for Laura has the dark eyes and black tresses of the tropics, and is as perfect a brune as her step-sister is a blonde.

Miss Morales is half Spanish by blood.   Her mother, a very pretty American girl, had married in the early "Fifties," when very young, Don Ramon de Morales, a Cuban planter.   But one year after his child's birth, during the great yellow fever epidemic in Havana, the great sugar planter had passed away, and her mother had returned to her home in New York, an extremely engaging young widow.

Quite shortly after this, she had been espoused by Alfred Carter Grayson, the banker of Wall Street, who was just commencing to lift his head among the leading financiers of New York.   To him she had borne one daughter, Blanche, and dying soon after, had left the big-hearted and cool-headed American business man to care for her other daughter Laura, who had no blood of his in her veins, but to whom he gave the love of a father, scarcely making a distinction between her and Blanche, his own offspring.

So the two half-sisters have grown up devoted to each other ; one element that oft destroys sisterly love being eliminated from this happy family—money !   For Señorita Laura Morales' estates in Cuba are magnificent in their extent and income, permitting Mr. Grayson to give his own ample fortune to his child, Blanche, knowing that his step-daughter, with her own money can purchase any earthly happiness to be bought by a long purse.   Thus, the two girls have grown up together, loving each other very dearly ; and now, when the younger has just come out into the gay world, they find themselves not only very popular with general metropolitan society, but also quite the belles of the little Cuban coterie that has naturally been drawn to Mr. Grayson's hospitable Fifth Avenue house by his step-daughter's interests and friends in Cuba.

Among the gentlemen who have become quite *amis de la maison,* are the two now leaning over the shoulders of the young ladies, Señor Ignacio Pasquale Ortiz and Señor Luis Vidal.

Vidal, a dashing young fellow of about twenty-five, is a Cuban patriot, and has already forwarded or accompanied several expeditions to the island. He is a man of mark in the insurgent ranks, being a relation of Carlos Manuel de Cespedes, President of the so-called "Cuban Republic," and an intimate of Vincente Garcia and General Quesada.

He has probably but two passions in this world as he bends over the beautiful girl in front of him, and looks at her as only Cubans look, with his soft, romantic, yet pleading eyes: one is to free his native land; the other, to make his own the beautiful being whose eyes tell him in reply: "You may dare! Though you are an exile; though you are an outcast, a price on your head; though you are poor; still you may love me, an heiress, for I love you!"

The other gentleman, the one who has taken Temple's place beside pretty Miss Blanche, is, though a Spaniard, known to be of strong Cuban sympathies. For, from the time of Señor Ignacio Ortiz' arrival in New York, some few years before, no one has been more engrossed in the Cuban cause, nor apparently more willing to sacrifice himself for it.

At first, perchance, looked upon with suspicion by some of the adherents of "The Ever Faithful Isle" that cluster about that well-known cigar store in Fifth Avenue below Twenty-Third Street, or the headquarters of the Cuban Junta in Beaver Street, as time elapsed, Señor Ortiz had blown all suspicion from him by joining an expedition that took arms and munitions of war to the insurgents. And, though the affair had come to a bad end, the landing being frustrated by a Spanish gunboat, Señor Ignacio Pasquale Ortiz had shown such gallantry, twice risking capture by Spanish

B

troops in his endeavors to enter the Cuban lines, that
no one stands higher in the esteem of the Cuban colony
than the gentleman bending over Miss Blanche Grayson
this night at the opera, and whispering to her : "I am
so glad you did not throw *my* bouquet to the tenor.
Poor Temple! *Dios mio!* if I thought that Capoul
grasped the flowers I had given to you, I should go behind the scenes and tear them from the Frenchman's
hand."

"Would you?" says the girl, biting her lips, then
bursts into an irrepressible flood of mellow laughter,
in which her sister, despite herself, joins.

So the conversation runs along,—though quite dis-
connectedly, for they all love music,—though once or
twice Señor Ortiz' whispers make Miss Blanche Grayson grow very red, and sometimes the ardent eyes
of Luis Vidal bring roses to Laura Morales' cheeks, and
happiness to her eyes till the curtain is descending, and
Mr. Grayson makes his appearance with Mr. Temple.

"You hardly greeted me as you passed me going
out, Howard," remarks the young Cuban, rising.

"Didn't I? Then, Luis, I greet you again, and remember, I mean it," and Howard Temple grasps
young Vidal by the hand, and gives it a warm-hearted
squeeze, that shows that the Wall Street man has not
forgotten his college athletics, though there is something in his eye that makes the Cuban say: "You
have some intelligence for me?"

"No."

"I was afraid you had bad news. Your face is not
as bright as it generally is."

"Oh, yes, bad news," says Blanche, lightly. "Lake
Shore down to 60. That is bad news enough. That
always makes Wall Street men look sad." Then turning her eyes to a lady near her, for the party is now
in the crowd of the foyer, Miss Volatile remarks,

"Good evening, Mrs. Livingston ! Didn't Capoul sing romantically ? He almost made me susceptible."

"Of whom, Blanche ?" laughs the society leader ; Miss Grayson has already achieved the reputation of being something of a flirt.

"Of the man nearest me, of course !" returns the young lady, archly, and the two, laughing together, pass down the broad stairs of the Academy. By this Miss Blanche artfully avoids the offer of escort either from Ortiz or Temple, the arm of the first she not caring to take, and foolishly wishing to punish the other for his having asked her father for her before he dared to petition her for her love.

So Temple and Ortiz come walking after her, chatting to each other, for they are very fair friends ; the young American conjuring his brain how to best break the news to Luis Vidal, who is just now taking care of the dark-eyed girl that he loves, in the crush of the vestibule.

For Howard has talked to Dennison, the young newspaper man, and he is satisfied that the *Virginius* has been captured, and furthermore, knows that Vidal's younger brother, Pedro, a boy of only seventeen, is on board the ship.

In fact, he has heard the same news discussed by one or two gentlemen in the corridors, though no one seems to pay particular attention to it ; the general public not at this time guessing the tremendous butchery that was to follow the capture—a tragedy that thrilled America to its center, both from the arrogant insult to the United States that was shown in taking a vessel bearing its flag upon the high seas, and, furthermore, the horrible assassinations, without legal trial, that succeeded it. An affair that, had not gold been poured out in Washington by the Spanish government with the same liberality that American blood was shed by it at Santiago, and the outspoken apologies for Spain of one well-known member of the United States Cabinet, there was indignation enough and there was power enough in America in that day to have given Spain its quietus in the Western world, and spared a later generation another and greater horror, that of the "Maine," and a grander revenge and a nobler justice, the one that has now come !

But, unthinking of this, the great audience of this November night of 1873 sweeps out of the Academy of Music, and apparently, no happier party strolls under the great porte-cochère on Fourteenth Street to their carriages than Mr. Grayson's, for they are all going to have a pretty little supper at Delmonico's, at that time located on Fourteenth Street and Fifth Avenue.

Apparently, Miss Blanche Grayson is as light-hearted as any of them. Pausing in front of her carriage door, one delicate hand draping up her trailing skirts about as pretty feet as have ever tripped out of the Academy, she extends the other, and says, coquettishly : "Señor Ortiz, won't you assist me ?"

"*Caspita !* Will not I !" and brushing the footman aside, the gentleman steps hurriedly forward, and with facile Spanish grace places the young lady in her carriage.

Luis Vidal has already played the cavalier to Miss Morales, and Mr. Grayson, accepting precedence by age, having stepped in, Ortiz, with Spanish common sense, takes the fourth place in the vehicle.

"Just tell the footman Delmonico's ; we'll meet you there !" cries Blanche blithely to Temple, as he stands biting his lips, not altogether pleased at seeing the lady of his heart ask attentions from others.

These directions being given, and the carriage being rapidly driven away, for many other vehicles are in the

waiting line, Mr. Temple turns to Vidal, who is standing beside him, and suggests : "Suppose we walk along
Fourteenth Street,—the night is very fine, and enjoy a
cigar?"

"*Gracias!* I prefer ——"

"Oh, yes, I had forgotten," interjects the American,
lightly, "your ever-present cigarette, Luis." So the
two young men light up and stroll along Fourteenth
Street towards Fifth Avenue, the night being a very
pleasant one, Temple glancing about sharply, as he
fears newsboys and extras may break the *Virginius*
intelligence too suddenly to his young Cuban friend,
for the two are intimates, and once or twice Howard
Temple has been able to do substantial favors for the
young gentleman who walks at his side. Fortunately,
no extras are about, the great newspapers of 1873 not
having got into the habit of issuing twenty editions on
days of excitement.

As the two stroll along, chatting together, the young
men are not so unlike ; though the Anglo-Saxon has
hazel eyes and the Cuban very black ones, both have
long moustaches, after the manner of that time, and
their figures are not so dissimilar, being about the same
height, though the American is more strongly built
than the lithe native of the tropics. Curiously, both
chat in Spanish, Mr. Temple having been for several
years the superintendent of Miss Morales' estates in
Cuba, and speaking the language like a native of the
island.

A few minutes afterward they walk up-stairs and
stroll into that pretty little Chinese room of old Delmonico's, where the party is reunited, and over oysters,
terrapin, cold partridge, mayonnaise and champagne
they apparently pass an hour very pleasantly. Though
Miss Grayson puts one or two more arrows into the
heart of Howard Temple, for the girl has got thinking

to herself, "I'll teach him to ask my father for my hand before he pleaded to me for my love! I'll show him that my preference is more important in such a matter than papa's permission! I suppose they were bargaining about me, French fashion! Ough! Did Howard dare to ask him what my *dot* would be?"

Yet all the time she guesses she is doing an injustice to a man she is very well aware loves her for herself, as has been shown on half a hundred occasions ever since she, as a little girl of fourteen, ran into her father's parlor where he was talking business with a handsome young fellow of twenty-four, and even in her short skirts got very close to the heart of a gentleman she at that time regarded as venerable.

And now a few unfortunate remarks of her father add to her chagrin; for the party having by this time broken up into little groups, she overhears Mr. Grayson whisper to Temple, "You'll give me your answer to-night?"

"Certainly!" replies Howard, "as soon as I have spoken to her."

"Ugh! bargaining about me again!" thinks the girl, who has quick ears. With this, she looks very engagingly at and talks most vivaciously to Señor Ortiz who is languidly manipulating a paper cigar between his cigarette-stained fingers, and gazing at her exquisite beauty in a way that makes the girl say to herself: "At least the Spaniard is romantic; no questions to papa about me first. Howard will speak to me to-night, will he? Not until I wish him to speak!"

Thereupon she proceeds to give Mr. Temple a very bad half hour of it, accepting attentions from anybody but him, eating philopenas with both Ortiz and Vidal, and telling these gentlemen they don't know what *pretty* presents she may give them, if they win.

Finally getting back to the matter of the bouquet,

which she knows is a sore spot with Howard, and
perchance not daring to tell him of her fib, especially
in the presence of Ortiz, whose posies she has sacrificed to Capoul, Miss Blanche remarks, "That was
an exquisite bunch of flowers you sent me, Mr.
Temple! I never shall forget the appearance of Mr.
Pompey Smith, your colored factotum, as he delivered
it to me. Talk about dandies! Sixth Avenue beats
Fifth Avenue in gorgeous attire! Check suit, red necktie, exquisite lavender gloves and gorgeous quartz
watch-chain! You must pay Pomp a good salary!
And then the ineffable darky grace with which he re-
marked to me, 'Mistah Temple's compliments to Miss
Blanche Grayson, and requests the pleasure that she
will receive the accompanying do-sewer with his compliments and all the regards of the autumnal season in
high society.'"

"Did the scoundrel translate my message *into that?*"
asks Temple, glumly. "I merely wrote my compliments on one of my cards and said to him, 'Deliver
this.' But you remember the message better than the
bouquet. I hope you kept the *card!*" There is a
sneer in his last sentence.

"Oh, good gracious!" cries the girl, "it must have
been tied to the bouquet when I threw it. Was there
a card?" and she opens her bright eyes to their full
extent. "I remember there was a *billet doux* with Señor
Ortiz' bouquet, but with yours? why, I must have forgotten it! Goodness, what must Capoul have thought
of your effusive compliments?"

At this Howard stifles an incipient curse, for, in
truth, there had been a tinge of sentiment in the brief
line he had written upon his pasteboard, which Miss
Blanche knows very well, as it is packed away in her
Holy of holies in her pretty chamber at home on Fifth
Avenue.

Then, though red and blushing as she thinks of this, she contrives to mutter nonchalantly : "But a girl gets *so* many cards and bouquets in the season ! She can't very well keep track of them, Mr. Temple, can she ? "

"So she throws them to tenors," mutters the gentleman with a sigh, "and then laughs about it to the sender afterwards ! "

" Pooh ! don't grow sentimental about a few posies and a *carte de visite !* " remarks Miss Elusive, then suddenly asks, rather pleadingly : "Come and see me and we'll talk the bouquet over to-morrow ! "

For now she is repenting, and has planned a great and pleasing surprise for him. She will show Mr. Temple that his beautiful offering has been kept very carefully.

"Thank you, I don't think I'll call to-morrow," answers the gentleman in grim politeness.

"Very well ! Some other day ! Any day will do. We don't leave town for Newport till next June, seven months away," remarks Miss Blanche with haughty nonchalance ; though her lips are quivering a little now, and her eyes are blazing. With this she rises, and, lifting her voice, suggests : " Papa, is it not about time to go home ? Mr. Temple looks tired after his Wall Street exertions."

But this is enough !

After the rest of the party have put on their wraps and are gone downstairs, Howard takes Mr. Grayson aside and whispers : " I will go for you to attend to Miss Morales' estate in Cuba ! "

"Good Lord ! she refused you ? " mutters the elder man.

"I have already learned my fate ! " answers the younger.

"Pish ! Blanche is an infernal idiot ! " says her

father. "I would have congratulated her on gaining you, Howard, as much as I should have congratulated you upon winning her, but of course I shall use no coercion in regard to my daughter's affections !"

"Don't humiliate me by suggesting it," shudders the young man.

"Very well then, go ! Next Saturday ! You must get off on the first steamer ! Perhaps a few months' absence may make the young lady know that she has missed a good thing. Humph ! when you ask her again——"

"I shall never ask her ! I know my fate !"

"Nonsense ! If you don't get a stock on first offer, bid again ! I asked her mother twice; but then she was a widow," mutters Grayson contemplatively. With this the business man coming up in him, he adds : "I'll see you at the office early to-morrow morning, for we must rush things to get you off. "

So, going down to his party, the old gentleman finds his daughters in the carriage awaiting him, with Señor Vidal sitting on the front seat. During the drive home Grayson *père* says nothing of Temple's contemplated departure from New York ; first, because he is annoyed with his daughter, who has played "fast and loose," as he thinks, with his junior partner; second, because he doesn't care to discuss a business matter with women.

As for the young lady, she chats pleasantly with her sister and young Vidal ; but upon arriving at her house, as soon as she can say "good-evening," runs up-stairs to her chamber, locks herself in, bursts into tears, and suddenly going to a magnificent bouquet of white flowers which has been kept most carefully soothed with ice-water, and bears Mr. Temple's card, kisses it passionately and mutters : "Howard ! Howard ! you foolish boy ! You don't know much about women !"

Then she wipes her eyes and says : "But I am glad of that ; it shows he hasn't had *much* experience !"

And this remark seeming to comfort her, Mademoiselle Blanche wipes her bright eyes again, tosses off her pretty raiment and finally goes to bed, looking a mixture of sylph and vestal virgin, to sleep and dream, and murmur between her rosebud lips : "Howard !"

CHAPTER II.

LA FLOR DE PASCUA.

A LITTLE before eight o'clock on the evening of Friday, the 7th of November, two days later, a gentleman of quick movement rings the doorbell of a very handsome residence on Fifth Avenue, and stepping into the brilliantly lighted hallway hands his card to a flunky, remarking : "Please give this to Mr. Grayson at once. I called by appointment.   He will understand."

Being shown into a gorgeous reception-room, Mr. George Dennison casts his eyes about and remarks to himself cheerily : "Wonder if journalism will ever lead me into this?   Did any man ever write himself from Bohemianism and a hundred dollars a week, to a palace on Fifth Avenue and an unlimited income ; yachts, horses, pictures and statues?" and goes to inspecting an elaborate photograph of Mr. Grayson's yacht, the *Hermes*, winning the New York Club regatta.

From this picture he turns with a start and exclaims : "Great Heavens, Pomp, is that you ?"

This is uttered as Mr. Howard Temple's body-servant, a darky gentleman of most exquisite air, enters the apartment languidly. a letter in his delicately gloved hand. Inspecting him the newspaper man adds, *sotto voce* : "By the Lord ! you *are* impressive ! "

"Yes, sah ! " replies the creature who is dressed like a Blacktown fashion-plate : lilac pantaloons, light checked coat and vest, expansive collar with red necktie, expansive cuffs with quartz sleevelinks, and bearing upon his breast a quartz watch-guard of heaviest gold setting ; the beauty of these adornments being emphasized by patent-leather gaiters of enormous size surmounted by white tops. His face is black as India-ink, contrasting strongly with the white of his immense eyes, big teeth and the water-melon ruby of his thick lips. His deportment is embellished by a most lazy grace and supercilious smile, the affectation of which is sometimes tossed away, as under great excitement Mr. Pompey Smith, forgetting the high-bred manners of the Coachman's Club and other fashionable colored coteries, becomes a first-class fighting ward-darky, with intense jealousy, big heart and extreme devotion to his indulgent master, to whom he looks up as the greatest swell in New York.

Excitement is now evident from Mr. Pompey Smith's vivid gesticulations as he continues : "Yes sah ! I *has* to be impressive. I am bidding de Sixth Abenue belles good-by. To-morrow Mr. Temple and me leabes for Cuba." Then, apparently a new horror coming into his mind, he mutters : "Good Lord ! Miss Rosa Sweetapple, Mrs. Livingston's lady's lady ! Dis will break her heart ! " and pathetically sighs : "Away from de Abenue in the bery acme of de season ! " clapping his lavender gloves to his frizzled and oiled hair with a despairing gesture.

"Ah, yes, Pomp ! " laughs the journalist, "I see ; you, the man of fashion ; I, the Bohemian ! "

Here astonishment strikes George Dennison as Mr.

Smith rejoins : "A Bohemian !   Dat's what my fader was !"

"The devil !"

"Yes, sah ! My fader come from Bohemey, way down plumb into the middle of Africa !" Then the darky exquisite scratches his frizzled head and crushes the Caucasian journalist with this remark : "You will excuse me, sah, but you is de lightest complected Bohemian I eber seed !" and turning to the door, mutters : "I must deliver dis."

For light steps are coming along the hallway, and Miss Blanche Grayson, entering the room, bears a beauty with her that makes the newspaper man start.

"You are Mr. Dennison, I believe," she remarks politely to the journalist's bow. "Papa asked me to say that he will join you in a moment !" Then she hurriedly ejaculates, seizing the billet presented by Pomp with his best salute : "A note from Mr. Temple !" and opening the letter appears not too well pleased with its contents.   For after glancing it over twice she petulantly tears the note up and says to the valet : "No answer is necessary, Mr. Pomp ; I won't detain you."

"Yas, we's got lots to do now." mutters the darky effusively, and Miss Grayson might get some curious news did she let Mr. Pompey Smith's tongue have full play.

But she cuts the valet short by remarking : "Of course, I understand ! Mr. Temple pleads urgent business for declining my invitation to dinner this evening."

Then the young lady turns away. and while the darky exquisite is smoothing, in the hall, the wrinkles out of a pair of lavender gloves over his big hands, and burnishing with his coat-sleeve his shining tile before making his exit to the street, Miss Blanche trips into a neighboring parlor and welcomes Señors Ortiz and Vidal, who are her guests at a little dinner party that is not exactly a banquet and all the more delightful for being informal.

A moment after, the blonde is joined by her half-sister, whose brunette eyes salute but sympathize with the young Cuban whose face bears an anxious look ; for Luis Vidal now knows, as all the world does, that the *Virginius* has been captured, though no further news has come to New York, the wires to Havana across Cuba from Santiago to which place the *Virginius* had been taken, for some curious reason not being in working condition.*

While the young ladies and gentlemen are chatting in the parlor, the young newspaper man in the reception-room is giving Mr. Grayson such startling news that he has sent a hurried note to Howard Temple, telling the district messenger boy he must find his junior partner, whether he is at the office, his club or his apartments, and to do it quickly.

"You are sure, Mr. Dennison," he says, rising from writing this, "that your information is correct?"

"So certain that I am going to Cuba myself in a day or two as war correspondent."

"You think, then, it means a rupture between the United States and Spain?"

"As surely as I believe in American pluck. Nothing but official cowardice or extreme sympathy in official circles for the Spanish government can prevent our revenging the dastardly crime both against humanity and our flag of which I have just told you!" remarks the American journalist, as he takes his departure and leaves the American financier muttering to himself :

* This was the only means of telegraphic communication with Santiago de Cuba at that time; the Cable to Cape Haytien not being then laid.—Ed.

"Good God, poor Vidal!" adding to this : "Merciful Heavens! Laura's estates and property! We must get that enormous sugar crop shipped in a hurry!"

With this idea in his head, and a horrified look on his face, especially as he glances at young Vidal, Mr. Grayson makes his way to the dinner party with very little appetite, and discovers that his charming daughter has very little appetite also. Though the girl is effusive, brilliant and vivacious, still Miss Blanche eats next to nothing of the delicacies placed before her.

Finally looking in a semi-pathetic way at the empty chair beside her, the girl murmurs to the obsequious butler, who is just serving the second course at the exquisite dinner-table: "Dodson, you need set no other plate. Mr. Temple is *not* coming; he has been detained at his office by business. O-oh! he *is* such a wonderful business man! Like most Americans, he lives to make money."

"As their daughters do to spend it!" mutters her father from the head of the table, then breaks out, rather testily : "Hang it, Blanche, don't be sarcastic! Howard is engaged on business of the greatest moment to your sister. Please remember that!"

"Oh, I know that very well, I've had to acknowledge and sign a power of attorney for Mr. Temple to-day!" remarks Laura *sotto voce*.

"So my step-sister's sugar estates necessitate an empty chair at our dinner-table!" pouts the younger lady, dallying with her fish.

"And an empty chair beside you!" laughs Laura, attempting to carry off the subject lightly.

"Ah, Señorita Laura Morales can be merry. She has a cavalier on either side of her!" returns Blanche significantly. Then with that affectation of coquetry which is peculiar to many American girls, and which

most American men regard as a jest, but which
foreigners sometimes imagine means a great deal,
she glances alluringly across the decorated dinner
table and suggests, invitation in her glance : "Supposing you, Señor Ortiz, sit beside me for the balance
of the *menu!* That will allow Señor Vidal to monop-
olize my sister and at least give me a cavalier ! "

At her glance the pure white complexion of the
gentleman addressed suddenly reddens.   His dark
sparkling eyes grow luminous.   He rises hurriedly.

"With all the pleasure in the world, my dear Miss
Blanche ! " he says eagerly ; then Castilian etiquette
overcoming him, he bows to the sparkling brunette who
is seated next to him, and murmurs : " With Señorita
Laura's permission, of course ! "

" You know you have mine, Ignacio ! " interjects
Luis Vidal.

" And mine also ! " laughs Laura, who prefers *tête-
à-tête* with the young Cuban to anything else in the
world.

The next moment Ortiz is at Miss Blanche's side,
looking at her snowy shoulders and rounded arms, of
which her evening dress permits alluring glimpses, and
gazing into the vivacious face whose sapphire eyes meet
his half mockingly.

Suddenly, the passion which has been growing in
this man for a year, more and more fervid, until, under
the spell of her beauty, it is now ready to burst its
bonds, flies into Ignacio's, heart, and the gentleman
murmurs : "*Dios mio!* To be at your side I would
leave even Heaven ! " Then noticing that the girl's
face becomes very red, and she bites her lips, and
turning away her face, gives him only one exquisitely
dimpled shoulder to view, Ortiz goes on to the company
in general : " Ah, Señor Grayson, it is a fortunate thing
for me that your step-daughter, the fair Señorita Mo-

rales, has estates in Cuba, otherwise I should not enjoy the place that was reserved for a man who is more fortunate than he guesses—Señor Howard Temple! *Sapristi!* he did not look very happy when he learned that the tenor Capoul had received his bouquet from your white hands, Miss Blanche!"

With this the Don chuckles contentedly and rather wonders at what the two girls are laughing, for at the mention of the bouquet Laura has burst into merriment and her sister has smiled also, though Miss Grayson's seems to be a rather yellow laugh, so much so that Ortiz continues: "*Caspita!* you are becoming serious, Miss Blanche! and you brought a light heart with you from the seaside. You left Newport bright, smiling and merry!"

"Oh, very merry! About as full of scandal as usual, and everybody talking about papa's yacht *Hermes!*"

"Which won one race gloriously!" interjects Laura, triumphantly.

"And lost half a dozen ingloriously!" jeers Blanche.

"But I won the *last* one," cries Grayson eagerly, "and the schooner is such a triumph that I think of taking a winter cruise in her to the West Indies, Spanish Main and Cuba; that is, if that accursed *Virginius* report—I mean if things—." He checks himself, but there is that in his face which makes Luis Vidal instantly ask: "You have heard news?"

"Not any that I—I think authentic enough to tell you!"

"*Dios mio*, you have some information?"

But the American puts him off by saying: "Nothing worth discussing, my boy. You see I am interested in this matter from a business stand-point. My daughter Laura's estates produce much sugar."

"Ah! but Luis has a brother on board and doesn't

look at it from a business stand-point!" remarks Laura, reproachfully.

"Yes, all Cuban patriots are my friends!" returns Vidal, but adds conservatively: "I have grown used to such risks, both for myself and others, and it is not a good soldier who cries before he is hurt!" With this the poor fellow strives to make the dinner party as light, pleasant and sociable as possible, whispering one or two Spanish love words into the ear of the beautiful girl who sits beside him that make her supremely happy.

So the conversation runs along quite pleasantly between the young gentlemen and the young ladies, though Grayson eats almost silently, and once or twice, when he hears a noise in the street, seems to listen in a half frightened way, until with the dessert comes a curious interruption.

"A card for Señor Ortiz!" whispers the placid butler, presenting the article ceremoniously upon a salver.

"*Santa Maria!* Domingo Mendoza!" This is whispered to himself between the whitest teeth in New York, and the black eyes of the gentleman look curiously disturbed as they glance over a flower piece upon Luis Vidal.

"'E says his business his hof great importance, sir," whispers the butler deprecatingly.

"He must have been told he would find you here," remarks Blanche. Then curiosity coming upon her, she asks: "What kind of a looking gentleman is he, Dodson."

"Well, I wouldn't call 'im a gentleman at hall, miss," returns the English butler. "'E looks more like the bandits they 'ave in plays. 'E 'as big, black, staring eyes and a hooked nose like ha heagle's. 'E is draped in one of those cloaks that highwaymen wear on the stage and 'is language 'as a Spanish haccent."

"*Santos !* perhaps somebody from Cuba ! " cries Vidal about to spring up. "Perhaps with news that we are anxious to hear."

" Yes, I—I will see him. Tell him I will see him in-stantly ! " remarks Ortiz stammering and rising hastily. "It will only be a moment ; you will excuse me, Señor Grayson ? " he adds and moves hurriedly to the door, apparently very much pleased to discover that Luis has no thought of accompanying him, as the young Cuban has settled himself once more in his chair and is again devoted to the black eyes of the beautiful woman who is looking with all her soul into his.

Passing hastily through the conservatory Ortiz is ushered by Dodson into a small reception-room.

Here a gentleman, pretty well described by the Eng-lish butler, but who has, in addition, a long black mustache, dark teeth and luminous eyes, rises to meet him. He has just removed from his head a slouch hat and taken from his shoulders a draping poncho, exhibiting himself in a florid evening dress of the tropics, and bearing in his buttonhole a beautiful spray of the *Flor de Pascua*, whose bright vermilion leaves and delicate wax-like buds in their shades of exquisite white and pink, show he must have plucked it on the "Ever Faithful Isle." This individual bows and mutters, "Don Ignacio, I kiss your hand."

To this Ortiz answers nothing, but quickly closes the door, then striding up to his visitor whispers, "Men-doza, you come from Cuba ? "

" A despatch ! " says the man shortly but guardedly, and hands to Ignacio a document, remarking senten-tiously : " From the Captain General."

" You brought this from Cuba in person ? "

" I did, Señor. Your report was entirely correct ; we captured the whole expedition."

"The newspapers have told me that," returns Ortiz, opening the letter hurriedly.

"The reward is satisfactory, I hope, Señor," mutters Mendoza sympathetically.

"*Diablo!* His Excellency is not as liberal as I deserved, but it is enough," murmurs Ignacio ; and thinks triumphantly : "Enough to give me the appearance of being rich till I wed the woman who will make me really so." Then his eyes become troubled as he whispers, "Was the boy on board?"

To this Mendoza replies, "Yes!" adding eagerly, "But the older brother—the reward would have been larger had the older brother been on board!"

"Sish!" whispers Ortiz. The elder brother is here in this house, and for that reason you must go away immediately. You should never have come here."

"Time was pressing Señor, I dared not visit you at your rooms where Cubans call at all hours—I thought at the house of this American, there would be little danger."

"You put great risk upon me."

"*Caramba!* and that is the way my good news is received, and my draft of money from the Captain-General?"

"Not at all. I am always rejoiced to see you, Mendoza, but you must leave this house at once!" Then Ignacio considers a moment and adds : "Wait for me at Delmonico's this evening. I shall be there sometime after twelve o'clock. I shall have a private room. After you have seen me go to it—ask for me. In the crush there of an opera night, you'll not be noticed."

"I understand, Señor!"

But as Mendoza is leaving Ortiz strides to him and whispers, "Have you any further message verbally?"

"Yes, I would have given it to you, Señor, had you not interrupted me. The Captain-General said : 'Tell

Ortiz not to forget that there is a reward of five thousand dollars for the capture of his intimate friend, Luis Vidal.'"

"Tell His Excellency," remarks the Spanish gentleman suavely, "that Ortiz never forgets *anything*, either in business, in love, or in art!" Then, his eye catching the beautiful flower of the Passion, he murmurs: "*A Flor de Pascua!*"

"Yes, Señor," replies the man, "the first of the season. I plucked it myself in Cuba, and brought it carefully. Permit me, Don Ignacio," and, drawing it from his buttonhole, the Spanish messenger presents to the agent of Spanish hate the flower of holy love and peace.

"Thanks, Domingo!" replies the Spanish dandy, placing it carefully in his buttonhole. "Remember Delmonico's!" then suggests contemplatively: "Luis Vidal leads an expedition to the island shortly; perhaps this *Virginius* affair may hurry him;" next asks savagely: "Have they executed any of them yet?"

"There was no news of them when I left Havana. But the wires were *down!* *Caramba*, you know what that means. The patriot General Burriel wishes no interference from the Home Government. Ho! ho! When the wires work again you will guess the happy news they'll tell of the American pigs!"

"I can imagine!" laughs Ortiz. "But let me show you out. If Vidal ever guessed, what would my life be worth among these Cuban conspirators—I, who am their friend, their companion, their dearly beloved—I, who am the agent of Spain, and betray them to death? Come with me!" And he escorts the Spanish messenger to the door, as through the open windows of the conservatory floats to them from far down the avenue the voice of the distant newsboy, calling, "Extra!"

Suddenly the two catch his indistinct words—perhaps because they suspect them : " *Virginius*—Murder ! Massacre ! Execution ! "

" *Diablo !* you've done your work well, noble Ortiz ! "
mutters Mendoza, and strides hurriedly out on to the
street to hear news that makes his savage Spanish
heart beat very high in joy and gladness.

CHAPTER III.

" THE LETTER FOR HAVANA.—SENOR TEMPLE ! "

As Ignacio turns to go back to the dinner-table, the
yell of the newsboy on the avenue catches the ladies'
ears in the dining-room.

Blanche comes rather excitedly into the conservatory, for extras were not as numerous in that day
as they are at present. Throwing up one of the windows, which opens on the cross street, and chancing
to catch a glimpse of a figure passing from the servants'
apartments of the house, she calls out impulsively :
" Pomp ! what is that extra the newsboys are shouting
down the Avenue ? "

" Don't know, miss ! " returns the darky exquisite
from the sidewalk. " Heard 'em say four men killed.
T'ink it must be a smash-up—a concussion on de
railroad ! "

" Quick ! run and buy a paper for me ! " cries the
young lady, who at this moment is joined by her
father ; Grayson coming in with a nervous expression
on his face.

For now several newsboys' voices strike the night
air in shrill staccato : " Death ! " " Murder ! " " Washington Ryan ! "

This is mixed with: "All about 'Ginius!" "Burriel!" "Jesus del Sol!" Whoop! "Bloody assassination!" Whoop — whoop — yell — yell! "Extree
extra!" All these making a confused blur of almost
indistinguishable sounds in the night air.

"Pshaw! I know what it is!" says Blanche, closing the window. "I heard 'em. Some horrid man
named Ryan has committed a murder in Washington!"
and she trips lightly to the Spaniard, who is watching
her graceful movements. To him she murmurs:
"Señor Ortiz, I know you are impatient for your
cigar;" then asks a little curiously: "Did your caller
bring any important news to you?"

"None but what I shall forget over my cigar," laughs
the Don, and lights his *perfecto*. Gazing on the delicate beauty of the girl, this gentleman voices to himself in soft Southern passion: "*Mi querida!*" then
thinks almost despairingly: "And but one man stands
between me and her."

A second after the newsboys' cries rise wilder on the
air; there are more of them: "*Extree*, Extra!" "All
about 'Ginius butchery!" "Washington Ryan!" "Burriel!" "Santiago de Cuba!" "Spanish assassins!" as
Laura comes running into the conservatory, followed
by Luis Vidal.

"Can you understand them?" she cries to the young
Cuban.

"No, but I hear enough to fear," he answers excitedly.

Just at this moment, however, there is a ring at the
front door, and Temple comes excitedly in, carrying
an extra crumpled in his hand.

Curiosity conquering both diffidence and anger,
Blanche runs excitedly to this gentleman as he enters
the parlor, and cries: "Howard! what is it?" For
the newsboys, having by their uproar attracted an audi-

ence, are now selling papers rapidly and making an awful din and pandemonium outside in the elation of successful business.

"Certainly I can tell you ! This extra proclaims an awful insult to our flag and outrage on humanity ! The Spaniards have just shot four of the prisoners cap- tured on the *Virginius!*" answers the young man in indignant voice ; then he pauses, a frightened look in his face, for Vidal has come hurriedly to him, followed by Laura, Grayson and Ortiz, the latter seeming es- pecially excited and crying : "Murdered them ? *Santa Maria*, the cowards !"

But the young Cuban whispers, tremblingly : "Temple, read me the dispatch !"

To this the American stammers : "I—I did not know you were here, Luis. I—I have told you all the paper says."

"Read me the *names!*"

Gazing at his interrogator, Temple feels compelled, and reads : "Havana, November 7th, 1873. By order of General Burriel, commanding at Santiago de Cuba, Barnaby Varona, Jesus del Sol, and—and General Washington Ryan were shot on the morning of the 4th !"

"You said *four* were killed ; you read *three*. You have omitted a name. Give me the paper !" cries the Cuban, hoarsely, and reaches for the extra ; but the American holds it from him and murmurs : "Vidal, my poor fellow, how can I tell you?"

But Laura, running to Temple and seizing the paper, gives a glance at it and half shrieks : "Luis ! Luis !"

"Laura, what is it you see?"

"Not from my lips—not from my lips !"

"Anything is better than suspense. The—the other name !"

"The other name," whispers the young broker,

"forgive me for telling you, is—is Pedro Vidal!" and grasps the Cuban to hold him up; for Luis is reeling and muttering: "Pedro! my brother! a—a boy but seventeen!" as Ortiz, looking at the paper, mutters: "Were shot to death!"

"That child was murdered because he bore my name. This will break my little sister's heart and kill my dear old father!" falters Vidal in broken voice, sinking into a chair; though Grayson tries to comfort him by volunteering: "There may be an error in the dispatch!" and Laura suggests: "Luis, there may yet be hope!"

But over these expressions of sympathy comes one of rage; that of Ortiz, who is remarking with vivid gestures: "I am a *Basque!* I would say *guerra à cuchillo!*"

"Don't doubt me!" whispers the Cuban. "I will avenge that boy!"

"For a man born in Spain," remarks Grayson, sympathetically, "your strong Cuban sympathies, Don Ignacio, make me know you have a tender heart."

"Not all tender. I, by living many years in Cuba, have become as much a Cuban as if I was born there; to the cause of the island I have devoted my life," answers the Spaniard, "so much so that it is arranged that I accompany Luis on his next expedition to the island!"

"And that shall come soon!" cries the young insurgent. "This news decides it. I leave for Cuba with the next expedition!"

"The true spirit!" assents his comrade.

But Laura, with tearful eyes, pleads: "Luis! think of your life! There is a price put on your head! Remember your father and your sister!"

"That makes my duty clear!" answers Vidal determinedly. "In their extremity I should be near them.

My father is an old man. This news may kill him; and then my sister, Maria, will be alone without a protector in a land distracted by a civil war that is more than barbarous. At such a time a brother's place is by a sister's side!"

"Still," suggests the old banker, "it may not be necessary for you, Vidal, to take such extreme risk. Mr. Temple leaves for Havana to-morrow morning to settle important business connected with Laura's property. He might bear a message from you to your family!"

But the old gentleman pauses, astounded by the look that comes into his daughter's face, for she is gasping to him: "Goes to-morrow to *Cuba?* Howard Temple?"

"Certainly! this news only proves my foresight. Howard's passage is already engaged. Temple, you know Laura's sugar must be shipped at once!" cries the Wall Street man whose business has risen in his brain.

But Blanche is not appealing to him now; she simply sighs: "Howard!" and whispers: "He must not go!"

"Nonsense, Blanche!" says her father. "Laura's fortune must not suffer! This news makes it imperative Mr. Temple should be on the spot. Six years ago he managed your sister's estates on the island. Conversant with the language, speaking Spanish like a native, knowing the ins and outs of our affairs, he will be able to ship the sugar away or sell it, while diplomatists talk, and so save a portion of your sister's property from confiscation or destruction, even though war should be the ultimate result of this atrocious outrage upon our flag!"

Then Grayson asks sharply of Temple: "You have everything ready?"

"Yes, sir!" replies the young man.   "My trunks are now on board the Alexandre steamer.   She has been delayed by repairs, but sails with the tide at day-break."   To this, he adds, determinedly : "I should be a very poor business man if I did not go *now!*"

"Not on my account!" cries Laura, generously, "if Blanche does not wish it!"

"Oh!" says that young lady, maiden pride rising up in her, "I do not presume to take such a *personal* interest in Mr. Temple's movements!"

At this, Grayson's junior partner gives her one search-ing look, then says : "Luis! write a letter of intro-duction to your family ; I will do all I can for them!"

Here the Cuban astounds them all with : "I shall do no such thing!"

"Why not?"

"Because any document bearing my signature would, if found in your possession by the Spanish troops, be a menace to your safety ; perhaps even your life," remarks Luis, simply.   "But if you visit our plantation, say to Juan Maria Vidal : Luis Vidal, when he left his father, twice kissed his lips and mur-mured ' *libertad*,' and he will know you are the friend of my bosom and trust you as such.   You may also tell him I shall not be long after you."

"In the meantime," suggests the American banker, "Mr. Temple can easily from Havana visit your plan-tation and do everything for your family that may be necessary."

"Certainly!" cries Ortiz, a sudden light flaming in his eyes, a strange ring of triumph in his voice.   "Mr. Temple can be of great assistance to them.   Your advice is good, Mr. Grayson!"

"Excellent!" sneers Blanche, then falters : "It places *two* men in danger instead of *one*."

"Nonsense!" asserts Temple.   "There is no danger

for me. I am an American. My business on the island is well known, and when I visit the interior I shall obtain a passport signed by the Captain-General."

Then seeing a wistful appeal in the beautiful face of Miss Grayson, that seems to have grown both spirituelle and pathetic within almost the minute, an ecstacy sets the heart of this young business man beating like a trip-hammer. He makes a step towards her, and she, catching his eye, grows strangely red and then suddenly pale.

But this is broken in upon by Grayson saying in commercial tones : "The power of attorney and all the other documents are prepared. I'll get them for you, Temple, and also your passport viséed by the Spanish consul, which came up this afternoon. Remember you must dispose of all salable and shipable property as rapidly as possible."

But Temple hardly catches his words. Having seen Blanche's face, he has no thought for sugar.

" Now I'll get the documents and give you a chance to say good-by to the girls," adds the American man of affairs ; so with a glance of sympathy at young Vidal, Mr. Grayson passes into his library.

"If you will excuse me," mutters Luis, rising, " I—I will take my leave."

He is about to stagger from the room, but his sad eyes light upon the flower in Ortiz' buttonhole. He pauses and mutters to the Spaniard : "You have seen some one from Cuba lately ?"

"Why—why do you think that ?" asks Ignacio, with a start.

"You have a *Flor de Pascua* in your buttonhole ! "

"Yes, one I—I received this evening in a—a packet from Havana ! "

Then suddenly the Cuban cries : "The flower my

brother loved ! " and going to it, kisses the posy on the breast of his brother's betrayer. "*Adios!* God help me ! Good-by ! " and he leaves the room, tears in his eyes.

But even in the vestibule of the house, a delicate hand is laid upon his arm, and a soft voice whispers to him words of a womans tenderest sympathy. For a moment there is silence ; then he speaks two words and Laura Morales is sobbing on his bosom. And when the beautiful half-Cuban girl returns to the light of the parlor, her passionate face is aflame and she has some of Luis Vidal's tears upon the lilies of her cheeks and some of Luis Vidal's kisses upon the roses of her lips.

But another romance has been going on in the parlor !

The joy that Blanche's anxiety for him has placed in Howard Temple's heart has not left it. In truth, it is being added to, for as he looks on the girl, he notes a strange, wistful bashfulness in her attitude, though a most alluring witchery in her lovely eyes.

Perchance in them there is penitence also, for something in the young man's face tells her, that since he left her side, he has suffered.

Catching this glance directed at Temple, Ortiz, as he gazes upon Blanche's beauty, snarls covertly behind his white teeth and goes into a short confab with Satan. For a moment, the agony of despair ripples over his pallid cameo features ; then a strange flush of unholy triumph lights his eyes ; he even smiles as he remarks in a suave voice : "You do a favor for Luis in Cuba, Señor Temple. Will you also do one for Ortiz ? "

"Certainly, my dear fellow," answers the American in happy voice. "What is it you wish ? "

"The communication I received from Havana within the hour requires an immediate answer. The mails are now closed. You sail at sunrise to-morrow morning. Will you take it with you and favor me by delivering it in person? It is of the utmost importance!"

"With all the pleasure in the world!" cries Temple.

"Then I will prepare it at once!" replies Ortiz. But turning his eyes upon his unconscious victim, as in the first flush of unhoped-for joy the young man gazes upon the woman he had thought lost to him, but now believes may yet bless him, the Spaniard hesitates. "A fine fellow! A generous fellow!" he thinks. "One who has done me many favors. *Diablo!* I'll give him *one* chance!"

"You'll find writing materials in the reception-room, Señor Ortiz," suggests Blanche, as she advances a step or two towards him, her white hand pointing the way in bashful yet eager suggestion; for perchance Miss Blanche divines that a *tête-à-tête* with Howard Temple will now be fatal to her.

"My swain looks very determined," she thinks, with a bashful flutter, as her eyes rest on Temple, who has turned from her and is glancing at a book, though whether it is in Hindostanee or Anglo-Saxon, he knows no more than a blind man.

Suddenly towards the fair girl, with directing hand, Ortiz takes one step. Then the beauty of the embodied loveliness before him puts fiery passion into his Southern heart. "For her," Ignacio thinks, "I would lose my soul!"

And if ever the possession of a woman would pay for purgatorial pain, Blanche Grayson now looks as fair and pure a bribe as ever Satan offered, and Lucifer, in his day, has given some rare beauty prizes to tempt masculine passion.

Miss Grayson is something over the medium height of women, but her lithe, graceful, girlish figure promises—nay, is already a grand maturity. The light tissues of her evening gown give sylph-like graces to the curves of Venus that they cover. Her white arms and dimpled shoulders spring, from the clouds of her costume, dazzling with snowy luster and chiselled in the fair proportions that Athenian sculptors gave to the women they loved.

But as Ortiz gazes—and he is a man full of that artistic taste which moralists call sensuous—it is the face that enthralls the soul! That face with pure, flashing, resolute, blue eyes and brow of intellectual power, yet made by lips of passion and chin of feminine subtility, of almost infinite possibilities of joy or sorrow; one that says to him: "To the man I love, I am a Juliet with modern reason! To the man I hate, I am a Medea, without mythological embellishments! But to both, I shall be always charming, alluring, bewitching, enchanting."

In after days Ignacio recalls the Medea part of this idea more strongly than he does the Juliet portion of his mental diagnosis.

Then, passion overcoming him, Ortiz takes from his buttonhole the *Flor de Pascua*, and whispers: "Permit me to offer you this flower dedicated to the Holy Virgin; the Cuban ladies wear it on their hearts!" tendering it to her with a pathetic appeal in his soft southern voice and graceful florid gesture.

But with northern directness Miss Blanche draws away and declines his offering coolly, perchance hurriedly, murmuring: "A flower from a sunny land should have a warmer resting place than on so cold a northern heart as mine, Senor Ortiz!"

She softens her refusal by giving Ignacio a graceful curtsey that adds to the piquancy of her beauty and makes his despair the greater, then turns eagerly towards Temple and cries archly: "Howard! Papa said

he would give you a few minutes to say good-by—to
—to the girls."

Gazing on this, Ortiz emits a subdued and sighing :
"A—a—ah !" drops the flower upon the floor, crushes
it under his foot, then grimly thinks : "*Diablo !* she
loves him but she's killed him !"

A moment later he remarks, suavely but impressively : "Señor Temple I take good care of the letter
I shall give to you. It is of great importance."

"Certainly !" answers Howard, politely, though he
doesn't turn his head ; for he now has eyes for but
one being on this earth.

A second later, the Spaniard having walked slowly
from the room, Temple impetuously says : "Blanche,
you ask me to say good-by ?"

"Yes I you are going to Cuba, are you not ?" murmurs the girl, archly. Then catching something in his
face that says to her : "I shall now dare !" she starts
bashfully from him, blushes like a rose, and takes re-
fuge in the big bay-window that is cut off from the rest
of the room by draping laces.

Perchance it is with intention that she seeks harbor
on this spot, for Temple, coming after and standing
beside her, suddenly starts and mutters : "By heaven I
the flowers I sent you that I supposed you tossed to
that screeching tenor !" For in all its beauty, pre-
served most carefully in moss, stands the bouquet he
had presented to Blanche Grayson the opera-night her
coquetry had driven him to agree to leave New York.
"So you—you tricked me !"

"You tricked yourself I" answers the girl, who is
now seemingly very stern with him. "The flowers I
tossed to the screeching tenor were the gift of another
gentleman ;" adding in ingenuous innocence : "But I
forgive you," and looks at him with noble dignity.

"You—you permitted me to think——"

"I was too proud to defend myself! But now that you acknowledge you are wrong, I will be very frank with you, Howard, and admit I acted abominably."

"Blanche, do more! Two days ago I asked your father for your hand."

"Ah! then, as his daughter, my *duty* is to listen."

"A *duty*, Blanche?" says the gentleman, sternly. "Then, I shall not exact it!" and he moves glumly away from her.

To this she falters, "You—you seem anxious to make your last hour in my company a short one. Will you not even say good night?"

"To *you*, I would never say 'good night.'"

"Oh, gracious!"

"Blanche! I offer you all a man can offer a woman; my heart, my name, my life! And you say your *duty* to your father *compels* you to listen!"

To this Miss Elusive whispers, droopingly with averted face: "You choose to ask my father for me as if I were a French girl, therefore I answer you as one. If you had come to me like an American—" she stands before him erect as Juno.

"Ah!"

"And said," the young lady is drooping a little now, "'Blanche Grayson! I, Howard Temple, love you,' the American girl would have said to you——"

"What?" He has caught her in his arms, but she, drawing from him, half laughs: "You have not said you loved me!"

"Then listen! I adore you! Every thought of my future is linked with your bright face; every beat of my heart is a love-throb for you. With you by my side, I am happy. Make that happiness eternal; be my wife! Now throw away pride and let your heart answer mine!"

Even as ne speaks, he reads his answer in her eyes.
"Howard, I will be your wife!"

Her words are driven back upon her fair lips by the
first kiss she has willingly received from any man, save
her father. For, until this evening, Blanche Grayson
has been haughtily distant to the other sex; perhaps
from an innate pride, perchance from a feeling that she
will give no portion of her heart to any man without the
whole of his.

And this feeling springing up in the girl's mind—
now she has taken her leap and has thrown herself,
heart and soul to the man whose caress gives her rapture and content—she murmurs: " I will be your true,
your loving, your devoted wife, Howard Temple!
Let that be your gauge of love for me! always, truth
entire! the same devotion as I give you—and I will
make you the happiest man on earth; that is, if you
love me as I love you."

Then she suddenly half screams, in astonished voice:
" An engagement ring? " for Temple has taken her little
left hand in his and is putting something on its dainty
second finger.

"Certainly!"

"And you bought it *before* you asked me? You
must have felt sure of your prey. O heavens, what
supreme humiliation!" and she breaks from him, with
indignant eyes.

But Temple is no man to lose a prize already won,
and his arm draws her to him commandingly, as he
sternly whispers: "Blanche! your pride is too sensitive."

"Ah! perhaps it is a relic of some old love affair?"
"It is."
"Oh, horrible!"

"This was my dead mother's engagement ring. In
the wild hope that you might perhaps be kind to me

D

when I was leaving you for a foreign land, I brought
it with me, hoping you might consent to wear it, knowing that months will pass before I shall again clasp
your dear hand to place another badge of my love upon
it. Blanche, shall I put this on your finger?"

"Yes! Forgive me! I adore you!"

But this tableau is punctuated by a kind of shuddering sigh, though unfortunately they do not hear
it.

So, a moment after, making some noise of entry,
Ortiz, whose face is white as marble, returns, bearing
with him a packet, and coming to the gentleman who
has a flush of happiness upon his visage, and the lady
who has most burning cheeks, murmurs: "The letter
for Havana, Señor Temple."

"Almost large enough for an official document!"
laughs Blanche, attempting that easy archness by which
young ladies confess kisses.

"You wish me to deliver this in person?" asks
Howard, reading the address: 'X. Zenon Martinez,
Numéro 57, Calle La Bouba, near the Café El Relam-
pago, Habana.'"

"Yes, Señor."

"Quite a curious address!" interjects Miss Grayson,
whose cheeks are becoming their natural tint.

To this, Ortiz, bowing, replies: "It is of great importance. Be very careful of that letter, Señor
Temple."

"I will!" answers the American, and places it carefully in his pocketbook, as Mr. Grayson, making his
appearance with passport and a bundle of business
memoranda, cries: "I hate to hurry you, my boy, but
you will hardly have more than time to make all your
preparations and get to the steamer at the hour for
sailing. It is now one o'clock."

"Good gracious! so late as that?" whispers Blanche,

her face growing pale, for now she knows the agony of parting is very near to her.

"Oho! the time seemed short to you, did it?" chuckles her father, but catching a very haughty but extremely curious expression on his daughter's face, he mutters a half affrighted, half astounded: " Holy Poker!"

This exclamation Blanche answers not, except by a sudden blush, but runs to her sister who is in the next room, and looking into the brunette eyes of Miss Morales, whispers: "Luis has spoken?"

"All that a man of honor should," replies Laura. " He loves me, but will receive no pledge of my hand until he returns!"

"Ah! and you said——?"

"What any woman who loves would have said! That if he returns I will be his wife, for richer, for poorer, for better, for worse, forever!" Then seeing the love-light sparkling in her sister's eyes, Laura whispers: "Mr. Temple has spoken to you?"

"Behold!" and the girl holds up a white finger blazing with the diamond ring.

But here Grayson, having earnestly impressed the last details of the Cuban business upon Temple, suddenly cries: "Good-by! God bless you, my boy!" and calls to the girls: "Blanche! Laura! come and see the last of him!"

With this, Miss Morales, coming in to Howard, whispers: "My congratulations!" and gives him her pretty hand, remarking, with attempted blitheness: "You'll be back soon, and then——"

But this thought bringing a sadder one into her mind, to cover her emotions, she half laughs, "I'll wave you adieu from the conservatory," and runs from the room, while Ortiz, wincing, for he very well guesses to what Laura's "then" refers, shaking Temple's hand, remarks earnestly : "I will do the same, Howard, my friend. We shall hardly have the luck to meet in Cuba !"

A moment after he joins Miss Morales, so as to see no more of Blanche's face, for it is now full of a passion that makes him shiver with jealous misery.

Grayson would now add some last business words about a thousand hogsheads of sugar at Santo Espiritu, but catching his daughter's eyes, which say to him : "The parting with the man I love must be alone !" with a last squeeze of the hand and a few hurried injunctions to Temple, he walks into the conservatory also.

So the two face each other—just betrothed, just to part—and have their last moments broken in upon by the advent of Mr. Pompey Smith, who comes striding in arrayed for the tropics, a large white sun-shade in his grasp, but with wildly excited eyes and somewhat pallid lips, apparently produced by a newspaper he carries crumpled in his hand.

This worthy remarks : "De carriage am waiting for us, Mistah Temple."

"In a minute !" answers his master, angrily.

"Dar's powerful more sanguinary news from dar. Dis second extree says it is rumored dat de Spaniards is gwine to shoot Cap. Frey and all de rest of de 'Ginius' prisoners. Butcher 'em like cattle, sah ! butcher 'em——"

"Don't come here with your foolish tales. Get out !" cries Temple, savagely, as he notes his sweetheart's face grow very pale and her delicate lips twitch nervously at Pomp's blood-curdling news.

"I shall hardly be over a month or two away, Blanche," he says, reassuringly.

"Make it as short as possible !" whimpers the girl. Then forcing herself to calmness, she adds ; "I did not tell my father of our engagement. That would have only brought discussion, and I have only time to bid you God-speed—for I know you must go!"

And he, looking at her, knows how brave a woman has given him her heart, for she is whispering: "You must not think of postponing your journey. My sister's fortune must not suffer for any selfish anxiety of mine."

"Had I guessed that I should ever have been blessed by you, Blanche, we could have found some one else to go to Cuba," remarks Temple, brokenly, for now he feels this parting tugging at his very heart-strings.

"Ah! so it was my miserable pride, my insensate coquetry, that sends you to a land from which such awful news has come!" utters the girl in despairing self-reproach. And some latent dread springing into her heart, she falters: "Howard! I feel as if I had gained you only to lose you!"

To this her sweetheart says stoutly: "I have youth, health, strength." Then, in the confidence of love, he adds: "With you to live for, Blanche, I shall return!"

"A compliment is no argument, even to a woman," mutters Blanche.

"You know I must go," he says, shortly; "no one can now be found to take my place. My business honor compels my being in Cuba as quick as steam can carry me. I have given my word."

"Then fulfill your promise, but give me your promise in return."

And suddenly some strange dread, coming into the girl's mind, she draws a ring from her finger, and says, commandingly: "Here is my ring that I place upon *your* finger. So long as I see it there, so long shall I know that I am first in your heart. And by this ring do you promise me, if in that unhappy land you visit, far away from home and friends, misfortune comes to you, that you will send for me for aid. If you cannot write, the moment I see this bauble I shall know it is your cry for succor."

"This *Virginius* matter has made you hysterical, nervous, excited!" interjects Howard.

But the girl cries: "Do you promise? You don't go to Cuba unless you promise."

"By this, I swear it!"

He is about to press his lips upon hers, that have grown white whispering to him, but she stops him and mutters: "Then I swear to you, Howard Temple, by my ring and by my love, that I will find you. Dead or alive I'll find you! and now——" Her arms go around him, she murmurs: "You can kiss me all you please!" and surrenders two rosebuds to his mustache with all the trust and love a woman ever gave to man.

Two minutes after, Temple going out from her into the calm Indian-summer night, steps into his carriage.

But even as he drives away and his coupé passes the conservatory. his affianced is frantically waving her handkerchief to him, and saying: "Good-by, Howard!"

In the strength of his young manhood, he returns her salute and cries: "Au revoir, Blanche! Be back in a month!"

But the Spanish gentleman, whose eyes flame as they seek the beauty of the girl whose loveliness he now regards as his, mutters: "*Diablo!* it is forever!"

Then, bidding adieu to his hospitable host and charming hostesses, Ignacio steps out of that Fifth Avenue house, and lighting his cigar looks up at the great mansion, and thinks: "A gilded cage, and in it a beautiful bird of brightest plumage!" Next smites his hands together in agony, and whispers: "*Mi paloma*, my dove! He kissed her! But it is his last kiss of her ! My friend, Howard Temple, goes to a land where military law implacable prevails. *Por Dios !* he has a letter in his pocket ! Ha ! a *little* letter in his pocket ! Her next kiss shall be for me."

And as he walks down the avenue, Ortiz goes to humming quite blithely the air of the despairing tenor, from Martha :

" M' appari tull' amor."

BOOK II.

THE BURNING PLANTATION.

CHAPTER IV.

A CUBAN WILD FLOWER.

There is no prettier spot than the plantation of Las Palmas in that isle of beauty—Cuba. Just on the borders of Puerto Principe and Santiago Departments, the beautiful Jobabo River flows languidly beside the fair estate of Juan Maria Estrada y Vidal, on its way to the Caribbean. The purple hills of the Alta de Rompe background it, their base covered with mixed thickets of feathery bamboo, lemon and wild orange trees, interspersed with occasional towering royal palms from which the hacienda takes its name.

These thickets, made jungle-like upon the hillsides by tangled bushes of mountain coffee, vines and parasites and fringed upon the higher slopes by a few scattering, stunted cedars, gradually run into grass lands on the crowning Sierra till burned up by the intense heat of the tropical sun, the dry mountain tops barren of herbage glow with the sterility of fire. Below, all is green —vivid green ; above are soft purple mountains and a sky, blue as azure and clear as ether.

Looking from the barred opening of his sleeping room, made airy by high walls and windows void of glass and free of fleas by cemented floor and absence of rugs, Howard Temple, who has just sprung out of his

54

hammock, lets his eyes wander from the surrounding balcony about which is the perfume of the house-garden, filled with flowers and tropic fruits, and a few plantation pickaninnies in the various conditions of nudity common to dark skins in torrid lands, to the valley below, where the rich savannahs of the Jobabo are made green by growing sugar-cane, and remarks : "It *is* beautiful, but hang it, I'd like to see an iceberg ! Four days more and I'll be at Santiago ; then New York in another week and—Blanche ! "

He re-reads a letter in a handwriting that has grown very dear to him, which had followed him to Puerto Principe, and is full of descriptions of New York winter gaiety, and better still—of love, and again mutters, with a longing sigh : "Blanche ! "

His face, which has been pretty well bronzed by two burning months, becomes bright and beaming, and he turns briskly to where George Dennison, arrayed in pajamas, is enjoying his morning cup of mountain coffee and sampling a big basket filled with tropic fruits—sugar pinas, oranges just plucked from the trees mixed with a few rose-apples to give them fragrance— the first meal of the day, and cries : "Two weeks more, and New York. Eh, George? New York ! "

For Temple, having finished his business in Havana and Santo Espiritu, and sold or shipped all the sugar, coffee and tobacco stored in the great sheds of Miss Morales' various plantations, has now but to make some additional arrangements with an English company prospecting an iron mine belonging to that young lady of extensive estates in the Sierra Cobre, in the Santiago Province, and also to take a glance at a plantation in the Coffee Mountains to be ready to turn his back on Cuba.

Chancing at Puerto Principe to meet Dennison, who is representing a New York paper on the island, the two have journeyed together, and for the last two days have enjoyed the profuse, the whole-souled, the Cuban hospitality of Don Juan Maria Estrada y Vidal and his daughter.

They are now in one of the great sleeping-rooms of the Hacienda Las Palmas, eagerly devouring the first meal of the morning, that is served at five o'clock, as Cubans get up early to finish the business of the day before its heat drives them to afternoon *siesta.*

"So!" remarks George Dennison, who is dividing his time between a sugar pineapple and an orange. "The humiliation of the American people has made your business on this island rather quick and easy!"

"Yes! The *Virginius* matter didn't last long," replies Temple. "Our State Department took water beautifully!"

"And there was never a more disgraceful act of diplomacy done on earth!" mutters the journalist. "Forced by the people, the State Department demanded: First, the restoration of the *Virginius*; second, the surrender of the survivors.—Burriel had butchered first and last nigh on to sixty of the innocent Jack-tars, coal-passers and minor engineers of a vessel with American register and captured on the high sea flying the flag of the United States; third, the compensation of the families of the murdered men; fourth, and probably most important, the punishment of the Spanish officials who had practically, without trial, assassinated them; fifth, indemnity for the future. But while General Sickles, in Madrid, had by threat of war, practically obtained from the Spanish Government consent to this, our secretary in Washington, in consultation with the Spanish Admiral Polo, was withdrawing from the essential points in demand. And what is the result? The *Virginius*, is returned in a sinking condition, the butcher Burriel promoted instead of hanged, and a few thousand dollars paid in indemnity for half a hundred Americans done to death!"*

"But it made Laura's business very easy for me!" remarks Temple, attacking an orange.

"True!" answers the newspaper man. "It made Miss Morales' sugar *safe*—for the present, but it has made the life of every American upon this island *less* safe than it was before. For now the foolish Spaniards think us cowards, and will murder us at their convenience!" Then he says, prophetically: "There will be a lot more of Yankee blood shed in this island before Spain feels the vengeance of the United States!"

"Well, I am going to get out of the island very shortly," remarks Temple, and turning to Mr. Pompey Smith, who is arranging a tropical toilet for him, for both the gentlemen are habited in pajamas though their morning meal has just been brought in to them by a pretty mulatto girl, Rosalia by name, habited in no more than a light combination of chemisette and short skirt, which display her superabundant bosom and her pretty bare feet and chocolate-colored ankles with prodigal liberality, he orders: "Pomp, you can pack my valise and saddle bags. To-morrow morning, I get under way for Santiago!"

"All right, sah!" says the darky valet, showing his teeth. To this, he adds, excitedly: "Reckon de gals am itching for us to get back to New York!"

"*Us?*" cries Howard.

"Yes, sah! I includes yo', sah!" assents the Sixth Avenue dandy condescendingly, and departs from the room in pursuit of the dusky Rosalia, whose feminine graces during their short stay on the Vidal plantation

* Vide, New York *Herald*, January 5th, 1874, which contains a full account of the matter in question, together with General Sickles' indignant letter of resignation.—Ed.

have put a fleeting yet tropic fire in the heart of this frizzled gentleman, whose tremendous manners and flashy toilets have made him both the Beau Brummel and the god of the darky young ladies of the Vidal plantation.

"I don't know whether Pomp is right in regard to New York," laughs Dennison, "but I have a strong suspicion there is a little girl here who is rather—you understand, eh, Temple?" adding lightly: "The sparkle of Señorita Maria's dark eyes on the veranda last evening convicted you to any inquiring mind!"

"The child has pretty eyes, hasn't she?" assents the other easily, though his manner shows concern.

"*Child!*" mutters the journalist, astounded.

"Yes! she's but sixteen."

"But in this sunny land of quick development," returns the newspaper man seriously, "where the bud of to-day is the tree to-morrow, the miss of sixteen may be a woman of a dozen romances—though I fear Señorita Vidal is only the woman of—*one!*"

"Good God! you don't think——" mutters Temple, hurriedly, almost affrightedly.

"But I do! An outsider generally sees most of the game. When you are not looking at her, she is looking at you. Her eyes, magnificent in ordinary, as they gaze on you become even more lovely. I tell you you have never seen the supreme beauty of Maria Vidal, Howard Temple; because when you have glanced at her she has not looked you in the face." To this, he adds philosophically: "And yet, even under normal conditions, Señorita Maria is about as pretty a picture of tropic loveliness as ever danced a man's heart out of him by twinkling feet at a *tertulia.*"

"Pooh! there can't be much danger in another day!" says Temple, trying to make light of the matter, though he now recalls something he had forgotten,

under the charm of the girl's childish innocence, that
what in America is considered merely a passing courtesy from a gentleman to a lady, is in Cuba considered
a most pointed attention.

"For *you*, no!" says the journalist, earnestly.
"For her, no, also! She loves you already!"

"Absurd!" mutters Howard; but a moment after
starts, as Dennison, finishing the last of his pineapple
and coffee and preparing to light a cigar, strides up to
him and whispers: "Would the fair one you call on
in your dreams say absurd!"

"Call on in my dreams! Who is she?"

"Blanche!" retorts the newspaper gentleman; and
to Temple's inquiring glance, laughs: "Our hammocks have swung very close together this last
week."

"By Jove! you sleep with your ears open, Dennison!" remarks Howard, his face growing red as the
flamboyants that cluster the ground in the garden
outside.

"Part of my business!" jeers the journalist.
"Apropos of that, I must get under way to-day for
Havana myself, for there is no news here. I have
been loitering about the island hoping to see a brush
between the insurgents and the Spanish troops, a
rather dangerous business, though exciting. But when
the rebels are in a plantation, the Spanish troops are
out of it; and when the Spanish troops occupy a village the rebels are generally upon the neighboring
mountains."

"Apropos of the dearth of news here," says Temple,
lowering his voice, "do you know, Dennison, that I
think that our hospitable host, Señor Juan Vidal and
his beautiful daughter are not yet aware that two
months ago one of them lost by murder, a son, and
the other, a brother."

"You are speaking of young Pedro Vidal, butchered on the *Virginius?*" asks George shortly and nervously.

"Yes! They have never mentioned his death to me."

"Impossible!" mutters the newspaper man. "Two months and the father and sister not learn of a crime of such import to them, a butchery that electrified the world?"

"But there are nearly four hundred miles of bad roads and poor trail between this spot and Havana. Las Palmas is fifty miles even from Puerto Principe. Few travelers are passing, no newspapers arrive. Neither the father nor daughter has ever spoken," says Temple. "Besides, Maria Vidal would be in deepest mourning, and her dress is as light as her laugh."

"And you have never hinted at their bereavement?"

"No! On giving him my message from Luis, Señor Vidal asked me most earnestly of its sender. I told him his eldest son was well, but did not dare to say 'Your youngest son has been butchered in cold blood.' It is not pleasant, Dennison," continues Temple, "to think of taking the light out of such eyes as Maria's, the joy out of such a voice, the radiance out of such a face."

"Be careful you do not take it from her when you depart from here to-morrow," remarks the newspaper man, earnestly.

But this caution is broken in upon from the veranda, by the young lady herself.

"*Aqui*, Rosalia! Isabella! Tema!" cries a liquid Spanish voice, soft and sweet as an Italian song. "Where's little Tado? Where's imp Tado? I want him to carry an umbrella over my head when I go down to see them gather flowers for my fandango this evening!"

This can be easily heard through the great barred openings of the room by the two gentlemen inside.

"Going to have a fandango this evening!" whispers the journalist, "and the brother of her heart murdered two months ago!"

"You see, they cannot know!" answers Temple, under his voice; then adds warningly: "Be sure you do not tell them!"

"A fandango! Ay, Ay! missie!" comes in chorus from several slave-girls, as they cluster around their pretty mistress in that familiar intimacy that slavery always brings between a family and its house servants.

"*Cierto!* A fandango in honor of Señor Temple and Señor Dennison, and my natal day!" laughs the voice with music in it. Suddenly it asks again: "Where's boy Tado?"

"Dat young imp," says Isabella, a trim and pert quadroon girl, who has the honor of being Maria's maid, "has been away all night."

"Chicken-fighting, I suppose. Tado is a naughty boy," laughs the girl.

"'Deed he is," assents Mr. Pompey Smith, who has apparently strolled out on the veranda—"Dat Tado is de most obnoxious brat dat I've eber encountered—Dat Tado absquatulated last night wid my new blood-red bandana hankerchief dats I wraps my head in at night to keep out de 'quiters."

"Stealing! I shall have to have Tado punished! The loss of that blood-red bandana handkerchief must have broken your heart, Señor Pomposo!" floats through the open windows in Maria's merry voice. "But may I ask you, Señor Pomposo, to carry the umbrella over my head as I look at the flowers; the sun is so hot!"

"Dat's part of my business, Señorita Maria!" comes to Temple in Mr. Smith's grandest tones. "In Newport, at de flower shows de gals didn't tink they was complete widout me to carry de polite. Laws-a-massey, dat Miss Morales and dat Miss Grayson, and dat Miss Libingston couldn't get into der carriages on rainy days widout my holding de rumbrell ober dem as dey picked up dar petticoats out ob de mud."

"Ah, Señor Pomposo! You are so dignified, I shall have to call you Señor Pomposo. You think, as my brother Luis wrote me, that the New York belles are very lovely?"

Temple notes the soft Southern voice is earnest, almost pathetic.

"Fair to middling, Señorita Maria!" this in his darky arrogance.

"Delightful!" answers the Cuban girl. Then she ripples on, a ring of joy in her tones: "Perhaps they are no more beautiful than I, eh, Señor Smith?"

"On de ground of beauty, Senorita Maria, you'd stand a fust-rate show; but when de New York gals calls in de aid of de champagne yaller on de hair, and de French white and de Paris rouge for de 'plexion, and de anti-fat for de figger, dey is purty powerful!"

"A-a-a-h!" A half sigh floats through the window. "And I presume Señor Dennison—and—and—Señor Temple are much favored by them."

"Ebry man has to speak for himself on dat topic!" says the darky, complacently. "Know I's had nothing to complain of de New York gals."

This brings a little whimpering giggle from Rosalia and Isabella, who have given their tender yet ardent hearts to the keeping of the gorgeous Señor Smith from the North.

"Just let me draw on my labender gloves, Señorita Maria, and light my cigar, and I'll carry that red sunshade ober your head in fust rate Manhattan style!" continues the Sixth Avenue exquisite.

"Here, Tema! Rosalia! quick! a bit of fire for Señor Pomposo's cigar!" comes to them in the liquid merriment of Maria Vidal, and there is a quick patter of bare feet as the slave girls run to do their mistress's bidding. A moment after she says, in eager inquiry: "Señor Temple is not dressed yet?"

"No, he gabe me particular fits about waking him up so early dis morning."

"Particular fits? impossible!" laughs the young lady; then adds, unbelievingly, "Señor Howard has a most charming temper."

"Charming temper!" ejaculates Pomp, savagely. "You'se neber brought his shabing water to him of a morning, has you, Señorita Maria?"

"Of course I haven't," laughs the girl; "but I—I have had the honor of lighting his cigar," and the voice grows trembling, yet tender.

"As Rosalia is doing for me now!" chuckles the negro exquisite. "De attentions of dese young ladies reminds me of Saritogey!" A moment after his heavy footsteps clatter down the stairs, apparently attending the patter of the prettiest little slippers in the world, as they trip into the tropic garden.

Here Dennison, who has been languidly strolling about the big apartment, puffing a cigar, suddenly utters a suppressed snicker, steps to Temple, and whispers: "Would you like to see what 'boy Tado' is doing? He's the most devilish, yet cutest imp, I ever beheld."

So he and Howard, walking cautiously to the end of the room, where they can get a view of the veranda on the other side of the house, and stifling their laughter, see a curious sight.

In a hammock, swung over the broad balcony, is a recumbent masculine figure of most picturesque Span-ish appearance and costume. His leather trousers,

adorned with silver buttons, are thrown open, Mexican
fashion, upon his high Cordova boots, which are
adorned with long, jingling, clinking silver spurs.
Around the tropic dandy's waist is wrapped a silken
sash of brightest red, tied in a loose knot and floating down almost to his feet ; a checked shirt, open at
the breast, displays a bronzed torso, but is covered
by a short velvet silver-buttoned jacket, which makes
romantic a by-no-means ungraceful figure.   The dark
face, though picturesque, is not attractive ; its thin,
cruel upper lip and thick, sensuous under one being
covered with long, drooping moustachios, waxed in
Spanish style. A broad-brimmed sombrero, adorned
by silver cord and tassels, has fallen from the hammock on which he lies, to the cement floor of the
veranda.   Apparently, the *caballero* is asleep, for his
eyes are closed, and a half-consumed cigarette issues
from his darkened teeth.

Bending over this resplendent sleeper, in lithe and
barbaric grace, is a negro boy, of about fourteen, nude,
save his breech-clout, as the day he was born.   His
eyes are sparkling with roguish yet malicious gleam,
his cheeks are laughing, his teeth are chattering with
devilish merriment.

In his hand is a long switch of feathery bamboo.
With this he is most adroitly tickling the ear of the recumbent caballero, and imitating with strange fidelity
the buzzing of a mosquito.

Apparently it is effective, as the sleeping man slaps
his face savagely, and mutters : " *Caramba !* Mosquito ! " and turns upon his side as if to avoid the pest.

But Tado, who has now his victim in the position he
wants him, chuckles to himself : "Mendoza damn
Spaniard !   Make him tink 'squito sting him ear ! "

With this, deftly pulling from his pocket a little
gourd, he opens it, and producing two bright red

ants, whose stings are fire, drops them into the ear of the sleeping Spanish dandy, with marvelous and tremendous effect.

With a wild, shrieking, howling yell, the victim springs like a jumping-jack from the hammock, and smiting his heavy boots together in agony, makes his spurs jingle as they strike the cement floor, as he shrieks: *"Carajo! Maldito! Diablo!"* Then his eyes glare about him in astounded anguish, and catching sight of the jibbering imp, who is imitating his contortions and mocking his anguish, he screams: "You, boy, I'll have your heart!" His eyes glow with a snake's hate, and he mutters: *"Santos y demonios!* I'll have your heart!"

"Hi, hi! Catch a 'squito before um kill um!" screams Tado, jibbering and grimacing like a monkey in wild delight, as he springs over the low railing of the veranda, pursued by the Spaniard, who fills the air with his shrieks of agony and execration.

But in some twenty flying leaps the boy reaches a tall cocoa-nut tree and scurries up its trunk with the agility of a ring-tailed monkey. From this place of vantage, perched on its tuft of crowning leaves, he plucks the growing fruit, and uttering wild yells of triumph, bombards with rifle accuracy, the besieging Spaniard who tries to swarm up after him.

Heavy green fruit full of milk, batter Tado's enemy and drive the Spaniard down.

"No catch you to-day, boy," growls Mendoza, "but to-night, lad, beware, I'll have your heart!" and so turns away, replacing in his belt his long, sharp Spanish knife, for this tree is one of quite a grove of cocoa palms, and he knows in their upper tufts he would have no more chance of putting stiletto into Tado, than he would have into a jabbering ourang-outang, of which the imp is a very good counterfeit, as he an-

nounces his triumph with shrieks, yells, grimaces and
Spanish cat-calls from the branches above.

"I have bigger game to look for than you, boy, now!"
calls Mendoza threateningly. Then he turns away
and mutters to himself these curious words: "Ortiz
keep me waiting long—one, two, three—four days and
nothing come! Perhaps to-morrow better luck. His
letter say one week!"

Here, chancing to catch sight of Temple, who in an
immaculate tropic toilet of light nankeens, whitest
linen, flashing patent-leathers and Panama hat, is
sauntering down the garden accompanied by Dennison, this Spanish dandy's eyes light up with greater
ferocity and more lurid fire than even when he glared
upon his boy tormentor. He snarls sententiously:
"*Diablo!* The *Americano rico* pursuing the footsteps
of Señorita Maria. He also hungers for her glances!"
With this, jealous anguish coming into his eyes, they
fill with Latin tears, he smites his hands together
in vivacious misery and moans: "Maria always look
at him; she never look at Mendoza now. *Infelis*
Mendoza, he who wears his bravest garments for her
eyes, no longer has consideration. A Castiliano of
purest blood is despised for an American pig!" Then,
in a low sighing breath of rapture, he mutters: "*Santos*, but she is beautiful! *Ojos Criollos*, ah, Creole eyes!
If I could but see the signal from the hill top. Then
I would know if to-night the plantation, and she, *O
Diablo, she*——!" and he sneaks off through flowering
shrubs and gorgeous trees to carefully inspect the purple mountain to see if it will not give to him from some
as yet unobserved point the signal of coming triumph.

And Mendoza *is* right. *Ojos Criollos are* beautiful.
At least Temple thinks so, as after strolling through
some long vistas of lime hedges and white blossomed
orange trees, Dennison and he reach a little glade in

the garden in which a fountain babbles coolly, and gaze upon a pretty picture.

Swinging carelessly in a hammock with one dainty foot from which the too-large slipper has fallen, poked coquettishly from it, is the young mistress of the plantation. Two big palm trees support the swinging couch and shade it with their graceful leaves. Fanned by one or two of her dusky maidens, and covered with gorgeous Cuban flowers tossed on her by the plantation field hands as birthday offerings, Maria reclines languidly in fairy grace surrounded by a pyramid of gorgeous color, that frames but cannot increase the loveliness it decks.

To this beauty is now added a strange emotion that makes Maria's dark eyes droop with modesty, and her cheeks glow with blushes, for she recognizes Temple's coming step—the step for which she is already beginning to long.

As Howard looks at her, Maria Vidal is the bud just beginning to blossom, the girl first feeling woman's passion—glorying in it, glorified by it, and yet afraid of its intensity—though it is as pure a glow as ever warmed a maiden's heart.

To her he has come, this prince of fairer mien, this knight of hazel eyes and sunnier hair than is common with the cavaliers about her.

No one since she has returned from the convent school in Havana has struck fire from her heart till this northern-business-prince, with liberal hand and manly beauty and happy manner, has come to make her think the land more fair, the sun more bright.

"Ah! awake at last, lazy *caballeros!*" she says eagerly, yet affecting nonchalance ; for with woman's passion comes often woman's subtility.

" I hope Pomp has not been slandering me ! " laughs Temple, giving an uneasy glance at his factotum, who stands with airy arrogance under his red sunshade, permitting himself to be admired by Rosalia and other dusky beauties.

"No, I hasn't giben you away *yit*, Massa Howard!" remarks Mr. Smith conservatively.

"But he is going to!" laughs Maria, "he was telling me how beautiful the New York young ladies were! He was also informing me what I hope is not true; that you, Señor Dennison, think of leaving us!"

"Yes, I am sorry I cannot remain longer, Señorita Maria," remarks the young newspaper man, "but there is no news here, and news I am after!"

"But couldn't you write a description of my fête and fandango. It is in honor of both you and Señor Temple and my birthday! Señor Howard, I am as old as that palm tree," she laughs. "Count its notches, and you have what I am told young ladies are anxious to conceal in colder climates."

"*Very* anxious to conceal it when they are but sixteen," says Dennison.

"Indeed, Señor?" rather haughtily.

"Yes, about twenty is considered the marriageable age in New York!" suggests Temple lightly.

"So *old* as that? What a *muchachuela* you must think me!" The girl turns from him; her eyes become full of tears. Suddenly she dashes these away, springs from the hammock, and standing before the Manhattan Adonis, courtesies to him and gives him the witchery of a glance made coquettish by deft Spanish use of fluttering fan. Then looking him straight in the face, with burning, yet pleading, orbs, she demands: "Am I a child, Senor Temple?"

"By Jove, no!" cries the young man astounded.

For this is what he sees!

Cheeks of ivory tinted by roses; eyes, like heart's-ease flowers whose black seems violet, yet glowing with vestal fire ; lips graceful as Cupid's bow, red as spring rosebuds, and dewy with woman's tenderest passion. The whole a face capable of a grand love and noble sacrifice, but made coquettishly naïve by a kind of childish archness that ripples over her features with every emotion of her soul—and she has many.

Beneath this is a figure of tropic beauty and development ; the graces of a girl, the outlines of a Hebe, with smallest feet and daintiest hands, and limbs rounded and bosom moulded as if they had been chiseled marble, and then, too fair to be inanimate, had been given the glow of most vivacious life.

All these charms are veiled in softest snowy muslin and draped about the petite, lithe and willowy waist with Spanish scarf of lightest, yet pinkest, gauze.

As he gazes, her face startles Temple, for Maria Vidal seems to have changed—even within the night. She who had bidden him *buenos noches* the evening before as almost a child, now seems to him a woman.

CHAPTER V.

"STRANGE, HE ESCAPED SO LONG."

MENTAL as well as physical evidences of this shortly become apparent.

Don Juan Maria Estrada y Vidal, the young lady's father, having joined the party to say *buenos dias* to his guests, likewise perceives it. This gentleman of Castilian punctilio, yet Cuban patriotism, after greeting the young men in the effusive manner of the island and remarking : "Señors, I kiss your hands !" casting his eyes upon his dainty daughter, laughs slightly and remarks: "Eh, Maria *mia ;* pink silk stockings and slippers of satin this morning? And yet before you came, *caballeros*," he smiles to the young men, "this little witch used to run about the plantation in bare feet!"

"*Mi padre!*" cries the girl haughtily, her eyes flashing. "Remember by the memory of my dead mother that I am sixteen years old to-day!" Then goes on with blushing face and almost tearful eyes to Temple: "My most honored father only remembers *before* I went to the convent where I learned to read and write and that ladies do not run about in *déshabillé!*"

A few minutes after, walking by Howard's side and looking wistfully at him as the party strolls back to the house for earlier breakfast than usual because of Dennison's anticipated departure, she murmurs archly: "What would you think of me, Señor Temple, in bare feet?"

"I should think the bare feet most charming!" mutters the young man, compelled to answer.

Her answer horrifies him: "*Santa Maria,*" laughs the girl, "then you shall see me in *bare feet!*"

And apparently having become a child again, she goes prattling to him of her school life in Havana convent, giving him some juvenile reminiscences with rare vivacity and artless ingenuousness, yet all the time showing to him this wild flower of the tropics has a lovely heart, exquisite sensibility, and impassioned temperament.

Suddenly Temple remarks astonished: "You—you are speaking to me in English."

"Why not?" returns the young lady. "At the convent I had an American young lady to share my room. Her father was in the tobacco business in Havana. It's easy as a child to learn any language—I speak English in compliment to you."

As they reach the veranda, Vidal, who has preceded
them, chatting with the American newspaper man, turns
about and says : "How shall I persuade Señor Dennison to remain with us ? "

"By feeding him on his regular diet, news, I
imagine ! " suggests Temple.

At this the party burst out laughing, as they stroll
in to a typical Cuban breakfast, its hospitable board
covered with luscious tropical fruits, its *olla podrida* of
meat, vegetables and the omnipresent garlic, its inevitable eggs and fried plantains ; and, in addition,
chickens, light claret and mountain coffee; the finest on
this earth.   Besides this, ever plentiful cigars lie convenient to their hands and the burning lignum vitæ
charcoal is always ready to give them fire.

As they sit down, their host, gazing out of the window, remarks : "In a few weeks more, if you will
stay with us, Señor Dennison, you will see the great
smoke coming from the chimney of my sugar mill in
the valley, and be able to write an article about the
flaming fires of bagass under my boiling kettles.   It is
a picturesque sight at night."

But here he is interrupted by an affrighted exclamation from Maria, who during his remarks has been
daintily inspecting the fowls, which seem both tough
and stringy.

She has just put her white teeth into a morsel of
pullet that is on the plate before her, and now screams
affrightedly : "That stupid cook !   I told her the best
chickens on the plantation, and she has ——"

"*Caramba!*   Murdered my two toughest and bravest game cocks ! " cries the Cuban planter, in a tone
of horror and dismay.

Temple and Dennison would burst out laughing did
not old Vidal's countenance show he feels the awful
loss.

A moment later, however, plucking up spirits again, he laughs himself, and remarks : "I think the whole plantation has gone crazy on account of Maria's fandango. She wishes to make it a great success for you gentlemen. I have gathered up the music of the neighborhood : two violins from Jose Reviera's plantation, only five miles away ; a banjo and guitar from Guiterez's hacienda, at a little greater distance. These with our local talent of tom-toms and mandolin, will make music second only to a band of wandering Spanish students."

"*O Dios !* it will be a great sight," cries the girl, " with all the torches in the palm trees. If but Luis and Pedro were here to enjoy it with me, then I would be indeed happy ! "

At the mention of her brothers, the journalist giving a significant glance at Temple, breaks in hurriedly : "But news is what I am after here, and news in this country means fighting." Then he goes on with the anxiety of a newspaper man for his pabulum : "I hear that the rebels—I beg your pardon, Cubans—are again active in this Eastern department."

"I believe so," returns the planter, his eyes lighting up. "Under Vincente Garcia they sometimes come as near as those hills."

"Then if I remain I may see some fighting, you think ? " asks Dennison eagerly, and would run on in this strain did not Maria turn upon him with flashing yet tearful eyes and ask indignantly :

"Do you love bloodshed and misery ? "

"No ! " answers George, " but I love news ; and news in this country means bloodshed and misery."

But at this moment wild cries come from the veranda. Mr. Pompey Smith is heard screaming in darky despair : " Laws a massey ! Look heah, Massa Temple ! Dat infernal yaller Tado has got your new tile that

you wore in Havana, and oh, good lordy!" there are
tears in the darky exquisite's voice, "Be insensible
villain has got on my new banana-colored kid globes!"

But Pomp does not need to report the matter, for the
grinning face of the negro imp, looking grotesquely
comical under a Fifth Avenue stove-pipe, pops into the
open entrance of the room, and Tado says with picka-
ninny directness:

"Say, Massa Temple, gibe me dis hat! I only took
it fer de fandango dis ebening; gibe um back to yo'
to-morrow mornen!"

"Yes, and a real to put in it!" laughs Howard, and
chucks a silver coin to the grinning ape who does not
enter the room, keeping discreetly out of reach.

Flipping this in his hand, the urchin cries triumphantly: "Say you, Pomp, won't we make it hot fer
de gals dis ebening?" and cuts a joyous caper.

"Pomp!" falters Mr. Smith, crushed by the familiar-
ity of his kickabout tormentor, "Yo please address me
as Mistah Smith, sah! And yo gibe me back my ba-
nana kids at once. Yo heah!" But the urchin with
many wild antics, skips off the balcony and dashes in
the direction of the negro quarters.

Still, quick as he has done so, Dennison has caught
a significant look from this wild boy thrown to his
pretty mistress, a glance that seems to say: "I have
news for you! Follow me!"

"I am sorry, Señor Temple," says the Cuban planter,
"that Tado has taken liberties with you; though,"
adds the old gentleman, laughing despite himself, "he
takes liberties with all of us. Of course, Tado should
be punished, but he is my dear Pedro's boy, and played
with his young master when the son of my old age
was a little fellow himself about the plantation."

"Yes, Pedro!" mutters Howard huskily, rising from
the table and strolls out on the veranda where Denni-

son joining him, he whispers : "Good God, they cannot know ! "

"And we must never tell them ! " mutters the newspaper man.

Then after the manner of men who have grown good comrades in their travels, the two say adieu, for George's horse, with a mounted servant provided by his hospitable host, to accompany him to Puerto Principe, is waiting for him at the door.

" Shall I mention you to Miss Blanche when I arrive in New York?" whispers the journalist significantly.

"Nonsense ! " laughs Temple. "I shall be in New York before you. You will find me at the Union Club."

"And you will find my club at the editorial rooms of my paper," remarks George, as the two clasp hands, and both mutter :

"God bless you ! " Temple suggesting earnestly :

" Have you got your passport safe ? "

" In this country, I always take good care of that," answers the correspondent.

With another clasp of the hands, and some farewell words to his host and young hostess, George Dennison runs down the steps, and mounts his horse.

This is watched by Temple from the veranda. To him Miss Vidal strolls out and adds waving handkerchief to his adieu. While doing this, though she chats easily to the gentleman at her side, telling him how she would like to visit the great world, some letters having come to her from her brothers proclaiming its wonders and delights, her eyes at times glance toward Howard, as if she feared that he also might say *adios* soon.

Noting this, and deeming this a good opportunity of breaking his news of coming departure, Temple cries :

"Good-by, again, George!" and as the journalist rides down the avenue of pretty lime-trees that leads to the dusty road he calls out after him : "Had you remained a day or two longer, I would have gone with you myself!"

Here the girl's pathetic, startled eyes stop him.

"Señor Temple, I—I had hoped," she falters. Then, her words choking in her fair white throat, Maria Vidal murmurs : "I did not think you would be a—a bird of passage!" and flits into the house, as if she feared this handsome young *caballero*, who has brought light into her life, may guess the secret that makes her heart throb wildly, and her soul cry out within her.

Gazing on this with perturbed eyes, Temple thinks : "I should have gone with Dennison!" and would take departure himself this very day if he could find convenient excuse in arriving telegram of hasty business.

But this dreamy spot is far away from the bustling telegraph world, so after a few hasty puffs of his cigar the young man goes to his room, and gives Pomp additional directions for their departure on the morrow.

Then, like all the rest of Cuba during midday heat, he turns into his hammock for an afternoon siesta.

From this he awakes, to hear the hum of negroes clearing out, for the fandango of the evening, a long, open, thatched shed, located under some big *palmas reales*, that stand quite near the house ; for as the sun declines, and the heat of the day passes from it, the plantation becomes a thing of life once more.

He steps from his room to the great shanty, which is open on all sides, it consisting simply of a huge thatched roof of leaves and grasses supported by the trunks of unsquared royal palms, and rafters made of the same wood, and carelessly watches the field hands decorating it with flowering vines and creepers, and hanging torches and candles about it for evening illu-

mination. Their joyous cries and excited African jabbering soon make the young man eager to get away
from their noise.

He strolls into the garden, instructing Pomp to bring
out to him one of the inevitable rocking-chairs of a
Cuban house, directs him to place it under the shade of
a big ceiba tree. Then lighting one of the far-famed
Yara Principes, that are peculiar in this region, this
young gentleman sees the image of his beautiful betrothed in the light wreaths of blue smoke that float
about him. His eyes gleam. He thinks: "When next
I travel, I shall have a companion."

But here Spanish eyes come to him and awake him
from his day-dream. A soft voice murmurs: "Your
friend has gone, Señor Howard. Are you not lonely?"

Looking up, the American sees Maria Vidal, in all
the glory of a Spanish evening toilet; a black lace
mantilla draped Seville fashion over her graceful head,
and held in place by a high Spanish comb that crowns
the glory of her soft tresses, the low-cut bodice of her
robe showing shoulders and arms of dazzling whiteness
and exquisite proportion; the short skirt permitting
glimpses of ankles of fairy mould and two little pretty
feet habited in pale silk stockings and slippers *de bal.*

"You see I am ready for my fête this evening,"
laughs the girl, waving her fan, and adding archly:
"But you have not said you are lonely."

"Well, I am;" remarks the gentleman, and, vacat-
ing his rocking-chair, he takes seat on a neighboring
bank of flowers as the young lady accepts his invitation.

"Tado is going to contest the honors of the fandango
with Mr. Pomp this evening, the boy tells me," she
says excitedly. "You must pardon Tado's liberty
with you to-day. He promises never to offend again.
You know he was the favorite of our little Pedro. So

we can't be very strict with him. But you don't answer—your head is turned from me."

"This is a very retired spot," says the gentleman,
in nervous enquiry. "Little news reaches you?"

"Very," answers the girl.

"But you have heard of the *Virginius?*"

"Oh, that awful massacre!" whispers the young
lady. "Papa sent to Puerto Principe for a newspaper."

"And in the list of executions?" ventures Howard.

"We saw the names of many dear friends, but
neither Luis nor Pedro, and then together my father and
I thanked God," says the girl, and, raising her eyes in
gratitude to Heaven, crosses herself devoutly, adding
a moment after in careless parenthesis: "The paper
had been a little torn by the lazy negro who brought
it. But what's the matter with you? Your face is
always turned from me, now!"

For Howard, with averted head, is thinking: "Poor
sister, poor father!"

Suddenly Maria cries lightly: "You shall look me
in the eye. I have news that will make you happy."
For all this time there has been a curious excitement in
the girl's actions.

"Little Tado brought good news from the insurgent
lines to-day," she whispers cautiously, almost tremblingly, "A message from Luis!"

"Ah, he is in the island!"

"Yes, *Capitan* Luis Vidal landed with the last expedition Quesada sent from America!" murmurs Maria
proudly. "Luis, your friend and my brother, will be
here this very night!" There is a ring of joyous excitement in the sweet voice.

"But is this visit to you safe for him?" asks the
American suddenly.

"We think so, or God forbid that he should come!

No Spanish troops have been here for several weeks.'
Then she adds nervously ! "But for one thing, I should
know it was safe—Mendoza is here ! "

" Who is that fellow ? "

" A Spanish adventurer who has been for the last
week or two hanging about this plantation," answers
the girl simply.

Noting a ripple of disgust run over Maria's vivacious features, the gentleman queries : " What brings
him here ? "

"Cuban hospitality forbids us to ask.   At times I
think he is a spy employed by the Spanish general at
Puerto Principe and comes on his business, and I fear
him.   At others," here the girl's face begins to blaze,
" I think he comes on an errand of his own, and then
I—I fear him and his mission even more."   The dark
eyes have tears of shame in them.

" Humph !   Has he ever spoken ? " queries Temple
angrily.

" *Diablo !* " cries the Señorita, her face aflame, her
bosom throbbing, "the accursed Spanish adventurer
would never *dare !* " and the American sees something
in Maria Vidal's face that tells him at proper times she
may do great things

But at this moment Mr. Pompey Smith, who has been
busy with valise and saddle-bags, comes hurriedly
from the house and shouts : "Say, Massa Howard !
Do yo' want dat shabing outfit packed into the saddle-
bags so as to be ready fo' de road to-morrow ? "

As he speaks the fire in the beautiful eyes dies in
them.   " The road to—to-morrow ! " whispers the
girl, a sudden misery coming into her face.

"Ob course, Señorita Maria ! Ain't I getting de
baggage ready ? "

" The baggage !   For—for what ? " the voice is very
low.

"De baggage fo' us to leabe to-morrow, to take the steamer at Santiago. Dat's what's de mattur!" cries the valet joyously.

"Put the shaving materials wherever you please!" mutters Temple savagely. He notes the curious agony in the beautiful face, and though he is no vainer than the rest of men, guesses.

"Anything else, sah?" this is from the negro valet.

"Nothing."

And the servitor returns to the house languidly, as Maria, who has started up as if affrighted, mutters: "You are going to—to leave us so—so soon?"

"I have over-stayed my time, already."

"But not your welcome. Howard—that is, Señor Temple, why—why depart?" and the girl is before him, a witchery of reproach in her eyes that might make many men forget.

But Howard Temple loves but one woman—can love but one.

The magic beauty of his fair fiancée in New York comes to him, and he returns perchance in kindly coldness: "Other duties call me away; I have to go back to New York," then adds, thinking to turn the matter off as lightly as possible, "In America I am a veritable slave."

"O Howard, a *slave?*" This in a tone of horror. Then the girl opening her eyes, laughs roguishly: "Tell me who is your master, and I will buy you; you shall be *my* slave!" and again sinks into the chair near him.

"Supposing it were a mistress?" suggests the young American.

"A woman, a *mistress!*" And Maria Vidal's orbs, blaze. "Then I will pay double the price!" she cries, and looking at his stalwart figure with admiration, remarks naively: "At how much are you valued?"

F

"Very highly !" laughs Temple, "but I am only a slave to my business." Then after the manner of men trying to apologize for leaving beauty in distress, for the girl's lips are twitching and her eyes have unshed tears in them, he murmurs : "It may not be forever; some day I may return."

With this her passion breaks out.

"Return—O Howard—*return!* I should go mad with joy !" Then modestly conquering rapture, she contrives to suggest : "I—I mean I should like to see you very much." But falters : "I—I am afraid !"

"Afraid of what ?" asks the cavalier, trying to make his tone careless.

"Afraid that when you return to great America," the liquid voice is soft as falling dew-drops, "to that land where, they tell me, the women are fair as the angels in altar pictures, that you will forget this—this deserted plantation and *me !*"

"Would you like a souvenir of my visit ?" mutters the gentleman, whose head had been averted, but who has noted the changes in the girl's voice.

"Howard, how kind you are !" She has turned upon him, a wild joy in her face.

"A—a little birthday present ;" he says lightly, "that is nothing to thank me for. Here, choose what you like !" and he holds out a watch chain, that according to the fashion of that day is embellished with several pretty little trinkets, rather congratulating himself he has acted quite diplomatically in the matter.

But Maria unheeding the baubles, suddenly pounces upon the flaming diamond on his hand, and cries : "I choose this one !"

At this, consternation comes on Mr. Temple, the diplomatist. Half starting from her, he mentally ejaculates : "By Heaven, Blanche's ring !"

Then, for her pretty fingers are on the trinket, he asks : "Why do you choose that one?"

"Because," says the girl in tender archness, "I know by the number of times you look at it, and the peculiar light that comes into your eyes whenever you see it—that you prize it so highly that some day you will be sure to return to reclaim it." And she tries to draw the circlet from his finger.

But he mutters nervously : "I— I cannot part with *that.*"

"You gave me my choice!" cries the young lady. "O Howard, do give it to me! I must, I will, have it!"

But here artifice comes to Temple, just in time, for her agile hands have half pulled the ring from his finger.

He says earnestly, yet cursing himself for the ruse : "Let me place another on your hand. This one, my seal ring, with my own monogram upon it—my own ring."

"Place it upon my finger, Howard."

As he does so, Maria Vidal looks at him with eyes that make him think : "It's lucky I am going away to-morrow."

Inwardly anathematizing himself for carelessness in a matter of etiquette that he should have looked at from the Cuban point of view, and with a dread that he will leave some sorrow in the heart of this beautiful girl, Temple, taking adroit opportunity of the sounds of jubilee and beating tom-toms coming up the avenue, remarks : "I'll just run down and see if the darkies are all ready for the fandango."

"Don't come with me!" he commands nervously, for Maria has risen as if to accompany him, "those pretty little slippers would have a poor time on that dusty road."

With quick steps he leaves the girl, who gazing with all her eyes at him, is wondering with feminine curi-

osity: "Why did he not give me the ring I chose?"
A moment after she half laughs to herself: "I'll ask
him!"

This ring business is also in Temple's mind. Away
from the young lady he thinks: "I'll put temptation
out of Maria's dark eyes by putting Blanche's ring into
my pocket," and removing the pledge his fiancée had
given him, places it with care and reverence in his
pocketbook.

While doing this he is passing with hasty steps along
a pretty little path between tropic wild flowers, vines,
creepers and palms, and in the dusk does not note a
pair of eyes that follow him, glaring like a tiger's after
nightfall.

These are Mendoza's, driven half mad by Spanish
jealousy and Latin despair. All this day, when not
employed in looking for the sign on the mountain,
the Spanish adventurer has been wandering about the
grounds of the plantation, communing with himself
and Satan, and now—having returned from a last view
in which he sees a signal floating from a distant palm-
tree that makes him think to-night will be a triumph
to him—he has chanced to put eyes on the ring episode
between the American he envies and this girl he desires
with that sensuous, insane and passionate jealousy peculiar to his race—this dainty yet haughty maid who
has disdained his beseeching glances as well as barbaric display of *caballero* finery.

Even as he looks after Temple, he hears a light tread.

It is Maria's footstep. She is calling: "Howard, I
will go with you!" and running after the knight of
her romance.

Suddenly she is confronted by Mendoza, who mutters hoarsely: "You shall not follow that *Americano*.
A Cuban girl should have too much pride!"

"She has too much pride to take advice from such

as you ! " answers the Señorita, a haughty light coming into her dark eyes.

"But if one like me could save you a great sorrow ! "
murmurs the man. Then he breaks out half piteously :
"O Maria, can you not be Mendoza's friend ? " And
passion coming into his voice he mutters : " You have
seen how I have watched you—loved you ! "

At this, a shudder of disgust that drives him to madness, ripples the girl's light frame. She says with
voice of cool contempt : " A Cuban girl may hate, but
she cannot love, the Spanish adventurer ! "

" But she might to save a brother's life ! "

At this Maria's face grows very pale. She falters :
"A brother's life ! What do you mean ? " But, as he
would place a hand upon her, she plucks her light
dress away, and mutters haughtily : " Let me pass,
Señor ! "

"Not till you have heard ! "

" You will stand aside, Señor ! "

"Oh, be not so cold to me ! " The man's hands
would clasp the being that he longs for, lusts for.

But she screams, " *Madre mia!* Do not dare to
touch me ! "

As she speaks Mendoza thinks a tropical hurricane
has struck him ; but it is only the grasp of an ex-col-
lege athlete. He is shaken until there is little breath
in his body, and thrown crashing down into a thicket
of briars. But their smart is as naught to the agony of
his despairing, jealous heart as this girl places her hand
in Temple's and says : "Thank you, Señor—for your
protection and your valor," and her eyes add : "I
adore you ! "

" Shall I thump this scoundrel, Señorita Vidal ? "
says Howard, who has heard her voice and returned to
her.

But Maria shudders : " *Santissima*, let him go ! "

for she has noted a gleam of steel in the Spanish adventurer's hand, and knows he will spring upon her cavalier like an adder, as in truth Mendoza would, did he not chance to see a small five-shooting Colt's revolver, that, with American common-sense, Howard has always carried with him on the island.

Then the girl turns and runs from them towards the house, knowing this is the quickest way to take Temple from this man she fears.

And he, with a few light, quick steps, overtaking her, whispers in astonished, yet sympathetic voice : "Maria, you are weeping?"

"My brother!" she falters. "The Spaniard said something that frightened me for him!"

"If there is any danger, Luis must be warned at once," whispers Temple with Yankee decision.

"Yes! Find Tado. Quick, find Tado!" whispers the girl.

And he would spring from her to do her errand but discovers he is too late; for down the broad steps leading from the veranda comes Mr. Pompey Smith and whispers, his eye gleaming with excitement : "Great news, Mr. Howard! Miss Maria! Captain Luis is in de house, an' his friend, Señor Ortiz!"

"My brother here? Luis! Luis!" and calling his name, Señorita Vidal runs hurriedly into the open doorway to seek her brother's kiss.

Stepping on to the veranda, Temple sees his old New York friend, Don Ignacio Ortiz, in dusty, travel-stained riding gear, and springs forward with outstretched hand to greet him.

But the other, at the American's welcome, suddenly starts and staggers from him, seems overcome—and mutters confusedly : "Señor Temple!" as if he saw a ghost, for his face is very white and his hands tremble slightly.

"Yes. Howard Temple, and mighty glad to put eyes on you, or any one else from New York!"

"Aha! Temple, my friend!" cries Ortiz, effusively, and wrings the American's hand, though this Spanish gentleman's fingers are clammy with perspiration, and all the time he is saying in his confused mind: *"Diablo! Strange that he escaped so long!"*

CHAPTER VI.

"THIS WILL BE A GLORIOUS NIGHT!"

GAZING at Temple, Ignacio passes his hand over his forehead in a dazed way, and stammers: "I—I supposed you in Havana!"

"No, I have been in the interior for several weeks," returns Howard. "And you?"

"Ah, you wish to know of my adventures? Well, Luis and I landed near Neuvitas, on the coast, something over a week ago, in Rafael Queseda's last expedition. With our party we made our way through the mountains and joined the forces of Vincente Garcia, operating in the Eastern Department. Of course Luis was on fire to see his father and sister, so, taking our first opportunity, we left our band of armed Cubans a few miles from here, and came secretly by a mountain path to the Las Palmas."

"Don't you think it would have been more prudent to have brought your escort with you?" suggests the New Yorker, a shade of concern running over his face.

"No!" answers Ortiz decidedly. "The fewer the men with us the less chance of the Spanish troops learning of this visit and burning the plantation. See,

even the negroes are entirely unsuspicious. I understand they have a little *fête* to-night."

For to them now come the sounds of darky merriment from the thatched slaves' quarters, and torches
are commencing to flicker and burn among the palm
trees of the garden, rivaling the light of the fireflies
and *cocuyos*. Above this, floats from the distance the
soft sound of violin, guitar and banjo, the music of
the Creole.

"Yes, in honor of Señorita Vidal's birthday!" mutters Temple, contemplatively; both gentlemen are
smoking.

"*Caspita!* You do not look *en fête* any more than
I," laughs Ortiz, gazing from his travel-stained garments at Howard's costume, which has been somewhat ruffled in his recent tussle.

"Oh!" remarks the young man, "I spoiled the
whiteness of my linen by throwing a ruffian into
a canebrake."

"Indeed!"

"Yes, a brute called Mendoza, who has been loafing
about here annoying Señorita Maria."

"Mendoza!" ejaculates the Spaniard, and his tone
suggests interest; then he says lightly: "Playing
caballero to another young lady, eh Señor?"

"No, only giving to my friend's sister the protection
it is usual to accord ladies in the United States,"
returns the New Yorker. To this he adds: "From
their fandango you can see Señor Vidal and his
daughter do not know of the assassination of young
Pedro. I must see the brother does not tell them.
To-night the blow would be too cruel."

With this Temple turns to go into the house, but
suddenly pauses and remarks: "By-the-bye, Ortiz, I
must return you that letter you gave me to deliver in
Havana. I tried the address, but the people looked

frightened, and refused to receive it, saying you were unknown to them."

"Ah, you couldn't find X. Zenon Martinez !" says Ortiz, contemplatively.

"I could not. Besides, Calle La Bouba was about the most disreputable street I ever entered. Women hanging out of every window and Spanish soldiers making love to them in every doorway," laughs the American.

"But the letter? You have it with you?" There is a strange interest in the Spaniard's voice.

"Yes, with my papers and passport in my traveling bag."

"That is good !"

"I'll get it for you?"

"At your leisure."

But Temple hardly catches the last sentence, for Luis Vidal has come hurriedly out of the house and is grasping his hand. The young man is arrayed in the usual costume of the Cuban insurgent officer—high riding boots, broad-brimmed straw sombrero, light cotton shirt, and carries machête and revolver in the belt that girds his waist.

"My dear Howard," he says, "to meet you here in my father's house is a joy. It reminds me of our happy days in New York."

And he would go on in his effusive Cuban manner, did not Temple, drawing him aside and speaking under his breath, ask : "Have you spoken to your father of the death of your brother ?"

"No ! The poor old gentleman was so overcome at meeting me, I could not bear to mention the assassination of our loved one," whispers the young man.

"Then keep watch of your tongue," says the American, shortly. "He does not know of your brother's murder."

"*Madre de Dios!*" cries the young officer, striking his forehead : "Must I be the first to tell him?"

"Not this evening—now that he is happy in seeing you again," whispers Temple; then suggests warningly, "Remember, your father is an old man!"

As the two men have held consultation on the balcony, Ortiz has murmured : "I will smoke a cigar in the garden," and strolled into the grounds.

"Strange, he has escaped so long!" he communes with himself, and goes about the shrubbery, which is now glowing with fire-beetles, as if seeking for some one whom he expected.

Suddenly a voice whispers at his elbow in the dusk : "Mendoza is here, Señor Ortiz!"

"Ah!" whispers the other, "I expected you. You are prepared?"

"I am! A company of infantry is in ambush in the grove of palms by the river bank, one mile from here. Two squadrons of guerillas are picketed in the deep jungle towards Yariqua, scarce half a mile away."

"Then," remarks Ortiz complacently between whiffs of his cigar, "we may gain the five thousand dollars for Vidal's arrest to-night. I have done my work. Now do yours. Bring up the troops!"

"There is an American here," says Domingo suggestively.

"Yes. Señor Temple. I was talking to him on the veranda," answers Ignacio contemplatively. He was boasting of having insulted you in the presence of Señorita Vidal."

"*Caramba!* Was he doing that?" mutters Mendoza savagely; then whispers between white teeth : "*Muerte de Dios!* How I hate him!"

"Ah! Enough to wish his death?" says Ortiz, slowly, as if rolling a sweet morsel under his tongue, and his eyes flash as brightly as the fire-flies in the plantain leaves.

"Yes!"

"*Por Dios!* At last!" sighs the Spaniard to himself. Then he remarks quietly : "I can do you a favor."

"I thought I heard a noise," mutters Mendoza, starting.

"'Twas but a *cocuyo*," returns the other. "But still, to be safe, let me whisper something in your ear. 'Twill make you happy, Señor Domingo Mendoza," and he places his delicate, clear-cut cameo lips near the thick ear of the Spanish adventurer, who calls himself a Castilian, but who has some negro blood in his veins, and whispers eagerly to him, giving him a few delicate details, suggested with rare skill by his commander-in-chief, Satan.

Listening to this, Mendoza bursts out in horrible triumph : "*Carajo!* I shall go mad with joy!"

"You understand me?" mutters Ignacio.

"I do, and I thank you, noble Ortiz."

"Quick, then! The troops!"

"*O Madre de Dios!* This will be a *glorious* night!" laughs Mendoza, and takes his way hurriedly through the garden and into the tropical jungle, chuckling to himself in bloodthirsty glee. For he has been saying to himself half the day : "Maria love the *Americano*," and has worked himself up into a vicious, unreasoning, crazy, jealous Spanish hate. And now, as Ortiz would have done to Howard Temple in New York for the sake of Miss Blanche Grayson, so will Mendoza do to him in Cuba for the bright eyes of Señorita Maria Vidal.

Over this all, comes the sweet melody of violins guitars and banjos, mingled with the barbaric thumping of tom-toms and the wild chatter of negroes who have had a day's rest and are going to make a night of it.

Dodging the advance guard of this festival, Ortiz, still smoking, strolls back to the veranda, to find old Señor Vidal with his son and daughter by his side.

"*Aqui*, Don Ignacio!" cries Luis eagerly, and introduces him, whispering: "My father, my sister. This is my friend."

"And a friend of Cuba's also!" says the Spaniard stoutly.

"Yes, we have heard of you," remarks Juan Vidal, stroking his white mustache. "Señor Ortiz, while you honor my house, everything in it is yours."

"My brother's friend is mine!" cries the beautiful girl. "*Beso los manos de V, caballero*," and she welcomes the comrade of Luis to her Cuban home with light tropic words and pretty Creole graces.

"I have sent Tado to the outskirts of the plantation with one or two other trusty negroes," says the old gentleman in low tones. "They will act as scouts. You need have no fear of being surprised, Señor Ortiz."

"Yes, we can sit here without thought of danger, and see the negroes romp in my honor," laughs the daughter.

"Still," remarks the son, "notwithstanding the vigilance of faithful Tado, whom I know of old as the most devilish imp of black skin on this island, I will keep my machête and revolver handy." With this, he sits down, his arm around his sister's waist, looking upon her with a brother's eyes, and murmuring: "You have grown into quite a young lady, *muchachita*."

"*Muchachita* no more!" pouts the Señorita vivaciously. "You must treat me now as a young lady of the world."

"Aha! A romance already!" jeers Luis. Then, noting the blushes that fly over his sister's features, he laughs: "Have I guessed right, Miss Red-cheeks?"

Perhaps these red cheeks are because Temple has just rejoined the party, having, with the assistance of his valet, brushed the dust off his clothes and donned another shirt.

"*Diantre!* but we will make a merry night of it," cries Ortiz, though he has winced at the mention of Tado scouting about the plantation.

Then he seats himself and lights another cigar as *refrescos* of light wine, sangaree, and the ever-present Yara *principes* are handed about by Maria's laughing maids, Tema and Rosalia, these dusky beauties being in great array for the fandango, wearing chemisettes and petticoats of whitest muslin, and being decked at waist and on their hair by gaudy-colored ribbons.

Even as these wenches flit about, their nude chocolate feet seem full of the music that is now near them, for the Cuban orchestra have just taken position in the great near-by shed that has been decorated and lighted for the negroes' dance, and are tuning up and thumbing their instruments, preparatory to the opening of the fandango.

"You have no further news, Vidal, from New York?" remarks Temple eagerly, as the gentlemen smoke together.

"Oh, of Miss Blanche Grayson and Señorita Laura Morales," says the Cuban, his eyes lighting up. "No. Only that the young ladies are well, and one of them very anxious for your return."

"Which one?" cries his sister, affecting levity.

Her brother notices that the girl's manner is strangely excited, vivacious, and peculiarly charming. A new light seems beaming and flashing in Maria's beautiful eyes.

"*Caspita*, I never tell tales out of school!" he laughs; then murmurs complacently: "For the first time in two years in my old home."

"Ah, if little Pedro were only with us now, our happiness would be perfect," mutters the old Cuban.

At these words his son starts up, an execration quivering on his lips. Were not Temple's warning grasp on his arm, some wild words of his would change the *fête* into a pageant of mourning.

Perchance the father would note the excitement on the young man's face, did not, at this moment, light, quick footsteps bring Tado cautiously from the house, his face lighted up with excitement, perhaps even terror, as he mutters to them : "*Caramba!* Dar's all de soldiers in Cuba surroundin' de house, Señor Luis !"

At this the party spring up, the men with muttered curses, the girl with a slight, sighing scream. But the American whispers with quick decision to them : "Remain quietly here, till I make sure !"

To this the young Cuban captain answers firmly : "I will go with you !" loosens his machête in its sheath, and draws his revolver from his belt.

"Stay where you are !" cries Temple. "Bid your father and sister good-by. There will be no danger for me if taken by Spanish troops," and calling Tado, he runs hurriedly through the garden, the little negro boy leading him cautiously into the by-paths of the surrounding jungle.

"I shall not be captured alive !" says Luis hoarsely, and would spring after Temple, but Maria's arms are around him and his father has caught his son wildly to his breast ; for Ignacio has muttered : "Captured, Luis ! *Diablo*, you know what that means !"

To this the Cuban answers : "Think of yourself, generous Ortiz."

"There is little danger for me," returns the other. "I am a Spaniard, not a Cuban. I served against Don Carlos a few years ago. These very officers here may recognize me. At the worst, they can only prove me to be a native of old Spain. But with you, with a price on your head, you know——"

To this, Maria has faltered with sighing pathos : "*I know !* Already I hear the fatal fusillade. O Luis ! Luis ! Have you come back to us for this ? "

Over the father's agony and sister's plaint rises the soft melody of Cuban music, and the negroes' happy voices, as with tom-toms sounding and wild jabber of jubilee, the darky crowd come up the avenue to dance in honor of their master's daughter, the mistress of the plantation.

A moment later Temple returns and whispers : " The boy's report is true." Then to the girl's answering sigh he adds : " But they will not be here immediately," and with American directness, says stoutly : "Now, Maria, your brother must be saved ! "

Then they all turn and look at Ortiz, for he has seconded the New Yorker with these curious words : " And only one man in this world can do it ! "

" Who ? " asks Temple eagerly.

" You ! " answers the Spaniard shortly.

" Me ? " There is astonishment in the American's face.

" Yes. You have been browned by the tropical sun. You are not so unlike Luis Vidal. You both speak Spanish as you speak English," says the Castilian, his voice clear-cut as a music bell. " You have a passport signed by the Captain-General of Cuba. Luis has none ! Give your document to Vidal, and with that paper he can pass through the line of death that is being drawn about this plantation."

" And you will gain the blessing of a father," mutters the old Cuban.

" And the eternal gratitude of a sister," pleads the agonized girl.

Looking on them, the American answers : " You do not know what you ask."

"'There is no danger," cries Ortiz enthusiastically. "You are an American. Your business on the island is known."

Here the young Cuban captain, breaking from his father's arms, cries : "I will not, I cannot—receive safety in such a way !" and would go on excitedly refusing, offering to take his chance with machête and revolver against the line of Spanish infantry that is closing around him.

But Ortiz, leading Howard aside, whispers to him : "One son is gone. Think of his father and his sister Will you permit the last——"

He gets no farther. The American interjects : "To be taken from them ? No !"

Then striding to the unhappy family, Temple commands : " Luis, come with me ! "

Still Vidal answers him : "You are accepting a risk for me—a risk I cannot permit you to take."

To this Ortiz cries : "To hesitate is to throw away your life. *Diablo !* Look !" and points off among the palm-trees, where some half mile distant under the moon which is now rising, can be seen the gleam of steel.

And Maria following his hand with eyes whose tears are quenched with horror, gasps : "The bayonets of the Spaniards who spare no Cuban prisoners !"

At this the old planter wrings his hands and mutters : "Luis ! My eldest born ! Not on my own hearthstone ! "

"Come !" cries Temple commandingly. "To hesitate is to throw away your life. Half a regiment surrounds this plantation. Then he whispers into Luis's ear : "Think of the girl who loves you in far-away America ! Come for Laura Morales' sake, if not for your own !"

"I—O God! Laura!"

"Come!"

And his father cries to him: "At once!"

And his sister's arms are round him, imploring him; she is sobbing on his breast: "You will kill my father if you die here."

So-half dragged by his family and by his friend, Luis Vidal is drawn into the house, and in Temple's room puts civilian's garments on him, Howard assisting him and pressing into his hand, despite his hesitation at the very last, the passport that will give him life.

On the veranda calmly looking at the negroes who are now trooping through the garden, and listening to their soft music, though casting occasional glance at the gleam of the steel that is drawing nearer to the Cuban homestead, Ortiz still smoking, murmurs to himself softly, purring in a cat-like way: "*Por amor de Dios*, AT LAST!"

Two minutes after, Luis Vidal, dressed as an American traveler, mounts a horse that is hurriedly brought to him and with saddle-bags strapped behind him, and the document that means to him safety from certain death, rides carelessly down the avenue to meet his Spanish foes.

Anxious eyes follow him from the veranda, the music rising about them seeming almost the dance of death, for the old Cuban planter has commanded: "Let the *fête* go on. It will allay suspicion."

Then after a few minutes' breathless silence that is punctuated by Maria's gasping sighs, catching glimpse under the moonlight some half mile away of a figure of a man on horseback, spurring along the dusty road, Howard whispers: "See! He is waving his hand. Luis has passed the Spanish cordon."

"*Madre mia*, my brother is safe!" gasps the girl, and turning dreamy eyes upon the gentleman stand-

G

ing beside her, whispers: ''Brave *Americano* our saviour!'' For her passion for this handsome young Northern knight, who has seized upon her heart, is now idolatry, and her eyes glow bright as the stars of the Southern Cross that is flaming overhead.

Then the old Cuban hidalgo, coming to his guest, seizes the young American's hand, and kisses it, leaving tears of gratitude upon it.

As for Temple, the thing has come about so hurriedly he is still half dazed—he hasn't been able to reason coolly as he has looked at a sister's agony, and a father's despair.

As for Ortiz, he is still smoking quietly and has just blown three rings of blue vapor between his sharp white teeth.

CHAPTER VII.

''DIABLO! HE'LL NEVER WALK DOWN FIFTH AVENUE AGAIN!''

BUT Temple, in his Anglo-Saxon way, says deprecatingly: ''Don't thank me. Please do not thank me, except by your happiness.''

A moment after, for all seem quite at their ease now except the American, who cannot help thinking though he has done a generous, perhaps he has done a foolish, thing, they go down the steps of the veranda and enter the great shed to view the fandango which has grown to its height, though they have scarce noticed it.

'' *Santos y angeles!* This will be a merry dance to-night, Señor Howard,'' laughs Maria, who with Latin mutability of emotion, is now a being of joy as she flits before him, light as a nymph, into the great shed that is bright with blazing torches at every point they can be placed among the sweet-smelling flowers and tropic plants that decorate the room, making the rude apartment graceful, even beautiful—though barbaric.

"How the music gets into my veins," she prattles as she takes a coquettish step or two.

And Temple, entering after her, gives a little exclamation of astonishment, for the field hands are dancing a plantation *Zapatero* with great Spanish style and much abandon. Huge Carrobalees negroes, some of them just from Africa, are doing their barbarous steps, big Congo blackamoors, less recently imported, are trying to outfoot the dusky belles of the cane-field.

Besides there is a select party of the house servants headed by pretty Rosalia, who with Tema and Isabella, Maria's own maids, their chocolate charms gleaming under whitest chemisettes and shortest petticoats, attempt the dances of a Spanish ball-room.

Above all this floats the soft music of Cuba from jingling guitar strings and scraping violins, mingled with the smoke of plantation tobacco, for even the pickaninnies have big cigars within their grinning mouths.

Upon this scene, Mr. Pompey Smith is gazing condescendingly, arrayed as a Sixth Avenue summer darky dude, with a straw hat decked with broad red ribbon upon his frizzled head, upon his feet patent-leather pumps of great extent and brightest shine topped by whitest gaiters, above these lavender-colored inexpressibles and check plaid waist and cutaway. One delicately gloved ebony hand is languidly occupied with palm-leaf fan.

"You are not dancing Pomp," says his master carelessly.

"No, sah. I had thoughts of trying de-dip-of-Bostoon, but none of de ladies' steps heah are quite up to dat of de Manhattan coterie. Besides," whispers the valet, "I has to draw de line bery sharp 'tween a citizen of de States of 'Mericay and low-down plantation slabes."

But here Pomp suddenly gasps : "Oh, laws-a-massey ; look at de ineffable villain !"

Tado is standing beside him, his hands inclosed in banana-colored kid gloves, stolen from his despairing rival, slowly waving a palm-leaf fan, in imitation of the darky exquisite. He also leans upon a cane he carries with the same imported Sixth Avenue grace.

Gazing on the boy, Howard laughs until the tears run down his face, for the imp is habited as to the upper part of his body in Temple's black dress coat and vest ; a shirt of immaculate linen, and high white choker collar, that nearly cuts his monkey throat, makes the boy's face seem blacker from the contrast. But from the waist down, save a breech-clout, red as crimson, the scamp has no covering. His ebony legs glitter with palm oil in simple nakedness, save that his long, skinny ankles are embellished by two white, high-topped patent-leather gaiters, likewise purloined from the American's valise. These, making great display above his claw-like feet, give to the urchin a kind of ostrich-like appearance, with tufted ankles.

"Oh, good Lordy ! He has your dress coat on, Massa Temple, and, so help me Heaven, my quartz watch chain ; and, oh, deah, if he hasn't made him breeches out ob my two new silk Sunday-go-to-meetin' bandana handkerchiefs ! De ladies will excuse the indelicacy of de impression," screams Pomp, and makes a grab at his despoiler. But with half idiotic chuckle, Tado springs from him, and commences a Voodoo dance of such wild gesticulation, such uncanny poses and effects, that he looks like barbarism personified. Then, uttering all the while Dahomey outcries and Congo shrieks, he whirls like a dancing dervish around the room, until the black tails of his dress coat stand straight out from his waist, and make him look like a black marble statue draped into decency by an anti-vice society that has not done its work very well.

Over the imp and his antics, Maria and her friends all get to laughing in their light-hearted Cuban way, Ortiz the merriest of the lot, the tears running down his cheeks, though once or twice he casts expectant glances about him, and mutters to himself: "They should be coming soon."

Temple is merry also. The joy of the beautiful girl gives him delight. To have removed the anguish from those bright eyes is a pleasure to him, though somewhat embarrassing, for once or twice the young lady in Latin fervor has slyly kissed his hand, and murmured: "Grand *Americano!* My brother's saviour."

So the musicians are playing triumphantly, and Tado is still in the midst of his unending whirl, when suddenly the boy, with a shrill yell of affright, dives through the crowd and disappears in the surrounding darkness, while into this comedy, as so often happens in this world, come stalking tragedy and death.

First, the sharp barking and snarling of the numerous curs common to a Cuban house, rises into the night air, followed by their shrieks of pain as they feel Spanish bayonets. A second after, with affrighted jabber, cries and shrieks, there is a rush of pickaninnies, who have been looking in upon the festival from the grounds outside.

Over this the tramp of marching infantry is heard. Hoarse-voiced commands ring out upon the quiet of the tropic night.

"Is every entrance and exit to the house and grounds picketed?" comes to them in sharp Spanish tones,

"It is, Major.   Likewise the garden."

"Very well.   See that no one leaves this plantation while the arrest is made."

As the words ring out, a platoon of Spanish soldiers forces its way into the shed, clubbing with the butt-ends of their rifles a few scared darkies who don't get out of their path with sufficient celerity.

Then, over all this assemblage, that was but a min-ute before joyous, happy and excited, seems to come the silence of fear, for every one, even the negroes, whose faces have grown ashen blue, know the mercy of Spanish troops upon a foray.

"Your reason for entering my house, Señor?" says the Cuban planter, a haughty defiance on his face.

As for his daughter, with a whispered: "Think, if it hadn't been for you?" to Temple, she has risen, her cheeks blazing, her eyes bright, as she gazes on the uniforms she hates.

"I am Lieutenant Gonzales, of the regiment of Ma-tanzas, and come in the name of Spain," answers the officer in command of the platoon.   "We have an arrest to make."

"That's your man!" cries Mendoza, who has guided them in.

He points hastily, and before Temple scarce real-izes what is done to him, he has been seized by two savage infantrymen, as the Spanish lieutenant says sharply: "I arrest you, Luis Vidal, rebel and traitor, in the name of Spain, and by order of the Captain-General of Cuba!"

"Me,—Luis Vidal!" gasps the New Yorker; then half laughs: "You are mistaken.   I am an American citizen."

"If you are an American citizen, your passport will show it," says the officer shortly.

As the Lieutenant speaks, Howard knows he has done a foolish thing.

"My passport is—is lost or mislaid by some accident of travel," he answers hesitating for a moment, but adding firmly: "I am Howard Temple of New York City."

While this is going on, Ortiz has thrown himself in apparent unconcern onto one of several hammocks that swing under the light palm-leaf thatch outside of the shed, and is smoking carelessly.

Upon this scene the old Cuban planter and his daughter have gazed, their faces growing more anxious with each word that has been uttered.

The negroes and musicians have fled or are crouching as far away from the Spanish troops as they can get.

"Howard Temple of New York passed through our lines a few minutes ago," replies the young Spanish officer with a sneer of unbelief on his face. "He has a passport."

"You, Luis Vidal, you have none!" jeers Mendoza.

"Pooh! This lie is to satisfy your grudge against me, you hound!" mutters the American who is now regaining his composure. "You know I am an American. I am Howard Temple of New York."

Addressing himself once more to the lieutenant, he asserts: "Give me an interview with your commanding officer, and I can easily prove it."

But at this moment the major of infantry, a veteran of punctilious manner and grizzled mustachios, who has personally taken care of each exit of escape, strides in attended by a captain of guerilla cavalry, and taking seat at one of the tables devoted to refreshments, claps his hands and calls: *"Aqui muchacho!"* to one of the house-servants who is crouching near him. "The best wine and cigars on the place. Champagne! You hear me!"

"Bring the gentlemen what they order," remarks the master of the plantation with punctilious politeness.

Then, as the two sit down, making themselves comfortable, lighting big cigars and quaffing betwixt them a bottle of "Veuve Cliquot" brought by the trembling negro, the lieutenant makes his report: "The prisoner claims he is not Luis Vidal, the insurgent, but an American named Howard Temple."

"His passport," remarks the major curtly. "This wine of the French is very good, Captain Mendez," he adds, as he takes another glass of sparkling Cliquot.

"The prisoner asserts it is lost, sir," replies the lieutenant.

"*Caspita!* A curious accident," sneers the major. And the captain bursts into a hoarse unbelieving laugh.

But Temple stepping to them, though the hands of the guard are still upon him, exclaims earnestly: "I can prove my identity!" then calls confidently: "Ortiz, you speak for me."

"Your papers would be the better proof, Luis," says the Spaniard suavely from his hammock as he smokes.

"Luis?" mutters Temple. "My name is not Luis!"

"*Diablo!* I meant Howard. A—a mistake," murmurs his Spanish friend as he snaps his fingers deprecatingly and takes another whiff of his cigar.

"An unfortunate mistake for the prisoner," returns the *comandante*, severely.

"Why don't you speak out like a man, Ortiz. You seem lukewarm for me!" cries the accused indignantly.

"Your papers would be the better proof," suggests Ignacio significantly.

"Then we must see your papers!" says the Spanish commander decisively.

"And they will tell you who and what I am," returns the American easily. "Pomp, bring my satchel!"

"Lieutenant, send three men with the negro, and go yourself!" commands the major, as Mr. Smith, his eyes very big and his white teeth chattering slightly, shuffles off followed by a squad of Spanish soldiers who, in their blue and white striped uniforms and Panama straw hats pinned up by the eagle of Spain in glittering brass, covering their sun-burnt and war-scarred features, seem quite romantic in the torchlight.

As this is being done, the guerilla captain, who has been pouring down the champagne, produces some papers from his despatch-box and shows them to his superior, consulting with him. Looking over these, and glancing once or twice at the American who is still in the grasp of the Spanish infantrymen, the major remarks: "The description of Vidal and you, sir, seem to agree."

But the captain interposes, with a Spanish oath: "From my little knowledge of their accursed lingo, you seem to speak English with a perfect *Americano* accent."

"Luis Vidal was educated in New Orleans," interjects Ortiz in a musing tone, as he passes the blue wreaths of smoke from his mouth.

"So, that explains his *Gringo* dialect," guffaws the guerilla officer, as the major sneers: "He upon whom you have called to assist you seems to make a very bad job of it, *Señor Americano*."

"Ortiz!" cries Temple, into whose mind has now flashed despite himself, some suspicion. "You are better in putting a man in a false position than in getting him out of it. But my papers will explain all." For Pomp, attended by the Spanish soldiers, has returned, carrying with him a black leather despatch-box. For this Howard would reach eagerly, but the captain, springing up, pushes him aside and seizes the box, remarking with military brevity:

"All the papers contained in this are yours, sir?"

"They are."

"Your key !"

And Temple selecting the proper one from his bunch and giving it to him, the guerilla officer unlocks the despatch-box, and pours out on the table before his superior the letters and documents Howard Temple has accumulated on the island or brought with him from New York, though one, a letter, falls upon the floor near them. But not stopping to pick this up, the two, over their cigars, go to examining his correspondence, the captain, who apparently reads English, interpreting to his superior.

As they inspect his papers, their suspicion of their prisoner seems to become gradually less.

"These seem to prove that you are Señor Temple of New York," remarks the Spanish major, and at his sign the soldiers release their grasp upon the young man, who cries joyfully, for he had felt the hand of death quite close to him : "The truth at last !"

Señorita Maria is pressing one of his hands, the tears in her beaming eyes, and her father is wringing his other silently.•

"Now, if you will explain how your passport has been lost or stolen, I will listen to you," remarks the *comandante* suavely.

But Ortiz, still lying in his hammock, suggests : "A letter that fell off the table."

"Yes, I saw it," cries Lieutenant Gonzales, and, picking it up, hands it to the captain, who reads slowly the address :

"X. Zenon Martinez, Numero 57 Calle La Bouba, near the café El Relampago, Habana."

"That letter is not mine," declares the American carelessly, still grasping the planter's hand.

"You said *all* the papers in the despatch box were yours," returns the guerilla captain.

"Yes, but that is the letter you gave me to deliver in Havana, Ortiz," answers Howard, in easy assurance.

"I—I don't remember any—such—letter." This comes from Ignacio contemplatively, and is answered by a start of surprise from the American.

"You seem to be anxious to escape the responsibility of this, sir!" says the commanding officer sharply. "It is addressed to a rebel name in a most suspicious locality. I shall open it." Breaking the seal, he glances hastily over the epistle and some documents, written on tissue paper in the smallest handwriting, that are enclosed within it.

"*Caramba!*" he cries, "we have him!" and commands savagely : "Arrest that traitor!"

In an instant Temple is pounced upon by half-a-dozen stalwart hands despite his protests that are answered by blows with clubbed rifles that half stun him. He is manacled and tossed down at the feet of his captor.

"What does it contain?" he gasps astoundedly.

"Despatches to the rebel leaders, a statement of the Spanish garrisons in Cuba in detail for their use, besides a confidential communication from the Cuban Junta in New York," guffaws the guerilla captain, merrily.

"Enough to kill a dozen men!" adds his commander severely, then sharply orders : "Search the prisoner!" and turns away chatting and laughing with his captain and paying but little more attention to his captive, who is now receiving Spanish mercy.

Among the agile hands that despoil the American of everything of value those of Domingo Mendoza are the quickest and the ablest.

A moment after, in answer to Ortiz' signal, the spy has glided to him and pressed into his hand something that glitters, muttering ; "This is what you wanted."

Inspecting the curious setting carefully, the Spanish recreant murmurs : "It is well ! I missed it from her finger, I knew she had given it to him."

"You *shall* hear me. I *will* explain !" cries the American faintly, for he has been bruised to semi-insensibility by his captors' blows.

"Silence! You are doubtless Luis Vidal," says the lieutenant, raising his sword threateningly

But the Cuban girl is beside him, her bosom flashing in the moonlight as it beats tumultuously, her face whiter than her bosom, her lips pale as the death that seems to be coming upon the man she loves, as she screams : "He is not my brother !" then begs : "Father, tell them—tell them the truth !"

And the old Cuban planter, stepping forward with Castilian punctilio, says, falteringly : "Major, a word with you. This gentleman is surely Señor Howard Temple of New York. My son, Luis Vidal, captain in the insurgent army passed through your lines but a few minutes since on a white horse. Pursue him but spare the stranger," and smites his hands together, for he knows he has brought peril on his son as he hears the quick commands given for a squad of guerilla cavalry to take the road towards Puerto Principe, and capture the man who has given passport to them, dead or alive.

Still the Spanish officers scarce believe him, for Ignacio laughs : "A father and sister would say anything to save the man they love."

"Ortiz, you gave me that letter," implores the American, upon whose brow is gathering the sweat of despair. "Tell them the truth ! Don't murder me !"

"The truth tells itself," purrs his betrayer, as he still smokes in the hammock.

Here, bursting from the throng of negroes that are

crouching about, Mr. Pompey Smith cries into Ignacio's sneering face : " If you is a white man, Ortiz, I's proud I's a nigger."

But he gets no further: A muttered, "Seize the escaped slave !" from Mendoza, and a couple of Spanish infantrymen club Pomp to silence with the butts of their muskets. For this is the beginning of one of those horrors common to that unhappy land where *pacificos* get slight mercy.

"Put a *candela* to this nest of traitors ! Order the troops below to fire the sugar mill and the negro quarters. The slaves and property of the father of a rebel taken in arms shall be our loot," commands the Spanish major, quaffing the last of his champagne, and lighting another cigar.

Accustomed to this business, half a dozen rough troopers seize the torches that were lighted for the *fête* and apply them to the dry thatch of the roof overhead, and, even while they do so, a scream comes from the surrounding women and children, for they see the red glow of their burning huts lighting up the palms and cocoanut-trees.

"It is easy to understand," mutters Temple to the Spanish lieutenant, who is still grasping him by the shoulder, "why that man implicates me. He is afraid of punishment himself."

"It is useless to try and criminate me," says the Spaniard springing up from the hammock.

And the major remarks : "Señor Ortiz is a trusted agent of Spain. His information brought us here ! "

" *Maldito tradidor !*" scream the girl and her father together.

But with an easy gaiety the Spanish adventurer smiles at the man whose life he has destroyed, and whispers to the Spanish commander : "Your prisoner might escape."

"Yes," cries Mendoza, "better shoot him on the spot?"

To this the major answers: "I will not take that responsibility. A court-martial must sit upon his case."

"But this one is as certainly dead," laughs the guerilla captain merrily, "as the younger son."

At his words the Cuban planter is in front of him muttering: "Pedro!" with staring eyes, "My boy—dead!"

"Captured on the *Virginius* and shot!" cries Lieutenant Gonzales; a sister's scream of agony greeting his brutal news.

"Pedro, my son! Temple! Answer, is it true? I have seen your face twitch at the mention of my little boy's name. Answer me! Is he—assassinated?"

But even in his own helpless misery, the American cannot say the words, and turns away his head from the old hidalgo, whose face grows white and whose limbs begin to totter. Suddenly he claps his hand on his breast, and mutters: "Pedro, the son of my old age! *Pasado por los armas!*" and falls stricken by the sudden shock at the feet of the Spanish major.

"Sergeant, take good care of your prisoner!" orders the *comandante*, and spurning the body of the Cuban planter out of his way, strides into the grounds, for the roof of the great shed is all on fire.

"Take good care of my prisoner? *Carajo!* Won't I!" mutters the sergeant, and in a jiffy, Temple's legs are corded together; then, trussed and helpless, he is dragged out of the blazing shed and tossed upon the ground outside, safe from the surrounding flames. For the place seems now like a burning Hades. The beautiful hacienda is flaming to the skies from every window. The wild cries of the negroes as they fly from their captors are discordant as the chant of demons. The hoarse voices of the Spanish troops and a little crackle of fire-arms where resistance is made, show that they are now banditti and are looting the house.

Near the spot Howard has been thrown, Maria, assisted by a shuddering field hand, has dragged her father's body. Over the dead planter his daughter is making reverently the sign of the cross, and whispering a Latin prayer.

Upon the ground the American lies stunned bodily, mentally; the flash of lightning has struck him from so clear a sky.

Over him stands Ignacio, still calmly smoking, though in his eyes there is the glitter of a tiger who has struck down his prey. "*Diablo!* you'll never walk down Fifth Avenue again!" he grins.

"Before God, Ortiz, you are guilty of my murder!" mutters Howard, from whose brow the dew of despair has been chilled by the certainty of sudden death. "You who have eaten of my salt, partaken of my bounty; you whom I once called friend, why—why have you done this thing?" And his eyes seek those of his erstwhile New York companion in dazed unbelief.

"Because," says the Spaniard slowly, his face lighting up with the triumph of success, "you are the only man who stood between me and the woman I love."

"You love—Blanche?" screams Temple with a shriek that startles Maria at the side of her dead father.

"Yes, and will marry her!"

"Never!"

"Never, when I have *this!*" and Ortiz holds up before his victim's despairing eyes the dazzling bauble his far-away sweetheart in that happier land had placed upon his finger, as he left her side.

"Blanche's ring!" shrieks Temple. Then agony greater than even that of death coming to him, the young man begins to plead to his betrayer : "Give it back to me !" His shackled hands clench themselves, as he implores : "She will think me untrue to her. Ortiz, I shall die here. You have my life, but for God's sake, man, don't make the woman I love despise my memory !"

"She shall forget your memory in another's arms."

"Not *yours*, villain ! Not YOURS !"

And as the Spaniard, made careless by success, leans over him, his victim struggling to his knees, smites him with his manacled hands upon the face.

The anguish in Temple's voice brings anguish to the girl who is kneeling near him. When the name of another woman as his love has been cried out in her ears, her heart that was hot with sorrow grows icy with another pang. She would scream : "Is this true? Do you, Howard Temple, who have taken my soul from me, love another?"

But at this moment she feels her white arm in a brutal grasp. Domingo, with triumph in his eyes and lust upon his face, his breath hot with passion and desire, mutters in her ear : "All have their reward save Mendoza. Now comes his turn. Thy sweet kisses, *niña de mis ojos*, shall make this night my heaven, *mi vida, mi quireda, mi alma !*" and the sneaking adventurer who has destroyed this Cuban plantation, reaches out to clasp unto his brutal breast its flower that she may grace his victory by her virgin shame.

But with that quick instinct that comes to women when their purity is assailed, the girl with a smothered shriek leaps from his grasp, flies through the soldiers busy with plunder, and lighted by her burning home, makes straight as an arrow for the jungle, crying : "*Vivo Tado ! Aqui Tado ! Pronto Tado !*"

While the fires blazes higher—*higher*—HIGHER ! the

great sugar mill becoming like the funeral pile of the family whose fortune it has been. Till at last its big iron smoke-stack topples over, and all grows dark and desolate.

BOOK III.

THE FORT ON CAYO TORO.

CHAPTER VIII.

ON THE DECK OF THE HERMES.

THE far-famed Coffee Mountains rise high above the eastern end of Cuba. From the rugged, purple-tinted Montes Seboruca, about which the balmy yet refreshing air makes it perpetual spring, they slope in unending beauty down to the gentle *lomas*—little hills—in which nestles the pretty village of Santa Catalina de Guaso,—somtimes called de Guantanamo,—surrounded by palms and cocoanuts that are ever green, and growing plantains that are ever fruitful.

From there some twenty miles of railroad runs between palms of unending species and flowering cacti, and, in some places, great mahogany woods, covered with *el jaguey*, that famous parasite of wondrous flowers, which at times grows into a tree itself, until the jungle becomes more tangled, the plantains and sugar cane thicker, as it crosses the low grounds that surround the inner bay of Guantanamo, and reaches the little town of Caimanera, whence a deep channel runs by the Cayos del Manati and del Toro, and some lesser islands, into the great outer bay. that gives passage to the little steamboats and sailing craft which flit in from the Caribbean to take away the coffee, sugar, and tropic fruits of this favored land.

Cut off from the rest of Cuba by the great mountain range of the island, the Sierra Maestra, the little town under the blazing sun seems to have gone to sleep one hot March day of 1874. Even the steamer, loading with bananas and coffee for Santiago, has let its fires go out ; the sentries on the old fort on the Cayo Toro murmur their "*alerta!*" drowsily ; the fishing boats hardly move on the water of the outer bay of Guantanamo. This is surrounded on its eastern side by the rugged hills of La Playa del Este ; though its western banks are chiefly low lands, that permit the planting of the sugar cane, till they also run into hills near the Caribbean.

In this blue water, a short three miles from the little town, just off Point Palmas, her arbor-awnings up from stem to stern, lies lazily at anchor a great white schooner yacht of sea-going dimensions. She flies the burgee of the New York Yacht Squadron and the flag of the United States, and is owned by Mr. Alfred Grayson, of New York, who is on board of her with his two daughters. Like its surroundings, this vessel seems also asleep. A few jack-tars on its deck lie under the forecastle, trying to get out of the sun. The only thing that will not rest this quiet day are women's tongues.

"O-o-oh, my goodness ! What a fatiguing place Cuba is !" The first is a stifled yawn ; the second is a rather languid sigh.

Miss Blanche Grayson rises nonchalantly from her reclining steamer chair upon the white deck of the *Hermes* strolls to the taffrail, and looks upon the great expanse of the outer bay of Guantanamo.

Beyond her, as the girl glances carelessly inland, is a deep channel running between the little town, and the Cayo Toro, which is crowned by its old-fashioned

Spanish fort. Back of this is a glimpse, through inter-
vening islets, of the big inner water, which is like a lake,
with its low banks and surrounding mangrove swamps.
To her right are the hills of the Yateras; beyond
them, to the north, are the purple mountains, on which
is Miss Morales' coffee plantation, the business of
which has brought them here. For Mr. Grayson,
after a cruise about the island, has dropped into this
port to attend to affairs that he fears have been neglected
by his junior partner, from whom he has not heard for
considerably over a month.

Carelessly noting a few fishing boats that are at work
off the Playa del Este, which are the only things of
life in sight, save some flamingos, whose wings are as
brilliant as bright clouds above them, a shark or two,
and half a hundred fishes that the clear water makes
easily visible, and, perchance, made petulant by the
burning sun, from which the yacht's awning scarcely
shields her, as it has now begun to decline in the west,
the young lady mutters: "This is as insipid as hot
lemonade."

"Blanche, you have had no spirits since we left
Havana—and yet you proposed the cruise," cries
Señorita Laura Morales, a tinge of reproach in her
tones.

Both young ladies are habited in the prettiest of
white muslins, made with Parisian *chic*, broad sashes of
ribbon gird their lithe waists and float over their fashionable panniers, though the girl with American blood
wears palest blue, and the maiden of dark eyes and
half Spanish origin, sports brighter and more gorgeous
pink.

"I found Havana uninteresting," remarks Miss Grayson, nonchalantly tapping her pretty white shoe with
the ferrule of a white parasol.

"No Howard Temple there," says the other, lightly.

A moment after, she whispers to her half-sister : " He must have passed us returning to New York."

"Then why didn't he answer my telegram *to* New York?" answers Blanche, savagely.

" It cannot be possible he is still at the Vidal's plantation," murmurs Miss Morales ; adding to her sentence a little gasp, as her blue-eyed sister turns upon her, and suggests :

"If anything has happened to Howard, I shall blame you, Laura ! "

" ME ! "

"Certainly ! If your father hadn't left your estates in Cuba for Howard to manage, he would have been with me now ! "

" Blanche, you are more than unjust ; you are ungenerous ! " cries her sister, indignantly.

" There's your Spanish temper again."

But Laura does not answer this. Her eyes grow sad. She murmurs : " If the man you love were in this island with death hanging over his head, as Luis Vidal is now, you would endure a slight disappointment more calmly."

"*Slight* disappointment ! I haven't heard from Howard Temple since we left New York." Then, Blanche's face twitching, she puts her arms around her sister, and pleads : " Forgive me, dear ; you are much more noble than I."

"Nonsense ! " and the two girls give each other a couple of exquisite kisses.

Just here, there is the noise of a steam launch churning the water up alongside.

The young ladies trip to the taffrail and find Mr. Alfred Grayson in white yachting-suit of duck is stepping on the deck, having run down from Caimanera, which is over two miles away.

"Girls," he says cheerily, "I have news for you."

Then noting their faces, and that Laura has a tear upon her cheek, he asks : "What's the matter?"

"Papa, I have just been making myself disagreable again," remarks Miss Grayson, attempting archness.

"By the Lord, I believe you!" mutters her father grimly. "Ever since we left Havana, Blanche, you have made the yacht a *very* lively craft. I had the gout ; the seasickness banished my gout. You've banished my seasickness, and hang me if I don't think you make me the most uncomfortable of the three!" His voice is savage, but his eyes as they look upon the beautiful creature standing in front of him, grow tender, and the old gentleman kisses his charming, yet *difficile* daughter.

"For shame, papa!" The pretty nose goes up in the air as she returns his caress.

"Contact in women," remarks the New York banker with a philosophy not acquired in Wall Street, "frequently changes the feminine into the feline."

"Oh Mr. Grayson!" This is Miss Morales' dissent.

"And so I have provided a traveling antidote."

"Nice to taste?" says Blanche piquantly.

"You will like it," chuckles her father dryly.

"What is it?" Both the girls speak together.

"Two fine young gentlemen," answers their father, "whom I have invited to make the return voyage with us to New York."

But in this case the antidote is not effective. The young ladies put two pretty noses into the air, and mutter nonchalantly : "Oh, men!"

To which Miss Blanche adds : "Neither of them shall have the cabin I've had prepared for Howard."

"Pooh! There are plenty of extra staterooms on board," says Grayson philosophically. "One is a Mr. Dennison, I met at Caimanera. He has done me some favors in the way of information. He has been here writing to the New York papers on the conflict between the insurgents and the Spanish troops, which has drifted gradually east until a great deal of the blood now being shed runs into the streams that flow from yonder mountains." The gentleman points to the high Sierras rising from the interior and background-ing the view.

"Ah, a newspaper man," remarks Miss Grayson sneeringly.

"A very pleasant fellow," says her father sharply, "and don't you put on any didos with him, my young ladies."

"Pish!" laughs Laura languidly. "Your young gentlemen do not interest me so much as my siesta," and, lifting her light skirts, the girl trips down the companion-way.

"By Jove!" ejaculates Grayson, gazing at his step-daughter's disappearing figure. "Neither of you have asked the name of the other young man I met in the town. You are the two most incurious girls I ever saw. It must be the heat."

"O Heaven! The other one isn't Howard?" cries Blanche in excited voice.

Looking at her eyes that are beaming with ex-cited anticipation, her father mutters slowly even sadly: "No," and she turns away with a sigh that goes to his heart.

"Blanche, you shouldn't think so much about him," says Grayson half sternly. "No answers to my tele-gram in Santiago. By Heaven, the fellow's perform-ances make me think he is not a good business man!"

"He's a—a *worse* lover," mutters the girl, in choking voice. "No letter from him for six weeks—just when he was leaving Santo Espiritu—the one in which he spoke of visiting the Vidal plantation." Then her eyes grow troubled ; she turns and murmurs : "Father, take me back to New York—*quick !*"

"Am I not going to do that to-morrow ?"

"Order Captain Pinnock to get the anchor up *at once !*"

"What ! and sail on half-rations ? Besides the American consul is away in the interior—and I can't get a clean bill of health from him till to-morrow. No, my lady, we will wait until we get our supplies and passengers on board. Here comes another boat from Caimanera."

"Pish ! It won't bring any news I want."

"No, what you want is Howard Temple," says her father grimly, chewing his mustache.

"Do you know I am getting anxious about him," says Blanche suddenly.

"Nonsense !"

"You must *have* some news of him ? "

"Not a bit," replies Grayson shortly ; and tells the truth.

But the girl in her excited nervous state scarce believes her father, and thinks affrightedly : "What is it he does not *care* to tell me?"

Just at this moment the sound of oars draws both father's and daughter's attention to the side of the ship. Looking over the railing, they see a shore boat propelled by two negroes stripped to the waist, their athletic muscles glistening under the perspiration drawn from their sable skins by the blazing sun.

Under a little awning at the stern of the boat, accompanied by a valise and traveling satchel or two, lounges the newspaper man in immaculate white duck, a bright sombrero de Guayaquil of lightest straw, shading his bronzed face. One hand made half black by Cuban sun, holds a palmetto fan with which he lightly agitates the stagnant air about him. For though George Dennison can rough it with any man in pursuit of news, he is very well pleased to take his *dolce far niente,* as occasion offers.

On him Grayson looks complaisantly. For in truth he is anxious to bring aboard any one, or anything, that may divert his daughter from the contemplation of a subject that has now commenced to weigh heavily on his own mind and spirits.

Some six weeks before this, the *Hermes* being announced by her skipper, a down-east Yankee, as ready for sea, Mr. Grayson, who has been contemplating a winter cruise to the West Indies, has listened to his daughter's pleadings that he take her to Cuba, from which Mr. Temple will very shortly be returning.

"Howard can join us, and come home with us," has said Miss Blanche.

"Humph! and when we get back to New York," her father has returned dryly, "I suppose Grace Church —that's the fashionable hitching-post at present."

"If—if Howard wishes it," has answered the girl simply, with beaming eyes and blushing face.

"Oh, Devil doubt him!" has cried Grayson proudly. "By Heavens, if Temple is not impatient with such a bride as you, he is not worthy of the goods the gods have given him!"

But on their arrival at Havana, where they had been received by the Captain-General, and where many hidalgos, both civil and military, had bowed down to the young American heiress and her half-sister, whose estates they knew were very great in the island, they had heard nothing of Mr. Temple, except he had left for Santo Espiritu on business connected with Miss Morales' plantations at that point. They had almost expected this, as Mr. Temple in his letters to Mr. Grayson and his *fiancée,* had spoken of visiting Santiago de Cuba, likewise the Coffee Mountains above

Caimanera on further business connected with Miss Morales' properties. From Havana they had sailed around the island *via* the southwest coast, but doing it leisurely in that dreamy, dawdling way that seems peculiar to the tropics both afloat and ashore.

At Cienfuegos, they had heard nothing of him ; but at Las Tunas, the port for Santo Espiritu, Mr. Grayson had learned that his junior partner had finished all shipping of sugar and tobacco, and sale of the same with very good results, and in a business manner that had pleased him. At Las Tunas they had also learned that Mr. Temple had departed for Santiago. But on reaching Santiago no Howard Temple had arrived.

Thereupon they had anchored the *Hermes* for a week while Mr. Grayson had run up to the iron mine at Cobre, and the ladies had lounged about the pretty seaport, receiving considerable attention from the *élite* of the town, foreign and native. But the agent of the English company at the iron mine, though expecting Mr. Temple, had not seen or heard of him. So coming back to Santiago, the American had frequented the San Carlos Club and had dined at the Café Venus, and though he had found the first hospitality itself, and the cuisine of the other remarkably excellent, had seen or heard naught of his wandering junior partner.

Inquiries had elicited nothing except that the mountain districts in the immediate rear of Santiago were being fought over by the insurgents and Spaniards with a bloodthirsty war such as Spain always wages ; though Miss Blanche's sharp ears had caught a rumor that Captain Luis Vidal had been captured in the interior after a desperate fight with Spanish troops.

This, however, was so vague and indefinite, that after consultation with her father she did not mention it to her sister, though her heart had grown very sore for Laura—the Captain-General Jovellar having openly proclaimed death to all prisoners captured in arms.*

So with a terror in both their hearts for the man of Laura Morales' love, they were anxious to leave Cuba. Their telegrams to New York and Havana having received no reply from Mr. Temple, Miss Blanche, who had grown nervously excited, had suddenly suggested: "Laura's coffee plantation."

"Yes, I might just as well run into Guantanamo. It is on our return voyage to New York, and there we'll perhaps find him," had been her father's reply.

"Of course, Howard must be there!" The girl had cried, her voice for the moment hopeful.

Thus it has come to pass that the *Hermes* two days before this has entered the Bay of Guantanamo. But at the little town of Caimanera its passengers have heard naught of Howard Temple. Though Grayson himself has journeyed to the mountain coffee plantation to interview the superintendent, he has returned with no news of his missing junior partner.

During their father's absence in the interior his daughters have dawdled about the yacht's deck, and then, to vary their *ennui*, when the land breeze has sprung up in the evening have been rowed up to the little town to receive the attentions of the few Spanish officers who have run over from the old fort, and some foreign merchants who have made themselves agreeable.

And each hour though Miss Blanche has flirted very prettily in pretended nonchalance at the absence of her lover, she has grown more and more *difficile*, her temper more variable and excited, until Grayson has groaned to himself: "By the lord Harry, I must get her mind off this fellow in some way."

* Under these orders the Spanish government admit the execution of 43,000 prisoners during the Ten Years, War.—ED.

So this day in Caimanera, having chanced to run upon Dennison, he has invited him to return with him on his yacht to New York. This, George has been delighted to do as his business in the island is finished.

After arriving at Havana *en route* for New York, the journalist had received a cable from his newspaper directing him to visit the eastern end of the island and write a few letters about the sanguinary conflict taking place through the highlands of Santiago between the patriots and Spanish forces. Of this he has seen about all that he thinks will interest the outside world, and is sick of the barbarous bloodshed of a murderous war, where prisoners, as soon as taken, are butchered, like sheep in the shambles. Therefore, he is very well content to take journey from Cuba in the beautiful white yacht.

Gazing at the coming boat Grayson is contented also. He says to his daughter quite cheerily : " My *first* young man."

"Oh, is he ? Ah, yes, I remember. I believe I saw the gentleman once in our house in New York for a few seconds."

A moment after the boat is alongside, and Laura having run up from the cabin, George, as he steps upon the snowy deck of the *Hermes* is introduced to two very pretty young ladies.

"My step-daughter, Miss Morales ; my daughter, Miss Grayson ; Mr. Dennison," says his host easily.

And the ladies returning his salute, George taking off his straw hat, remarks : "Your cavalier for the voyage," then adds : "Mr. Grayson, Colonel Villalonga asks me to tell you he is detained by unavoidable official business, but will call for the young ladies to take them to the fort as per promise at five o'clock."

"We are very much obliged to Colonel Villalonga," replies Blanche ; "but I hope he will not trouble himself to come. I am too anxious to see our anchor up to care to go on shore again."

Looking at her and noting her striking beauty, the journalist remembers he has seen her in her father's house. Though having been introduced to her as Miss Grayson, and not being a society man, he has no idea her Christian name is the one Temple had murmured in his sleep as their hammocks had swung side by side.

"Now you have met all of your *compagnons de voyage* except one," remarks Grayson. "He will be here sometime this evening. So I will leave you, Mr. Dennison, to the ladies, and write a telegram in the saloon to forward for transmission to Santiago. Hold your boat, please, so that I can send it back to the town. You will find liquors and cigars and everything else below. All you have to do is to touch the bell and the steward will do the rest," he adds hospitably, and is half way down the companion ladder.

But Dennison says: "It will be unnecessary to detain the boat. You'll have no chance of forwarding a telegram from this port this afternoon ; the Santiago steamer will not sail for two days.*

"But she should have gone to-morrow : Ah, those lazy Cubans ! " mutters the man of business, here he checks himself, restrained by a flash in his step-daughter's eyes ; then laughs : "Mr. Dennison, if you make yourself very agreeable, you will probably be able to talk yourself into the cabin that should have been Mr. Temple's, had we not missed him in Havana." And

* In 1874, the cable had not been laid between Playa del Este and Cape Haytien—though a submarine wire from Santiago de Cuba to Jamaica was working,—the one over which the dispatch was sent in 1873 that brought an English gunboat commanded by the gallant Lampton Lorain to save the last of the *Virginius* crew from massacre.—ED

steps languidly down into the saloon, in search of a cooling cocktail.

"I spent a very pleasant week, a month ago, with Mr. Howard Temple. I presume you refer to him, as the name is an uncommon one in Cuba at least," remarks the newspaper man. "We may have a mutual friend."

"Certainly," replies Blanche eagerly. "Won't you sit down?" For the young ladies have already sunk into reclining steamer chairs.

"With pleasure," says George, and makes himself comfortable on the rail of the skylight.

"You met Mr. Howard Temple in Havana, I presume?" a sudden interest in her voice.

"No, at Vidal's plantation in the interior of Cuba. Ah, thank you." This is to the steward who has brought him up some cigars.

"He left before you, then?" asks the girl eagerly.

"No; business called me away. Pleasure detained him. But he expected to leave shortly after me."

Here Miss Morales asks, her voice deep with earnest inquiry: "You have heard nothing from him or the Vidals since?"

"No; I did not again visit Puerto Principe, returns the newspaper man, "Since the United States government has permitted the murder of a lot of its subjects in front of that blank wall in Santiago de Cuba, it is not so safe for an American as it was before. The Spaniards never loved us, but at least they had respect for us as a nation until that. Now they not only hate, but they sneer at what they call the American hog. I feel much safer here than on those mountains."

"Then Mr. Temple should have been in Santiago long ago," cries Blanche, a shade of anxiety in her tone.

"He may have remained longer."

"Impossible!" There is a little sob in the girl's heart. She thinks her lover should be as anxious to meet her as she to greet him.

"Impossible?" laughs the newspaper man, a slight query in his voice ; then he suggests lightly : "with the *attraction?*"

"What attraction?" Blanche is very much interested now.

"You are acquainted with the Vidal family?" says Dennison easily, as he lights his cigar.

"We know the son Luis." This comes from Laura Morales.

"Ah!" George puffs out lazily a little whiff of smoke and suggests : "Then you do not know the daughter?"

"The *child*, Maria?" remarks Miss Grayson carelessly.

"CHILD?"

"Luis Vidal described her as a child," says Miss Morales taking up the conversation, for she sees her sister's pretty lips are twitching nervously, and her fan is moving agitatedly, though Blanche has turned her eyes from George who goes on, in an explanatory way :

"She was a child two years ago, when, I presume, her brother last saw her. At sixteen, developed by the sun of the equator, Señorita Maria Vidal is a most charming woman."

"Ah, *she* was the attraction!" falters Blanche, half laughingly.

"Judge for yourself," replies the journalist. "I am about to describe her in my very best style. A true Cuban beauty, exquisite dark eyes, beautiful figure bounded by the outlines of Venus though willowy as a nymph's, lily hands, fairy feet, the ankles of Seville——"

"I understand the true style of Cuban beauty," mutters Blanche, then attempting to conceal her torture she laughs : " I have but to look at my sister to realize your description."

" Blanche, you are embarrassing ! " cries Laura, and turns away with very red cheeks, permitting Miss Grayson from this moment to have the conversation pretty well to herself.

" So Mr. Temple was interested ? " Blanche says, despite herself, there is a quiver in her voice.

" Hard to tell," smiles Dennison, " but when every look of dark eyes was at him, and every gesture of the beautiful hands was for him, amid waving palms and cocoanuts, and the odor of white lime hedges and jasmine flowers, a man would have little heart——"

" If he did not fall in love with the possessor of such transcendent charms," cries his listener, cutting short a speech that is driving her half mad, and rising nervously, she turns away, walks to the taffrail, looks over the water that is throbbing against the ship's side not half so rapidly as her beating heart.

Just at this moment through the open skylight, Grayson calls from the cabin : " Blanche, send Mr. Dennison down to me ! I want to show him what a cocktail the steward of the *Hermes* can make."

" Blanche ! Good Lord, so this is Blanche," thinks the newspaper man with a sudden mental start, and looking at the beauty whose little foot is now tapping the white deck, he remembers that Blanche is the name Howard had whispered in his dreams as their hammocks had been side by side. " I will be with you, Mr. Grayson," he cries, and, rising, walks to the companionway, glumly communing with himself : " By Tophet, how Temple will bless me for this ! " But he wisely attempts no explanation.

" We will excuse you," says Laura, her soft voice slightly icy to this man who has been unwittingly putting poisoned arrows into the heart of her dear sister.

This is broken in upon by Grayson again : "I see your legs half way down the companion hatch. Come, along quick. Cocktail is getting hot." Then he laughs in masculine humor : "Have you talked yourself into Temple's cabin ?"

"No," cries George, and steps down the companion-ladder cogitating ruefully : "But I am very much afraid I have talked poor Temple out of it."

As the gentleman disappears, the younger girl turns to her sister and mutters bitterly : "So Howard Temple is in Cuba with dark eyes gazing love into his."

"That is at best a guess," whispers Laura. "Mr. Dennison's very profession teaches him to draw the long bow."

"Pish ! It was merely a plain statement of fact. I might not believe one of Mr. Dennison's sensational newspaper paragraphs, but I do credit his word."

"Mr. Dennison says Howard intended a month ago——" interjects Laura.

"To leave that plantation," cries Blanche. "Then, if in Santiago, I should have seen him. If in New York he would have seen and answered my telegram. Ah, Laura ; ever since then I felt that there was something wrong."

"Good Heavens ! You think him false to you?" asks Miss Morales, in indignant voice.

"No," answers the other simply, "When I think Howard Temple untrue to his vows to me, I shall cease to think of him forever. When I gave Howard my ring, I felt it bound him as this binds me," and she holds up the diamond that Temple placed upon her finger in New York ; then sighs : "And yet I *know* he is in Cuba. Ah, Laura, at times a great fear comes into my heart."

I

"Of what ?

"I do not know ; I cannot tell, but it is *here!*" And the girl wrings one beautiful hand slightly, and presses the other to the light draperies above her beating heart as she walks about the deck, an indescribable dread upon her beautiful face.

———

CHAPTER IX.

"HAPPY ORTIZ!"

To this, the hand of fate soon adds a more definite agony.

The cries of negro boatmen and the splash of oars proclaim another shore-boat is alongside.

"Blanche, restrain yourself, for Heaven's sake!" whispers Miss Morales; "some one is coming on deck." And, stepping to the taffrail, Laura starts with surprise, for Señor Ignacio Ortiz, his cameo face bright with expectancy, his costume of tropical white made romantic by a bright red silken sash, his little feet decked in patent-leather shoes and silken stockings, upon one of the fingers of his slight yet muscular hand glittering a diamond bauble, as he tosses a silver dollar to the boatman, is stepping up the side-ladder to the *Hermes'* deck.

"Aha, Señorita Morales," he cries, "Mr. Grayson, in Caimanera, two hours ago, had the goodness to invite me to take passage with you to New York, and I am here." He hastily orders the negro boatmen to put his luggage on deck, and then catching sight of a graceful figure that is turning to him, his face lights up with passion and he exclaims : "*Madre de Dios !* Señorita Blanche ! Ah, now I am indeed happy !"

But Laura's hand is on his arm; she is speaking to him eagerly: "Where did you leave Luis Vidal?"

"Hush! Safe!" He puts his fingers on his lips: "Safe in the insurgent lines. I dare not tell you more in this nest of his enemies. The negro boatmen even now may be listening."

He glances cautiously about.

"God bless you for the words!" whispers the girl, her face beaming, radiant, and gives him a patrician hand, whose delicate fingers he presses to his lips in Castilian style.

"And now, Señorita Blanche——" He is stepping eagerly towards her.

"How do you do, Señor Ortiz?" and Miss Grayson holds out her hand nonchalantly to the gentleman, who, seizing the fair ungloved fingers, lifts them to his lips, in so extravagant a manner that the girl starts back, a pretty little blush tinging her cheeks, which have been pale.

"You had not heard of my coming? It—it was a surprise—I hope a joyous one!" he ejaculates nervously.

"No, papa attempted to tell us, but was prevented. However, your stateroom is prepared for you, I believe. The steward has orders," remarks the young lady, rather coldly.

"Ah, yes; if you will permit me, I will light a cigarette," returns the Spaniard. "I met your father only two hours ago. I had been called here on some—some military business——" He pauses abruptly, his face grows pallid, though his eyes are gleaming. "Since I learnt you were here, I—I have been a little excited. A cigar calms my nerves."

"Ah, excited at the thought of meeting old friends!" says Laura, her voice and her face happy with the tidings that he has brought to her.

"Yes, of—of course.   Have I your permission?"
And the Don produces an elaborately ornamented
cigarette case, taking from it a paper cigar.

"Of course; you know we love smoke," says
Blanche, more cordially, as if anxious to soften the
former coldness of her greeting.

"A-a-ah!"   The Spaniard's face is aglow.   "Permit me to offer *you* a cigarette," and he extends the
little case towards her.

"Thank you.   I am not Spaniard enough for that,
yet," remarks Miss Grayson, lightly; then suddenly
starts and glances earnestly as his jewel flashes under
her eyes.   A moment later she murmurs, as if anxious
to throw something off her mind : "Now, sit down,
and tell us your adventures on the island."

"I dare not," whispers Ignacio, cautiously, "until
I have left it.   But everything is all right—all right—
very right!"   He emphasizes this last by a curious
longing, yet possessive, glance at the younger sister
then asks eagerly : "We leave here immediately?"

"Yes, the *Hermes* sails to-morrow morning," an
swers Laura.

"*Dios Mio* that is well!"   There is a sigh of relief
in his tone.   "There is talk of yellow fever in the town."
He makes gesture of caution to Miss Morales, and the
diamond on his finger flashes again.

But Blanche seems not to hear his mention of the
dreaded pestilence of Cuba.   "You have added to
your jewelry," she interjects nervously.

"Blanche, you have sharp eyes," laughs her sister.

"It is a—a peculiar ring."   The girl's gaze seems to
follow it as if she can't believe what she sees.   "At
least, it looks so from here," continues Blanche earnestly.   "Can I—can I examine it?"

As she has spoken, a strange light has flown into the
Spaniard's face.   "With pleasure," he answers, and

taking it from his finger, presents it to her with an elaborate bow.

"A very—a very fine diamond," gasps the girl, and holds it up to the light looking searchingly upon its inner circle. Seeing there initials that she recognizes, her face grows white and frightened. Turning away, she looks over the blue water and it seems to make her brain reel. She puts a hand to her brow, which is cold as ice, and shivers slightly though the day is burning.

"It is a handsome ring," remarks Miss Morales, somewhat astounded at her sister's emotion.

"Yes," replies Ortiz, carelessly. "Cuban ladies sometimes have very beautiful jewels."

"Cuban *ladies ?*" cries Laura.

"Certainly! I picked this up in a little *monté pio* at Puerto Principe," he remarks as he smokes, his half closed eyes studying the pliant figure of Blanche who, her head turned from him, is drooping over the railing. Then looking down the open skylight, Ortiz calls cheerily: "Aha, *buenos dias !* Señor Grayson, I hear the clinking glasses down there ; I will be with you in a moment."

But a light hand is laid upon his arm, and turning he sees a beautiful face, strangely pathetic, looking into his. To him, fair lips that are pale are whispering : " Puerto Principe ? That is near the Vidal plantation, is it not, Señor Ortiz ? "

"Yes. Not a great distance for Cuba : some thirty or forty miles. Cuban belles are extravagant at times. A young girl had sent the diamond for sale."

" A young girl—pawned it ? "

"Well—you would call it pawned. But when the families of patriots ruined by the war pledge jewelry, they seldom redeem it. The Jew pawnbroker knew it was safe to sell it to me at a moiety of its value, and

I—well, I am a Spaniard—barbaric in my tastes, if you like—I bought the diamond."

"A Cuban *girl* ?" repeats Blanche, as if she could hardly believe, her voice growing cold.   Suddenly she asks : "You heard her name ?"

"*Dios mio*, yes ! She is a sister of Luis Vidal. Maria, I believe she is called.   That is one reason I bought it : that I might return it."

"The sister of Luis Vidal !" cries Laura, excitedly. " If he needs money——"

"Sh-h-h ! Don't mention his name here. Those negro boatmen have not left. They are discussing what they will do with my dollar," whispers Ignacio, rolling his eyes.

"Maria Vidal," shudders Blanche, a curious strain in her voice, that now seems artificial.   Then she says : "I have a fancy for returning to Miss Vidal her ring as well as you, Laura.   Can I—may I— ? "

" Be permitted to *purchase* it ? " cries Ortiz, shrugging his shoulders indignantly.   "No ! Accept it as a souvenir of our coming voyage, dear Miss Blanche."

"Not without a return," says the girl, in tones so cold they seem to chill her lips that have grown white. " Permit me to replace it by this one ! " and she draws from her finger the ring Howard Temple had placed upon it in New York the night he had left her.

"Blanche, that's your— !" cries her sister.

But Blanche's eyes stop Laura's tongue.   Miss Grayson repeats : "My souvenir de voyage, Señor Ortiz," and laughing airily, turns away, leans over the railing at the stern and wonders if she should jump overboard would a shark kindly end her anguish.

"Ortiz, your cocktail is ready ! " comes up from the companionway in Grayson's voice.

"I—I am with the cocktail ! " cries the Spaniard. "Ladies, I make my adieu."   And looking at the girl whose heart he has stabbed, he mutters : "A proud spirit," then sighs in mighty relief : "She has not heard. God is helping me, she has not heard !"

"Come down, Ortiz !" cries Grayson. "It's a long time between drinks."

"*Dentro de poco*, and I am with you," laughs the Spaniard. Casting one quick glance at the beautiful creature he has stricken, he notes the girl in all her grace standing proud, erect and haughty, her blue eyes beaming bright as sapphires but cold as icebergs, and mutters : "The proper desperate spirit to make her toss her beauties into my arms. Oh, happy Ortiz !" So stepping down into the handsome saloon of the *Hermes* no gentleman on board is so happy as the gentleman who has left despair behind him on the yacht's white deck.

Laura gliding to her sister whispers in voice full of reproach : "Blanche, you have given Ortiz, Howard Temple's engagement ring."

"And behold the return !" cries the girl, holding up her hand. "Look at it ! See my initials within it ! "

"O Heaven ! The ring you gave Howard !"

"The one he swore to keep till death, but gave to Maria Vidal. Oh, she must have loved him dearly : she *pawned* it. But Mr. Temple shall know that light faith makes light troth." And the girl bursts into a laugh, melodious yet despairing and sneers : "How I will flirt with dear old Colonel Don Quixote Villalonga at the fort this evening. He bows to the American heiress."

"Blanche, we must not go on shore," whispers Laura.

"Why not ? The officers are pleasant ; I can improve my Spanish ; the evening will be cool."

"Because. Did you not hear Señor Ortiz say the yellow fever had broken out ?"

"Yellow fever! Delicious; that makes the place more inviting. I love Yellow Jack," jeers Miss Grayson bitterly. "He is the only man that is not inconstant. He seldom deserts you till death. Besides," she is speaking desperately now, "I've got to get away from my thoughts! Anything to forget! Something to make me believe this is a dream! Oh, don't think I do not know it is a fact!" she cries to her sister's half-horrified gesture. "Have I not learned from the words of two men that Howard Temple has stayed by another's side."

"Impossible! I cannot believe it!"

"Neither would I if facts did not tell the same story. Howard did not meet me because he preferred to be with her. Otherwise we must have found him somewhere. Don't tell me that a man so well known as Mr. Temple, with such enormous business interests as yours to make him prominent, could disappear, even in this barbarous island, and leave no trace behind him. But I won't think about it. Colonel Villalonga, or some of his gallant younger officers shall make me forget at least for the moment. Now, Laura, come to the fort with me!" Anything to get away from myself. If you don't come with me, I go without you!"

"Remember Creole convenances!"

"Oh, I know Havana would consider it social perdition, but what do I care? I leave this hated isle tomorrow!"

"Indeed, it will be enough of a social solecism if we go together," replies Laura. And looking down the skylight she would call into the cabin below, where the gentlemen are apparently chuckling over some story of Dennison's.

But Blanche's hand is on her sister's arm. She whispers: "Don't tell papa. He might forbid our excursion,"

"If he has heard Ortiz' yellow fever report, he certainly will."

"Then not a word to any one. When Villalonga comes we step in his boat and away we go. Besides, I don't want Ortiz or that newspaper man with us. *They* would remind me. Their story would keep ringing in my head. The true Cuban beauty with form of Venus, lily hands, fairy feet, ankles of Seville. My God! Laura, you remind me of her *too!*" gasps the girl in tragic voice. 'Yours is a *Spanish* beauty!' And with her great eyes bright as brilliants and blue as steel but desperate in their anguish, Blanche Grayson strides the deck, her mien frightening her sister.

*   *   *   *   *   *

All this time the gentlemen are very merry in the cabin; for Ortiz is at his best. He whispers a few little confidential news items of the Cuban war into the correspondent's ear that Dennison thinks will be interesting in type. He tells so good a story that his host holding his sides, cries: "We will have a rattling voyage!"

This starts George, who gives the others one or two rattling anecdotes that make Grayson shout: "Bravo! more cocktails!"

So the steward brings more cocktails, and they smoke and chat, for the air has become cooler now, and is floating in through the open port-holes and down the skylight. But after some hour of this, the father suddenly says: "Those girls are very quiet up on deck."

"Whispering secrets," laughs the newspaper man.

"With your permission, I will go up and see," suggests the Spaniard, thinking of the beauty that is above him, that he fondly feels now is very close to him. He runs lightly up the companion-way, for he is anxious to again look upon the face for which he has been long-ing ever since he last saw it in New York.

A moment later he is upon the deck, and gazing around finds it deserted.

Stepping to the Captain, a New England sea-dog from Gloucester, Massachusetts, who is tramping forward unconcernedly, he asks : "The young ladies ?"

"Went ashore some fifty minutes ago with an opera bouffet colonel and a kiss-your-hand Dago officer. Miss Morales said something about yaller fever. But the Spanish colonel cried : 'Yaller fever in *March?* You're crazy !' They are going to do the old fort, I heerd 'em say," returns the mariner. Then he suddenly screams : "What's the matter wid ye? Gol darn it, has Yaller Jack got hold of ye?" For Ortiz has uttered a little affrighted cry, and is reeling with both hands clasped over his white forehead.

"No," mutters the Spaniard. "No, but the sun is —is hot even now. I— there *is* yellow fever ashore. Say nothing to the father. I will go and bring the ladies back. Order a boat, quick ! The fastest one !"

"Yaller Jack ! Great Gosh ! Is Yaller Jack ashore ?" gasps the seaman, who knows very little about the hygiene of the Cuban dry season, but has heard of Yellow Jack as being the dread enemy of sailors in these islands. "Good Lordy, give 'em the steam launch, Jim ! She's got fire in her boilers yit ! And look alive !"

In less than a minute Ortiz is in the stern sheets of the swift boat that is darting for the landing of the old fort on Cayo del Toro. He shades his brow with his hands and thinking he sees white garments fluttering on the battlements, mutters to himself : "*Diablo!* If she should see him—if by some accident of the ac-cursed fate that brought them here, *she should see him !*"

His face is so pale as he steps upon the rocky landing at del Toro that one of the men in the launch to
whom he cries : "Hold the boat for me here ! " remarks
to his companion : "Jube, that *Dago* looks as if he
had the black varmint in his umbellicals ! Damn
it—he's reeling now."

And Ortiz from his apparance might be stricken by
that dread disease, but it is only a sinking heart, a
mighty dread !

———

CHAPTER X.

THE UNKNOWN PRISONER.

"DIDN'T we dodge papa nicely, and—mercy ! what
a romantic looking spot, Colonel Villalonga ! " cries
Miss Grayson, in languid enthusiasm, as she sits in
a little embrasure of the outer battery of the fort on
Cayo Toro and listens to the lazy waves that wash its
coral foundations, the music of a Spanish infantry
band, coming from the parade ground in a quaint little Andalusian melody, seeming to give accent to the
rhythm of the waves.

"In your presence, Señorita Blanche, romance comes
to every one, even to an an unfortunate who has
sweltered here for two long years next Holy Week,"
remarks the old Spanish colonel, who stands by her in
military erectness, his manner suavely gracious, his
eye, bright and undimmed by sixty winters that have
whitened his head, and thirty hot summers that have
dried his skin to parchment during the time he has
served his country in the West Indies and Spanish
Main.

To this compliment the girl only returns a slight
sigh, for though Miss Grayson's manner is affable, her

mien nonchalantly vivacious and her bearing easy,
this day's news has brought to her a very sad spirit.

"Ah," laughs the colonel, "your sigh is that of romance. The soft music of my country brings sentiment to your young heart. If you were an old cam-
paigner like me, you would understand what it is to
lounge here and look upon those mountains and know
your brothers in arms are fighting up there, though to
you has only been given military police duty to perform, and sometimes——" The old martial hidalgo's
voice trembles slightly as he mutters : "sometimes an
execution to superintend."

"O goodness, this is not a military *prison* ?" half
gasps the girl.

"No more than any other fortification is in Cuba,"
answers the commander, his voice growing stern ;
"where there are rebels to be punished. A few drift
in here, some are brought here, and a court-martial
does for them, as in Santiago, Bayomo or Havana.
But we won't think of the most unpleasant duty of a
soldier—not on this day which is bright to me, the
brightest I have spent in the West Indies. I hope my
hospitality has pleased you."

"Oh, very much," says Miss Blanche gratefully.
"You have treated my sister and myself *en princess*.
The guard-mounting, the parade were beautiful, military, romantic. Your bronzed infantrymen looked as
if they might have fought under Pizarro, but you yourself were the most martial of your command."

"*Dios mio*, Señorita Blanche, you flatter me," says the
old soldier, bowing before young beauty.

In truth, Colonel Don Pablo Guiterez de Villalonga
looks like an old *Conquistadore*. His step is firm and
vigorous, his spare figure, drawn up with military erectness, is wondrously agile for a man of his years and
service ; his uniform is spotless in its glory ; his lac-

quered boots shine with a lustre equal to that of the sun just sinking below the mountains.

"We will have more music here, for the band has been ordered out early this evening for you and your sister's sake, then a little refreshment at my quarters, and after that I will escort you to your yacht as the band plays the sweet music of *la retreta*," he murmurs, relaxing slightly and bending a little over the graceful figure and face that is even more enchanting than of yore, for a veiled pathos adds a strange tenderness to the lovely eyes.

"Ah, indeed. That is very kind of you. Your Spanish music is so lovely," remarks Blanche, "and the surroundings add to it." With a pretty wave of her parasol she indicates the little fortress that is at her back.

And she is right!

There is no more romantic fortification in all Cuba than the tumbled-down fort on Cayo Toro. Originally built to defy pirates and buccaneers, its earthquake-crumbled walls would make but short resistance to modern artillery. All is old, medieval, barbarous, save two batteries that have been built of more modern construction, in white wings along the rocky slope that is lapped by the soft waters which are narrow here in this passage which connects the inner and the outer bay of Guantanamo.

Facing the strait, and cut off by it from the town, the fort stands on a little rocky eminence some mile from Caimanera, whose lights will soon sparkle across the inlet. It is on a kind of promontory of some little elevation and isolated and remote from the commerce of the town; beyond it are one or two hills, not high, covered with palms and undergrowthed with the densefoliaged thickets of the tropics, that decline sharply to a little *caleta* or deep indentation in the rocky coast some half mile from the fort towards the east, one of the many little fingers of bright water that run from the outstretched silvery hand of the outer bay, cutting into the tropic hills and making unending beauties in the landscape of Guantanamo.

The two batteries, being works with guns of recent construction, look more like modern fortifications. In an embrasure of one of them is seated Miss Blanche ; in another not far away lounges Señorita Morales, two or three handsome young officers lingering about her bright eyes and subtle graces. For, like the military gentlemen of other countries, these boys, sent to give their lives for Spain by war and pestilence, have discovered Miss Morales has great estates upon the island, and are devotion to beauty linked with wealth.

Behind these batteries, shaded by a few palms and cocoanuts, is a little parade ground from which the band is still discoursing the music of *el Relampago*, that vivacious Spanish opera whose scenes are laid in Cuba, whose choruses are sung by plantation negroes.

Behind this are the officers' quarters, low buildings of painted adobe, surmounted by the red tiles common in all Spanish America ; in front of them runs a long and pleasant piazza where lazy lieutenants swing in hammocks and smoke eternal cigarettes, and dream during siestas of eternal señoritas, and cry out to their *muchachos* for eternal *refrescos*.

Back of these buildings, deep in the edge of the jungle, yet within the fortifications, as if the authorities wished to keep its moans, stench and misery as far as possible out of their ken, is the military prison, a stinking pen, on two sides stockaded by heavy posts, its other boundaries being a one-story, stone building, which contains cells, from whose barred windows that face only upon the open pen, captives groaning with the heat, filth and vermin of a Spanish prison, stare out with straining eyeballs, and sometimes parched lips and tongues, swollen from lack of water, upon gangs driven shackled to the transports for life-exile in African penal settlements, or else marshaled for death, kneel, their faces to that low adobe wall, while a firing party at word of command sends them to eternity, by volleys of musketry fired into their writhing bodies at regulation distance, the sergeants following up the fusillade by blowing out the brains of those who still have breath by their *fuego de gracia.*

Even as the setting sun, scarce half an hour high in the heavens, casts its lingering rays upon this place of agony, a chain of prisoners are being driven out from the barred cells to hear the military sentences of a quick-acting court-martial, while a lieutenant stands in the shade of a little tiled guard-house carelessly handling the findings that give life or death.

To him comes hurriedly a figure arrayed as a Spanish dandy, and, doffing his sombrero, asks eagerly : "Number 93 ? Señor Lieutenant Gonzales, what have they done with Number 93 ? "

" *Caramba !* Still anxious about your friend Mendoza," laughs the officer as he glances over the documents ; then adds : " You have got your wish."

" Death ! *Gracias à Dios,* that is good ! Death ! *Carajo,* I could eat his heart ! The court-martial kept me waiting long."

" Yes, there is some doubt whether the fellow is an American," remarks Gonzales. " That is the reason they postponed his sentence and execution till the American consul had left Caimanera for a day or two. Ortiz' evidence decided it."

" A great man, that Ortiz," chuckles Mendoza.

" Yes ; you and he have got the reward for the capture of *El Capitan* Luis Vidal of Vincente Garcia's insurgent forces ! " grins the officer.

"And you also your share, Lieutenant Gonzales,"
guffaws the spy. "Not a dangerous game. In
this lonely fort, cut off by the mountains from the rest of
Cuba, there is little danger of his Government hearing."

"*Par Dios!* What do we care for the American
Government anyway," sneers the lieutenant.

"*Caramba!* We slaughtered sixty or seventy of
them in Santiago not four months ago, and what did
they dare to do about it? *Nada!*" cries the informer.
"And Burriel for doing his grand work, what have we
done about it? Made him a bigger general than
before! *Santos*, I like the blood of those *Gringos!*
But the dogs are coming. *O Madre de Dios!* I want
to see him when you tell him it is death."

With this Mendoza chuckles merrily as the manacled
wretches are driven into line by the butt-ends of muskets and the brutal hands of their guard, and stand in
their rags and filth and vermin, a few of them half-
dazed by the light of day, some half-crazed by misery,
savage hatred in most of their worn faces, and the fire
of patriotism that the fear of death cannot destroy
beaming in many of their haggard eyes.

"Each prisoner will advance two steps as his number is called," commands the Spanish lieutenant, stepping to the front of them, the sentences in his hand,
and anxious to get through his job, for a pretty girl of
Caimanera awaits him with words of love on the outer
battery. "Numbers 41, 53, 76 and 47, being convicted
of treasonable sympathies with the insurgents, are
forthwith by the judgment of the court sentenced to life-
imprisonment with hard labor in chains at Ceunta," he
reads in a careless sternness; then cries sharply:
"Silence in the ranks! Sergeant, compel silence!"

For at his words, that bring to them a fate as cruel
as death, Numbers 41 and 76 are muttering in a half-
crazy monotone, and Number 53, a boy of some

sixteen years, with a hectic flush upon his sunken cheeks, and the soft curls of youth clustering in matted locks about his eyes, from which even the hope of youth has gone forever, is groaning : "You are destroying me because my father is a patriot."

But these beaten to silence, the lieutenant goes sharply on : "Number 93, being taken in open rebellion to the Spanish Government, the sentence is that he be led out at sunrise to-morrow and shot to death by a squad of infantry, in front of the wall. By order of the Court : Juan Valdez, Captain ; Lieutenants Flores, De Noro and——"

He pauses astounded, for a creature of hollow eyes, whose clothes that were once garments of fashion and are now rags, whose hair has grown long and matted, and whose eyes are bloodshot with despair, has cried hoarsely : "You *dare* not do it !"

"Silence, prisoner ! "

"I am an American. I demand to see my consul. You *shall* hear me. Some day my country will reckon with you for the murders you have done!"

"Silence, Number 93 ! " and the sergeant has raised his clubbed musket to strike the culprit down, when suddenly the wretch mutters : "They are laughing in the lower battery. Ha ! ha ! ha ! do you hear them—laughing in the lower battery! My God ! I used to laugh once ! " adding wearily and brokenly, "but that's a—long—time—ago." Then his ears made acute by agony, he screams : "I am delirious. I hear *her* laugh !"

"Silence, Number 93 ! " *Incomunicado* for this ! Gag him if he utters another word, and to-morrow morning shoot him gagged, if he dares to proclaim himself an American hog ! " sharply commands the lieutenant.

And Number 93, helpless and manacled, is seized

K

upon, battered to obedience, and thrown into a little cell, whose barred window opens upon the prison-pen where they will do him to death as the sun rises bright, smiling and burning, on the tropic morrow.

Here he, falling prone in the little vermin-haunted place, mutters : "My God, she will never know! I thought they might take me to Santiago. There I might have had a chance. But he was too subtle —. In this lonely fort—I shall die—and she—oh, God, not in *his* arms !—That would be too cruel a fate—for her I love !" and he sighs out between his parched lips those mighty sighs that come to us when hope has left us.

In the prison-yard outside, as the sergeant had struck Number 93 with his musket, a battered straw hat had fallen from the head of the prisoner.

As the lieutenant turns away, the Spanish dandy, who has stood behind him, has cried : "That does me good ! That makes Mendoza's heart happy !" and has picked up this straw hat. Looking in it, he has seen a picture of the American eagle, and screamed : "*Caramba!* Curses on the crow !" and, joyously and excitedly, has shied the dirty, tattered and worthless piece of straw, with jeering hand, over the stockade to the outside world. "Would you like to see another Americano citizen, Gonzales? A nigger I am teaching to shriek '*Viva Espana!*' with my cowhide," he chuckles.

With this, he strides off, merrily, to some low, thatched sheds a hundred yards away, where he throws himself into a hammock, and cries : "*Aqui pronto!* El Señor Smith ; bring me some *aguardiente*, and look quick about it, my Americano citizen !"

At his words, to him comes tottering a dejected figure in tattered Sixth Avenue dude clothes, the remnants of one lavender-colored kid on his trembling hand, and mutters : "Say, what dey gone done wid poor Massa Howard ? "

To him Mendoza bursts forth in jeering laugh : "*Diablo !* It is death ! "

"Oh, my Lordy, what'll dey say in New York ? "

"They won't say anything. They'll never hear. You'll not go back to tell 'em," chuckles Domingo. "I don't think you'll try to run away after what you got the last time from your kind new master. Eh, slave ? " And the ruffian grins as the ex-darky exquisite writhes and shudders at the dread recollection. "My *aguar- diente*, quick, you loafer ! "

"Yes, sah."

"Say, 'Yes, Massa,' you scoundrel. You seem to forget."

"Yes, Massa, you scoundrel," mutters the miserable one. "Pomp don't forget."

And as he turns away, there is an awful devilish, Dahomey flash in his white, rolling eyeballs that shows that Pomp don't forget, though Mendoza had better remember.

* * *

CHAPTER XI.

"TO-MORROW MORNING THEY SHOOT ME."

But while military barbarity is going on in the prison-pen, military gallantry is doing bravely on the battery by the water.

The Spanish colonel is bending most assiduously over the American heiress, and telling her his brightest anecdotes of life in Madrid, when he was a junior officer of the Guard, and a very wild young gallant of the Don César de Bazan type.

To these confidences the girl has laughed, archly : "I am afraid you have not yet forgotten high life in

Madrid, Colonel. Even in the tropics, you look as if you had had many flirtations." adding, lightly : "Per haps, here is one of them coming now ? "

For approaching the little rock landing-steps, which the waters lave almost below them, is one of those dugouts made by natives from the great ceiba trunks— a craft that is a mixture of boat and canoe. It is pad- dled by a Cuban girl, aided by a negro boy of curious gesticulation and wild and excited grimace.

"I do not think I have ever seen her before," answers the colonel, shading his eyes and looking earnestly. "But *Dios mio,* she is beautiful as a cygnet !" He strokes his moustachios with a Ruiz Blas manner, and runs over in his mind some amourettes he has had in Caimanera without adding to his knowledge of the lady, for he mutters : "I do not remember her."

As this has been spoken, the girl, whose great beauty is exquisitely displayed by a simple dress of deep black, has sprung out of the craft, run lightly up the landing steps, and having spoken to the sentry, who has stopped her at the water gate, is being conducted by the sergeant of the guard to the old adobe buildings.

"*Santos,* they are taking her to my quarters !" cries the old soldier, apparently surprised.

"Ah, I am beginning to grow jealous," laughs the American girl. "She is such a pretty creature."

"Jealous ! That would be the delight of my life, Señorita Blanche."

And gazing at the loveliness that is before him, gal- lant words come to the ancient colonel's lips, and he curses under his breath with many fierce Spanish oaths the intruding sergeant who here steps up to him, and, saluting, announces : "A girl at your quarters, Señor Colonel, begs you to honor her with a word."

"On what business did she come ? "

"That she did not state, sir, directly. She simply

said on an affair of life and death, and one concerning the honor of the arms of Spain."

"The honor of the arms of Spain always commands me," answers Villalonga shortly. Then turning to Miss Grayson, he adds : "Some appeal from the inhabitants of the country for protection against the insurgents, perhaps. But it will not take long. You will excuse me if I send a bright-eyed boy lieutenant to your side."

"Oh yes ; send the lieutenant—any one," cries Miss Grayson carelessly. "No, I mean come *yourself*," she adds, seeing she has wounded by her careless words a gentleman who has been very polite to her. So she giving him a pretty glance, the old officer salutes, and followed by his sergeant strides up the little shell-path that leads to his quarters.

Then Blanche gazes pensively over the rippling waves and seeing far down the bay the white awnings of the *Hermes* a deep sigh escapes from her rosy lips, for, she is thinking : "To-morrow I shall be on my way to my northern home," and a little shudder quivers through her graceful frame as into her mind flies : "Home— without *him*."

But conquering this, she mutters : "Pish ! He is not worthy of a thought—and yet he seemed noble and true to me—but facts say other things about Mr. Howard Temple. A blow to your vanity, eh Blanche? Tra-la-la ; I am strong enough to rise above it. O Heaven ! what's this ? "

For an excited vivacious darky voice is saying almost in her ear : "O laws-a-massey ! *Santos y demonios*, ain't dem lobely boots you's wearing." And a negro boy, dressed more completely than many of his race in Cuba, for he wears a striped cotton shirt and pantaloons of Mexican cut thrown open over his claw-like naked feet that glisten in the sun's rays, and on his head is an enormous, but battered sombrero with gaudy tarnished silver band, is inspecting her, from white os- trich-plumed hat to extravagant pannier and looped-up skirt,—from head to heel, as it were, chiefly the heel at present. For he has put eyes of excited admiration upon two extremely high-heeled French bottines of white satin, tightly laced over the graceful ankles and topped off, as was the fashion of that day, with very fetching silken cords and tassels.

But before the girl, who is rather appalled by the suddenness of his address and the admiration evident in his tones, can say a word, he bursts out : "Say, gibe me one of dem tassels on dem boots. Good lordy, you beats de band. I wonder if you's like one of Pomp's gals in New York."

"What do you mean, you little atrocious wretch?" cries Miss Grayson savagely. "Where did you get such fearful American slang, you little Spanish negro?"

"From Señor Pomposo Smith," cries the creature. "Say, you comes from New York, don't you? You knows Señor Pomposo Smith?"

"Señor Pomposo Smith. Who's he?"

"What! Don't know Señor Pomposo Smith. Why he said eberybody in New York knowed him."

"I am not acquainted with Señor Pomposo Smith," answers Blanche sternly. Then she suddenly says, a tone of interest in her voice, "You are the boy who came in the boat a few minutes since with the girl in black?"

Here the urchin astounds and horrifies her.

"Yas, I'se Tado," he laughs.

"Tado what?"

"Don't know. Señor Vidal neber gabe me no udder name."

"Señor Vidal?"

"Yas, I'se Señorita Maria's boy now since her bruder

got cotched by de Spaniards and——." He checks himself suddenly.

"Her brother! Señorita Maria Vidal is at that officer's quarters?" gasps the girl. "For what does she come here?"

But Tado suddenly grows half idiotic and chuckles: "Say, gibe me a real to put in dis hat?" and he shoves before her the dilapidated thing he has taken from his woolly head.

"Ten *reals*, if you answer my question."

At this suggestion, the boy, his face becoming more leering and imbecile, cuts a caper or two before her, and guffaws: "Say, gibe me dem tassels on yo' boots!"

Here the girl astounds him, for she cries: "Ten *reals* to keep your mouth *shut!*" and tosses the silver into his astonished hand.

"Hush, not a word!" she mutters, and springs hurriedly up, her face growing pale. For into her mind has flown: "The boy said her brother had been caught. If so, Maria Vidal is here about him. If harm has come to Luis—O God of mercy—Laura!"

Her sister's light laugh coming from the neighboring embrasure makes Blanche tremble. She thinks: "I must see for myself. I must know before I strike her heart!" and flits hurriedly up the shell walk towards the colonel's quarters, the negro urchin strolling after her and every now and then cutting a caper and uttering a wild guffaw as he chinks the silver in his pocket.

Miss Grayson's light steps soon bring her to the veranda fronting the officers' quarters. No military gentlemen are upon it; the sun's heat having passed, the junior officers are, most of them, on the battery with some ladies of Caimanera, who have come over to listen to *la retreta*, and use their eyes and fans upon the hearts of martial gallants.

As Blanche puts foot upon the balcony, words float through the open door and windows to her that make her pause affrighted, and *know* she has guessed the awful truth.

"I can listen to you no farther, Señorita," comes to Miss Grayson, in the curt though polite terms of Villa-longa.

"For the sake of the Virgin. You do not know. Life and death hang upon my seeing him." The sweetness and pathos of the voice would enchant Blanche, but these tones in caressing potency have lured her lover from her side. Even in her agony for her sister, it brings another despair to her.

"Impossible," returns the *comandante*. "Lieutenant, you will show this lady from the fort! No, no, I can listen to you no further." For apparently the girl has made some entreating gesture.

A moment later, a graceful maid, her face deeply veiled, perchance to conceal the tears that are in her eyes, perhaps to hide its beauties from the leering glances of Spanish soldiers, steps falteringly upon the veranda. Then, with a sudden impulse, she would turn back as if to plead again, but Lieutenant Gonzales stepping after her, says harshly : "Girl, leave this fort ! "

Turning upon him for one moment, the Señorita throws up her veil, and gives to Blanche a glimpse of a face of pathetic southern beauty though its dark eyes are lighted with contempt and passion, as she says : "How can I expect mercy from the race that murdered my poor little brother ? "

The lieutenant, with a snarl stretches out a brutal hand to seize the girl and shove her from the place, but the colonel stepping hurriedly from his room, interposes observing : "Gonzales, remember we do not war with women."

Then, bowing with prim yet knightly courtesy, he takes off his cap, and remarks : "Señorita Vidal, your brother is the enemy of my country, but I remember I also have a sister in far-away Castile," waves his hand to indicate he can say no more to her, for she has made another appealing gesture.

Seeing that there is naught before her here, the girl cries suddenly : "Tado, come with me !" She has already stepped from the veranda, and is upon the shell walk, when Villalonga turning, ejaculates : "Miss Grayson, you here?   This is a happy surprise."

But the American girl does not answer him, her mind being engaged upon a mighty problem.

So he goes on effusively : "Ah, Señorita Blanche, I am happy you have not listened to my bright-eyed lieutenants, but have deigned to honor me with your attention again.   In your great New York.——" Villalonga's voice grows low and soft as he whispers a little plea into the fair ear that the drooping head places so convenient to his tones.

Catching these words the Cuban girl gives three quick shudders.   " Miss   Grayson—Blanche !—New York !—Oh, *Madre doloroso*, she who has his love—she who has everything—she who, my brother Luis has told me, wears the ring of promised marriage on her finger from him !   She has come to save him !" and makes a turn as if to come to the veranda again.

But Gonzales is by her side.   He has taken her hand. and is whispering brutally : "Leave the fort !   These are the orders.   Obey them !   Leave the fort !"

And his superior's head being turned from him, for the *comandante* is now saying some pretty complimentary Spanish things to the American girl, Maria Vidal with one more quick glance of envy and despair at the beautiful creature who has won the heart she loves before it ever reached her side, mutters sadly :

"Come, Tado. I have other work for you now," and stepping down the little walk, leaves the parade ground followed by the urchin blackamoor who has been playing catch-penny with his silver coins despite the dangerously longing glare at his treasure of a near-by sentry.

Gazing after her to be sure she will not return, Gonzales steps back to the veranda, and approaches his superior, who is still doing most of the talking to Miss Grayson, for his guest is only answering him in short monosyllables, though her lips quiver and three is a far-away look in her eyes.

Saluting the *comandante*, Gonzales remarks : " Pardon me, Señor Colonel, if I suggest it is necessary to sign——" He hesitates here.

" Sign what ? " cries Villalonga sharply, for the American beauty's distrait and preoccupied manner have made him somewhat testy.

"Sign the order for the execution of Number 93 to-morrow morning."

At this, Blanche gives a horrified shuddering start, faltering : "Good Heavens ! You are going to put that prisoner to death ? "

But Don Pablo does not answer this directly. He turns sharply to his lieutenant, and says : "See how you have startled Señorita Grayson." Then, bowing to Blanche, he adds : " Perchance Gonzales is mistaken, but in any case don't think me cruel for doing what I must—my duty as a soldier. I will return to you very shortly."

Accompanied by his lieutenant, to whom apparently he is speaking rather sternly, for Blanche hears him mutter : "Don't you see how you have frightened her," he disappears into his quarters, leaving the girl with white lips and panting bosom, gasping to herself : "Number 93 ! I must remember that ! Number 93 ! "

Suddenly the quick thought of the Anglo-Saxon flies through all the misery in her brain. "I must be sure Number 93 is Luis Vidal—to act for my sister. I shall be cooler than Laura. She would be frantic with agony. I must see and be certain! How to do it?"

Then she thinks hard: "What plea is the surest, what bribe the most alluring to the average Spanish officer?" The answer to this comes sharp, strong and convincing: "Gold!"

She has seen how the love of pelf has worked upon Spanish custom officials in every port they have been in on this cruise. She remembers how they have whispered in her ear: "For an *onza* placed on my eye, I am partially blind. For two *onzas*, one on either optic, I shall see nothing." So she cries to herself: "Gold!" and putting her hand in her pocket, finds her purse is full of its equivalent—United States greenbacks.

She steps hurriedly but lightly to the end of the veranda, looks through the little path that she can see leads through the graceful shrubbery of the tropics to the stockade. Along this she trips quickly; and at the gate of the prison pen, whose odor would at any other time have made her retrace her dainty footsteps, sees the sergeant of the guard, the omnipresent cigarette between his black teeth, and a drowsy sentry who paces before the wicket in a languid, perfunctory way.

"*Aqui!*" she calls, bringing her Spanish to bear, and waves the non-commissioned officer to her, slipping behind some plantain trees that take her out of eye-shot of the sentry.

For a moment the sergeant looks astounded; then, remembering her as the lady his chief has delighted to honor this day, he comes to her, salutes respectfully, and is delighted as the girl produces a well-filled purse.

Taking from it most of its contents, Blanche says :
" You understand this ? "

" Si, Señorita—*Dinero* of the *Americanos*."

" Good in Cuba ? "

" Good as Spanish gold ! "   The man's face lights
up, and, marvelous to relate, he tosses away his
paper cigar.

" Behold ! "

" Aha !   What would you, honored lady ?   It must
be of great importance," answers the sergeant, his
eyes growing big ; for the amount of money placed
before him astounds him.

" The prisoner, Number 93, condemned to death—I
must see him ! "

" Impossible !   *Santa Maria !*   You ask my life !
He is *incomunicado*."

" *This*, for two minutes' interview ! " she whispers,
and counts out all the money in her purse with trembling fingers and pleading glance.   " You are the
sergeant of the guard ? "

" Wait here ! " whispers the man, and reaches for
the bills.

But with quick instinct, she answers : " No !   The
money *after* I see the prisoner ! "

Then Blanche gives a hopeless sigh, for the sergeant
has hurried from her.

A moment later she hears him giving orders to the
sentry.   Apparently it is the hour of the change of
guard.   She hears a bugle sound, and, looking at her
watch, notes it is nearly the even hour.

A second later the sergeant, with quick steps coming to her, mutters : " While I change the guard—before the relief—there are two minutes."   And opening
the gate of the stockade, he pushes her into this place
of filth, dirt, offal and hideous smells.   Then, pointing
to a little barred opening, he whispers : " There ! the

second from the door! Quick! Speak to him if he is
not crazy, speak to him!" and turns hurriedly away.
The gate closes on him. She can hear the sergeant
outside of the stockade arranging the sentries of the
relief.

Then, knowing she has but little time, with two
quick sighing steps, her hand upon her heart, and
muttering: "Pray God, for Laura's sake, it is *not* her
lover," she is at the opening. She places her fair face
against the bars, and, gazing into the darkness of the
foul-smelling cell, whispers with trembling lips: "Luis
Vidal!"

A deep-drawn moaning sigh answers her.

"Luis!" She is speaking desperately now. "I
come to see you—to save you. Luis!" Her eyes
are sparkling with excited dread, the setting sun illu-
mines and halos the delicate loveliness of her pallid
features.

At her words, a creature gaunt with famine, whose
faced is lined with misery, whose blood-shot eyes stare
at her blinking and unknowing, whose hair is matted
with the filth of a Spanish prison, rises up before her.

Not a foot away they gaze, eye to eye, and face to
face, his feverish breath playing on her sweet lips.
Suddenly, the red sun's rays tinge and make vivid his
agonized features, and she cries: "Thank God, it is
not Luis Vidal—this crazy convict!"

For he is muttering: "The face I have prayed to
see." Suddenly he utters a heart-breaking laugh and
gasps: "Yes, their tortures have driven me mad.
Blanche!"

But the girl has answered this with a low moaning
sigh: "I am crazy also."

"And yet she swore to me!" cries the man, his
emaciated hands reaching out and seizing the white
arm of beauty ; then, looking into her face with glances

that burn like red-hot irons into her heart, mutters:
"And yet she swore to me, by her ring and by her
love, I'll find you, Howard Temple! Living or
dead, I'll find you!"

"Those words I gave to but one living man, and
but one living man can give them back to me!" Her
voice is as maniac as his own.

"Blanche!"

"Howard!"

The fair arms plunge into the darkness of the cell
between the bars, and strain him to her. The fair lips
reach the grating and on them are placed the fevered
caresses of love struggling with despair, of hope fighting against death.

Then he, growing calmer first, whispers: "By
Heaven, I knew you'd find me! I was arrested on
the Vidal plantation as Luis Vidal."

"Oh, don't talk of that," shudders the girl. "I forgive that. Tell me how to save you, for——" she falters
here.

"For to-morrow morning they shoot me."

"Through my heart first!" and her arms are round
him; in the agony of his coming death she has forgotten the agony of her loss of love.

Then the man speaking quickly and sharply, whispers: "You must get word to the American consul!"

"Impossible!" moans Blanche. "He is not within
reach."

"Telegraph the Captain-General!"

"How—with no wire nearer than Santiago!" she
gasps, wringing her hands.

"Then to-morrow morning before that wall——"

"O God, no! Tell me—teach me how to save
you."

And he, thinking for his life, mutters: "There is but
one—one little chance."

·" What's that ? "

" Gold ! The same means that doubtless gave you access to me."

" Yes, they can be bribed," whispers the girl, a spasm of hope flitting over her face.

" Contrive in some way to get me means to leave this place. Have a boat from the yacht. You came in the *Hermes ?* ' "

" Yes, yes ! "

" Have a boat off that cove," he waves his hand towards the rear of the place, " outside the fort. A path leads from this prison down to it. I have noticed —I have watched—had I had money I might have been free myself. But the guerillas stole all that from me."

" And you will meet that boat ? "

" Yes, at twelve o'clock to-night ! They change the guard then. "

" You will he there ? "

" Or be dead ! "

" No ; no !—That means my death also."

To this he whispers hastily : " Don't let the memory of a poor fellow who died because he loved you——"

" Who shall live because he loved me ! " cries the girl who has forgotten everything save that the man she has loved—ay, does love still—is dying.

But suddenly a hand is fiercely laid upon her arm. The sergeant is whispering and cursing: " No more! Quick ! The last sentry is being placed. *Santos* ! Quick ! or I am a lost man ! " and is dragging her away from the opening.

Even in the daze of her agony Blanche knows she must not be seen communicating with the prisoner. That might destroy his one chance ! She passes her hand warm as with fever over ner brow chilled with despair, and mutters : " To save him I must control my•

self," and staggers through the gate of the stockade.

But sighing words are floating after her, that she
does not hear: "O God of Heaven, I forgot to warn
her of the villain who betrayed me!"

BOOK IV.

THE MOONLIGHT SURPRISE.

CHAPTER XII.

"TRUST ORTIZ!"

BLANCHE has placed the reward in the Spanish sergeant's outstretched hands, and is staggering through the little tropical pathway unheeding its thorns and briars and trailing branches. The sun is in her eyes. Half dazed with misery, she scarcely sees.

To her comes a light voice as she reaches the end of the shrubbery. Miss Morales is saying in elder-sister tones : "Blanche, you should be more careful ! What have you been doing about that horrid prison pen ? Colonel Villalonga has been looking for you everywhere."

Suddenly Laura pauses and starts, a chill of dread running through her veins. For Blanche has clasped her hand convulsively, and whispered wildly : "I— O, God, I have seen *him !* They shoot him to-morrow morning ! "

"Shoot him ! Shoot *whom ?* Speak !—O Heaven, you mean Luis ! " And Laura reeling also, is gasping : " If my love is in their cruel Spanish hands, nothing can save him. He is the insurgent leader whom they hate."

159

L

"Not your love, Laura ; but my love !" whispers Blanche, who sees the awful misery in her sister's face. "Not Luis Vidal, but Howard Temple !"

"Howard Temple ? "

"Yes, Howard Temple, who is a prisoner in that hole," repeats the girl, her voice harsh and discordant. "Don't you understand me ? " For Laura has started back, thinking her sister crazy. "They—shoot him— to death—in that pen—in place of your lover, Luis Vidal. Help me to save him ! "

"You are mad ! "

"O Heaven, if I were ! "

"Howard Temple is an American ! "

"But by some awful chance mistaken for Vidal, the Cuban leader."

Then, passing her hand over her brow, which is cold as ice, her brain within it throbbing and dizzy, Blanche mutters : "I must play my part. Colonel Villalonga must not guess that I have been admitted to see a prisoner *incomunicado*, and found him—O Heaven, the man I love. Go to the yacht, Laura ! Bring my father here. Tell him as he loves his daughter's life and reason, to come quick. Tell him," she jeers hysterically, "as a business man he must save his junior partner."

"And you ? "

"I stay here to try and regain my self-control driven from me by this awful shock. For God's sake, get my father here that I may consult with him. Then she cries in desperate command : "Quick ! To my father ! "

So Miss Morales, shuddering, yet overcoming herself, turns and makes her way as rapidly as possible towards the water-gate of the fort, hoping to catch a boat to take her to the yacht.

But at its very archway, she meets Ignacio, whose face

is as pale as her own, gives a fervid exclamation of joy, runs to him and whispers : "Ortiz, God has sent you to me ! "

"*Santissima*, I hope so," he mutters, and, taking out his handkerchief, wipes his brow, which is covered with the perspiration of haste, or fear, or some other unknown emotion.

"Yes, Blanche has seen Howard Temple, who is *incomunicado* in that prison."

"Seen Howard Temple ! In that prison ! " These are two faint cries from the Spaniard, whose face has grown even more pallid than before.

"Of course you do not know. O Heavens, who could guess such horrors ! Howard Temple ; they shoot him to-morrow ! You know the Spanish officers ? "

"Intimately."

"Then come with me, quick ! You know Temple is Blanche's affianced husband."

"*Madre de Dios*, yes ! "

"Come before she faints."

With light steps, Laura leads Ortiz hurriedly through the parade ground, and in another minute they are at the side of Blanche, who has been crying to herself : "I must be cool, collected, diplomatic," and yet shuddering : "How can I be calm when my heart is breaking ? "

To her Laura has uttered : "I have brought Ortiz who knows the Spanish officers ! "

As he has come Ignacio's agitation has increased. He is as trembling as the girl who turns eyes full of awful unshed tears upon him, and whispers : "They shoot Howard Temple to-morrow morning," then cries : "Don't look as if you doubt me ! *I have seen him !* "

At the words the Spaniard's face grows bloodless as

marble as he stammers : "*Caramba!* And—and you know—?"

"Everything!"

"*O Dios de mi alma!*" There is a horror in his voice.

"Don't look at me in that dazed way !" cries Blanche desperately.   "They shoot him to-morrow! Howard was arrested as Luis Vidal on the Vidal plantation by some horrible mistake."

"Impossible !   He—he is an American citizen."

"Impossible? When his bloodshot eyes have gazed into mine ! When his breaking heart has beat against mine ! When he has told me with his own parched lips !"

"Told you *what?*" This is a shriek of dismay from her listener.

"That they kill him to-morrow morning. Shoot him to death by a file of soldiers. Ah! you are trembling for him. He is your old friend. You are a Spaniard and know the Spanish officers. Help me to save his life !"

"I do know the Spanish officers. I will help you to save his life with my own !" cries Ortiz, enthusiastically. Confidence seems to have replaced fear in his heart.

"God forever bless you !" falters Blanche, and, seizing his hand, she wildly kisses it.

Here, fire running in his veins from the first touch of her lips, this unutterable villain thinks with a spasm of joy and hope: "*Diablo!* Temple has not told her *all.*" Then he says quite calmly : "In order to aid you efficiently, make me your confidant; tell me everything."

"Yes, Ortiz must know," whispers Laura.

Then to him Blanche falters out her piteous story, once or twice with little flutters of her hands when the agony is too potent, and all the time her eyes have in them those awful unshed tears that show she has little hope.

And he, listening to her and looking at her beauty, which has grown, even as she speaks, more spirituel in its pathos, more alluring in its anguish, thinks in his subtile analytical mind : "Now she is mine beyond a doubt ! If not her love, surely her gratitude will give her to me."

Then he speaks to Blanche and his confidence lifts her up, and makes her for the first moment feel some hope of success. " These Spanish officers," he says, " have all been my friends for the weeks I have been here. There is probably only one way to save Señor Temple, his execution comes so soon."

At this, a shuddering sigh racks the girl's graceful frame.

"But don't despair," he whispers. "The one way I speak of is gold, of which you have sufficient."

"Yes, any sum—any price."

"I will investigate. How much have you with you ? "

"I have given the sergeant all," says Blanche showing an empty purse.

" But here is mine ! " cries Laura, and she tosses into his hand a wallet bulky with bills, adding some half dozen glittering rings she strips from her delicate fingers.

"With what I have with me, this will surely be enough to begin the matter," Ortiz returns easily. "Now, for Temple's safety, we must all notwithstanding our anxiety, play the diplomatist. Come with me back to the parade ground. Listen to the music ; flirt with the colonel. That's what you were doing a few minutes ago, I believe, Señorita Blanche. Meantime, I will investigate." Then he asks anxiously : "Have you the strength to play your part ? "

"For his sake I have," answers his victim, with an awful attempt at firmness.

But Laura mutters : "In the name of Heaven, don't trust her. See, she is drooping now! Quick something to revive her—Ortiz, for God's sake !"

For the music from the band is being wafted faintly to the suffering girl—some soft melody from Martha.

Catching its strains, into Blanche's mind flies the recollection of that last night at the opera, when, had she been true to her love, and not to her pride, he who is dying here would have been safe with her in far-away America. This torturing thought overcomes her and she is gasping : "Home—without *him!*" in a way that makes this scoundrel who looks upon her now as his very own, furious with jealous rage against the dying man who causes her heart to bleed.

Scarce able to control his temper, he says hastily : "Leave all in my hands. Miss Blanche, remain with Señorita Laura ; I go for something to revive you."

And the girl answering him by a nod, for she can scarcely speak, he hurries from her, but out of her sight stands thinking as if for his existence.

Suddenly he laughs : "*Caramba*, Mendoza ! *Dios mio*, what a grand coup ! *Mi querida* who is sighing there shall worship me as the hero for her soul. Then there will be no more sobs for this dead man, but kisses for me, the living. Ah, happy Ortiz !" and steps briskly away towards the hut of the Spanish spy, whistling a lovely little chanson very merrily.

Two minutes afterards he comes hurriedly from under Mendoza's thatched roof and mutters, his brow clouded, his hands trembling a little : "I must remove her from every chance of seeing that accursed negro."

So Blanche, wondering if it is not a dream from which to-morrow she will awake and be happy, stands clasping the trunk of a cocoanut tree to hold herself up, awaiting Ignacio's coming. But the sound of hammer and hatchet in a neighboring shed makes her know it is reality, dreadful and awful. The hammer seems to strike her heart. Thank God she does not guess its import!

Three minutes after, Ortiz returns bearing some *aguardiente* in a gourd. "It was the best I could get, without explanations," he remarks; as Laura half forces some drops of this down Blanche's throat, the fiery liquor seeming to strengthen her.

With this, Ortiz suggests: "Señorita Laura, you had better lead your sister out of the fort to keep her away from contact with Spanish officers for a little while. Just step along that pathway that leads to that little cove."

"The one where I have promised to have the boat for him to-night?" whispers Blanche suddenly. "Remember that!—That is his chance!"

"Yes."

But Blanche doesn't seem to hear him.

The hammering in the shed has suddenly ceased.

She has started to her feet with a low gasping moan.

"See!" She points to some men who are carrying a rough wooden box into the prison pen, laughing and joking over it. "Oh my God! His—his coffin!" and reels and would fall to the earth were not Laura's arms about her. "Quick, take me from this fort, whose horrors drive me mad!" she cries with eyes filled with agony. "Take me away before I run to Villalonga and scream out to him for justice or for mercy."

"That would probably destroy Temple's only chance!" murmurs Ortiz—"Quick, Miss Laura!"

At this they both hurry Blanche along. But having passed the fortifications, Ignacio who seems well acquainted with the place and to be known to the sentries, remarks: "I will go back and make a quick

investigation.   Laura, remember on your sister's giving
no sign depends our success and Temple's life."

"Don't fear me," answers Miss Morales, with flashing eyes.   "Don't you see how much calmer I am
than Blanche.   It is not to be wondered at.   My lover
is not dying there."   She waves her hand towards the
prison pen, then falters : "My sister, lean on me.
O mercy, you are staggering !" and takes the sufferer
to her heart.

"Now I must go," Ortiz adds suavely.   "It is
necessary that I know Temple's exact status.   When I
return, Señorita Blanche, be sure I shall bring you
hope !"   With these words which again lift up the girl
and give her greater fortitude, Ignacio steps hurriedly
away, and passing the sentry, re-enters the fort.

As he has suggested, Laura supporting her sister at
times, for Blanche stumbles over trailing vines, and
little inequalities in the tropic path, they wander into
a scene of beauty ; but heed it not.   For their steps are
hedged by the brightest wild flowers of the equator, red
cacti blooms, orchids and ferns, and creepers covered
with blossoms of varying yet vivid color, and about is
the great green tropic forest, overspreading palms and
feathery bamboos.

But nature's charms are as naught to Blanche.   She
stumbles on, but one thought in her soul : "Howard !
will Ortiz save him ?"

Soon footsteps follow them ; and this man to whom
she now looks for every good of life is once more by
her side, and whispering eagerly : "I have arranged
it !   *Madre de Dios*, dear Señorita Blanche, I have
arranged it !"

"You—you mean Howard's certain safety ? "

"Yes !"

"God's blessing on you !"

"'Tell us, quick !"

The first comes from Blanche, the second from Laura, and both the girls are about him with eager words and impassioned gestures.

To them he whispers: "Come with me. We must not be overheard." So, taking Blanche by her white hand to aid her faltering footsteps, he leads her down the path that grows in tropic beauty as it enters the little cove, and by a quick descent along rocks, bedded in wild flowers and creepers, reaches the white wave-lapped beach.

Upon Ortiz' face is the radiance of proprietary love, as he looks upon the loveliness that he at times supports, for Miss Grayson's steps are still uncertain, and once or twice, O happy joy! the touch comes to him of the glorious contour of her figure, as the rough rocky steps of the path jostle her against his protecting arm.

Then, the trail descending sharply, he springs in front of both the girls, and at a high boulder from which Laura would have scrambled down, he swings Miss Morales lightly to the lower shelf of rock, and she, tripping ahead of him, he turns to assist Miss Grayson.

But Blanche's beauty makes him pause. He gazes in rapture at the drooping figure that stands above him. His eye lingers on the exquisite loveliness that is even now, he thinks, within his hands. In careless attitude the girl stands, with one outstretched hand seeking his support; with the other, unconsciously, she has gathered up the clinging skirts of her gauzy robe. His eyes catch the delicate feet, cased in the petite white boots, laced high over tapering ankles and decked with the fashionable tassels which had excited Tado's admiring wonder. Above them is a glimpse of rounded limbs, perfect in their graceful contours and molded like those of Venus, the slight web of silken stockings permitting the dazzling sheen of her fair flesh to tint them.

She murmurs : "Aid me, please?" And his glance flies to her face with its blue eyes that once or twice scintillate like sapphires with nervous anguish, and then becoming teary are veiled by their long, drooping lashes as the red lips that are pallid now, but still beautiful in the sensitive delicacy of their expression, quiver with latent anxiety.

Her hand is still extended to him. As he looks on her, he notes the gleaming whiteness of her admirably modeled arms and shoulders that glisten like polished marble, cool and snowy, through the light tissues of her tropic costume.

In his imagination, he sees these beauties all his own, he hears her call him husband, he feels the clinging caresses of those sweet lips as they acknowledge him their lord and master, and for one instant his fervid temperament gives him a vision of paradise.

"Aid me, please, dear Señor Ortiz?" pleads his lovely victim.

And he, awakening with a start, suddenly takes Blanche in his arms, lifts her tenderly to the lower rock, and leads her carefully down the deep descent, speaking in softest voice words of sympathy and aid, for he wants her to feel that he, and he alone, has power to guide her through this day and—ever afterwards.

But his touch is so ardent, his voice so passionate that at any other moment in her life, Miss Grayson would know it is not sympathy for Temple that is in this man's heart, but love for her, burning and fierce, that Spanish love, which says : "You shall be mine—mine only ! Let him beware who stands between your kisses and my lips."

But there is only one thought in this girl's mind : "Save him—I must—I will ! Howard shall live though all the powers of earth are raised against him ! For if he dies my life ends also ! "

So they come down into a little cove that seems nature's fairyland. The high cliffs in rocky terraces descend to the ripples of the Caribbean, now and then being broken into erratic and greater beauties by rocks and crags covered by wild flowers or growing tree ferns.

Over them twine creepers decked with vivid tropic blossoms, and above all wave giant palm trees of tufted feathery green, in varied species, royals and cocoanuts. From one ferny cliff a babbling spring sends a cool cascade over an arched rock, to meet the soft rippling waters of the sea that have floated in from the great Bay of Guantanamo over coral reefs to lap the white sand beach.

This—tinted by the sun's declining rays, that now, as they are leaving this deep retreat, have tinged rocks and plants and water-fall and waves with the bright crimson of a tropic sunset—glows carmine.

"O God," falters Blanche, "the place seems blood."

But Ortiz sharply commands : "Drive such hysteria from your mind," then whispers : "Now far away from the stronghold of his enemies, where no chance ear can listen to betray us, I can tell you how we will save him."

"Quick !" cries the girl. "You have kept me too long. My anxiety has been too great ; too awful. In God's name what have you done ? "

"I have discovered," says Ortiz tenderly yet confidently, "that there was enough evidence against Temple to convict. A court-martial has sentenced him."

"Yes, yes ; I know all that ! "

"We cannot apply to the American consul, for he is absent. We cannot telegraph to the Captain-General, for there is no telegraph."

"But there is a wire from Santiago to Havana!" cries Laura.

"Yes, and in this light wind it might take a day to travel the forty or fifty miles from Caimanera to that place. Then the delay of sending and receiving answer from Havana. At best, with a leading wind good, strong and full, you could not be sure of the *Hermes* bringing return message within the twelve short hours that mark his span of life."

"The steamer unloaded at the wharf!" cries Blanche, a sudden ecstasy illuminating her features.

But this dies out as Ortiz speaks. "Only half un-loaded. The consignees to be found; permission to be obtained; charter to be made; permission of captain of the port to sail; her fires not lighted. Besides, after she reached Santiago, it would be hours before answer came from the Captain-General. The steamer, if you could make arrangements, even with all the money at your command, would be too late."

"Yes; yes,—it is his life! I—I dare not take the risk."

"Furthermore, it would be known why the vessel was chartered. That would prevent the slightest hope of Temple's escape in any other way; extra precautions would be taken; his guards be doubled."

"Then I shall appeal to Villalonga!" screams Blanche, hysterically.

"A sure way to prevent Temple's escape," whispers Ortiz. "None save the Captain-General can stay this execution. Colonel Villalonga has a soldier's iron heart; he must and will do his duty."

"He dare not do it. My affianced is an American! My father shall threaten Villalonga with the vengeance of my country——"

"Did that save the *Virginius* captives?" sneers Ortiz, "When your State Department permitted their

slayer, Burriel, to live in honor ; from that moment
Spanish officers no longer feared the vengeance of a
country who let its flag be captured on the high seas,
and its citizens be executed under its consul's eyes,
without reprisal."

"Do you think I will remain and let Howard Temple be slaughtered? I *will* do something !" cries the
girl, desperately ; and though half fainting, she turns
to run up the path.

But Laura has clutched her frantically by the arm,
and Ortiz is whispering : "I *have* done something !"

"What?" His victim is gazing upon him—her hand
upon her beating heart.

"The officer of the guard is my friend. If he is assured a sufficient reward, he will permit Howard Temple to escape to-night."

"Is this true?—for God's sake don't trick me. It is
easier for me to know the worst !" sobs the girl, though
no tears are in her eyes.

"It is as true as Heaven !"

"Then money will buy him?" asks Laura, eagerly.

"Like many Spanish officers, Manuel Gonzales loves
gold better than duty."

"Tell Manuel Gonzales," whispers Blanche, "that
if Number 93 escapes to-night, a fortune in America
awaits the officer of that guard."

"He may doubt," answers Ignacio. "He must
have proof. Ten thousand dollars."

"The diamonds my mother left me are on the
Hermes. You remember, Laura, I wore them at the
Captain-General's reception. My sister, go on board
the yacht. Give them to Ortiz. They are worth a
little fortune. Gonzales must believe them."

"He shall have mine, too," answers Laura, her eyes
on fire.

"Thank you !" cries Blanche.

But the generous girl, whispers : "I but do for you what you would do for me, if Luis Vidal were in Howard Temple's place."

"May I also be permitted to add my mite?" suggests the Spaniard, insinuatingly.

"If more is needed, ask my father!" cries Blanche, commandingly ; for on learning that the guard can be bribed she has become as one inspired. "Tell my father, Laura, as he loves his daughter's life, to have the yacht ready to sail, and the boat off this cove, at twelve o'clock to-night."

"You are not coming with us?" asks Laura, anxiously.

"No, no! Not now! I should feel I was deserting *him!* I do not leave this shore till I know that he will live. Oh, don't fear for me now. when I am fighting with hope in my heart for Howard Temple's life!" whispers the girl. "I am strong enough to play my rôle. Colonel Villalonga would think it strange if I left without bidding him adieu. Send him to me."

"At this, Ortiz, who has made a step up the path, returns to her, and whispers, warningly : "You must say nothing to him. If Villalonga suspects me of bribing that guard, I shall fall by the side of Temple."

"True friend," answer his victim, her eyes gazing gratitude and friendship into his. "True comrade ; for Howard's sake, you endure danger, also." And she extends to this successful villain an eager and a grateful hand, which he, seizing, kisses with rapture.

Looking upon her, Ignacio feels Blanche is surely his, and murmurs, decisively : "Quick, Señorita Morales, come with me! And now the diamonds for the doubting Gonzales. Dear Miss Blanche, I'll bring you word before you leave this place that Howard Temple will surely live! Trust Ortiz!"

And she cries back in words that make him happy:
"With my life!"

Up the path, he laughs to himself, a very curious con-
cert in his wily Carthagenian brain: "*Diablo!* How
Blanche will love me when she knows I have risked
my life even to bring Temple's dead body unto her."

CHAPTER XIII.

THE LETTER OF LIFE.

As her sister and the Spaniard disappear among the
beautiful ferns which hedge the rocky path that leads
from terrace to terrace on the cliff, Blanche mutters:
"Villalonga must not see that my cheeks have been
tear-stained. I—I must appear to him the Blanche
Grayson of the afternoon."

She runs to the little cascade. Bathing her face with
its cool waters, and drinking from its refreshing stream,
the girl finds herself more hopeful and more fitted to
fight the battle for her lover's life than she has been
since Howard Temple's fevered lips had whispered to
her of his coming death.

But others than Villalonga are coming to her.

For, since Ortiz has turned away from Mendozas
hut, a negro, whose black face is ashen with misery,
whose rags—the tattered remnants of Sixth Avenue
fashion—betray that he was once the most debonair
exquisite that walked its pavements, has glided cautiously after him. With many glances of shuddering
fear that he may be pursued by Spanish soldiers, and returned to the mercy of the inexorable Mendoza, Pomp
has skulked along the tropic pathway, following the
footsteps of the Spaniard. When he has seen Ignacio
join two young ladies in dresses of New York fashion,

his teeth nave chattered in his head from supreme astonishment, he has uttered a little muffled cry of joy, intense—but astounded. The whites of his eyes have grown big, as he muttered: "Miss Blanche and Miss Morales! How dey git har? O Gosh almighty, has dey come to sabe me! What'll dey do when I tells 'em!"

But shortly the negro hears footsteps following him, and quick exclamations in the Spanish tongue he has learned to dread—like death. So Mr. Smith, with a shudder, disappears in the dense undergrowth to let those he supposes his pursuers pass him.

For a moment, dreading the awful reckoning that has been given him with the cowhide several times when he has attempted to escape, Pomp would return and slink back to the thatched hut of his tyrant, but, pausing under a plantain tree to watch, he sees a girl in black, accompanied by a negro boy, whose gestures are vivacious, whose mien excited, whose chatter is incessant, who cries to his mistress: "Señorita Maria, I seed de American gal wid dem tassels on her boots go dis way!"

At this Pomp mutters: "Tado!" and would run out and catch the boy and his companion, but their gait is too rapid, for they fly along the path with the steps of youth.

Suddenly, they too, just at the entrance of the little cove, disappear with a sudden cry and gesture, in the tropic shrubbery and undergrowth, and Señor Smith, taking warning from them, darts through cacti and Spanish-bayonets, unheeding their thorns, and hides himself once more, then mutters: "Golly, dat war a good t'ing. Dat was luck! Har comes dat damned hellion ag'in." And his eyes grow bloodshot with Dahomey hate.

For it is Ortiz, who is returning with Miss Morales

along the path. To her the Spaniard is whispering :
" Have no fear. It is arranged. The money will make
Manuel Gonzales true to us and true to Temple.
Gracias a Dios ! Number 93 is safe as I am."

So it comes to pass as Miss Grayson, feeling herself
strong enough to do her work, turns from the little
waterfall, and even now is about to ascend the rocky
trail, thinking to meet Villalonga with light words, as
if this had been but a careless stroll, pauses and gazes,
astonished.

Two figures are running down the path to her. The
one in advance, a negro boy, comes on with wild gesticulation, crying : " Dar she is ! Dere am de gal wid
de tassels on de boots. You told me to track de American señorita and bring you to har," then mutters, his
eyes big with delight : "Cracky, ain't she a stunner !
Caramba ! She's purtier den a bull-fight ! "

But, at a gesture from Maria, he wanders away along
the shore, amusing himself by catching a few land-
crabs, that have incautiously ventured from their holes
as the sun has ceased its burning.

With hurried steps his beautiful mistress trips, agile
as an antelope, down the rocky path, waving her hand
and crying in English : "I must see you—don't turn
from me ! You are Miss Blanche Grayson, of New
York ? "

For, catching a glimpse of the beauty, in its untram-
meled grace, of this girl who she thinks has stolen from
her the love that made life happy unto her, Blanche
remembers with a shudder that, in the shock of
Temple's coming death, she had forgotten his dis-
loyalty.

" How do you know my name ? " answers Miss
Grayson, sharply ; and facing Maria feels she is in the
presence of a rival who might cause any woman to fear.

Before her is a vision of youth, loveliness, and

M

piquant archness, with eyes that plead and woo and cajole, and form of fairy grace, which is now displayed in all its native beauty by a light clinging gown of poor black muslin, whose very poverty and scantiness add to the girlish charms ; for a short skirt reveals feet light as a nymph's, and taper ankles of exquisite mold that swell into the rounded contours of a form whose curves are so graceful they would enchant eyes of man, ay— even to holding the hearts of many of them. Still, the face is the supreme beauty of the girl ; the pallor of her cheeks is now tinged with that beautiful brunette blush that gives an ivory transparency to the skin ; the lips are delicately sensitive ; the eyes black and wondrously pathetic ; the brow frank and open ; and over all is a sad nobility of expression that tells of great sorrows patiently endured and bravely met.

Were she aught but Maria Vidal, Blanche would be sympathy itself. As she is Maria Vidal, each grace, each charm, each beauty is a new horror to the American.

"My brother has often spoken to me of you."

"Your brother ? Ah, you mean Señor Luis Vidal?" remarks Miss Grayson, with icy politeness.

"Yes, Luis."

"Then you are Maria Vidal ? "

"Yes, señorita ! "

"Ah, I remember now," jeers Blanche. "The true Cuban beauty, whose dark eyes looked love."

This is muffled in so deep a sigh that Maria does not hear it, and says simply : "I have sad news for you."

"*Doubtless ?*" The covert misery scarcely hides the sneer in the voice of the American.

"Howard Temple, the gentleman you love, is a prisoner in that fort."

"I decline to discuss Mr. Temple with Señorita Maria Vidal."

"Not when I come to aid him—to aid *you* ?"

"A late time to aid him, when Howard Temple is to be shot to-morrow for your brother, who should be in yonder prison in his place!" answers Blanche savagely, indignation in her tone and gesture.

"Shot to-morrow!" gasps Maria, turning white to her very lips. "*Madre de Dios!* They—they didn't tell me that!" then moans : "Shot to-morrow! O *misericordia!* Must I then use this letter ?" and places a trembling hand upon a panting breast, that is beating as if to break forth from the robe that conceals its beauties.

But the American girl has grown strangely impressed, and is now whispering eagerly : "What letter? Has it aught to do with Howard's safety ?"

"It is his life—but my brother's death," answers the Cuban. "This letter," she draws from her bosom a little note in a coarse envelope, "my brother gave me, with these words : 'Discover if Howard Temple is to be executed. If he is, swear to me by the Holy Virgin that you will immediately deliver it to the Spanish authorities! He who so generously gave me his passport shall not lose his life to save mine!'"

"Oh, Heaven! Let me see it!" With a quick grasp Blanche has the document and, recognizing Luis Vidal's handwriting, whispers : "This is addressed to Colonel Villalonga—and you swore to deliver this ?"

"My brother made me swear."

"Then keep your oath!" commands the American girl.

But the Cuban shudders : "I cannot——" then cries : "I will not! That letter contains an offer from my brother to deliver himself to the Spanish if Howard Temple is set free."

"God be praised! But—but your brother is not·

near enough to fulfil his promise by to-morrow morning ? "

"He is not eight miles away, in the Yateras hills. You can see them from that cliff," answers Maria simply. "Luis Vidal is there, with a band of armed Cubans. That letter contains directions how to reach him." Her feet tremble, her eyes fill with tears, for she is thinking of her brother at the mercy of the Spaniard —in imagination, she sees the firing party and the burial trench.

But the other is speaking, her voice ringing happy and triumphant : "And the *real* Luis Vidal is worth to the Spanish government a hundred of the *false* ones ! This is Howard Temple's *certain* safety !" And Blanche gazes at the letter as if its dirty envelope contained the joys of Paradise.

Here a loosened stone rolling down the path shows some one is approaching, though still far up the cliff. On this, Blanche whispers in hoarse command : "Do you hear that officer coming down that path ? This letter is addressed to him. Remember your word ! Save Howard Temple ! Fulfill your oath ! "

"A sister cannot be a brother's executioner ! "

"Then I will deliver it for you ! " The American girl is springing towards the little path along which the swaying and rustling ferns tell her the Spanish colonel is hurrying to her side.

But Maria has seized her hand and is imploring : "Not if Howard has a *single* chance on earth. For when that letter is delivered my brother will not have one."

" He has—several ! "

" Then give it back to me ! "

" But this letter is his certain safety ! "

" I *will* have that letter ! " Maria Vidal is struggling wildly for it.

"Never!" And Blanche holds the paper high in air.

"You are robbing me of my brother's life!"

"As you have robbed me of Howard Temple's love!" laughs her rival.

"Think of my brother!"

"What do I care for your brother," jeers the American girl; then calls desperately: "Colonel Villalonga, I have something for you!"

"Think of *your* sister!"

"My sister!" the flush of triumph leaves Blanche's face, which becomes white as marble. "Laura!" Staggering back, she gazes half-dazed at the girl who has put this dagger into her heart.

"Who loves my brother as truly as you love your adored!"

"Y—e—s."

"You know that!" whispers the Cuban. "And could you ever say: 'Laura, my sister, behold *my* love whose life is bought with the death of the man *you* adore. Howard Temple is alive——'"

"But Luis Vidal is dead," cries Blanche, taking up the tone, a weird horror in her voice. "And I, your sister, have sacrificed him! Would Laura do this to me? No, no! Not from my hands. Take the letter; fulfill your oath!" And she is pleading to Maria.

But Señorita Vidal cries with a shudder: "No; use it yourself. Destroy your sister's happiness. Destroy my brother's life, but not if Howard Temple has the chance you say he has."

"Let me think," falters the American; and into her mind flies one convincing thought: "Ortiz, said the officer of the guard would *surely* take the bribe." Then looking at the letter gloatingly she mutters: "O Laura, how I am tempted."

Here another voice breaks in upon this zigzag of passion. It is the gallant Spanish colonel calling from some little distance up the cliff: "Señorita Blanche!"

The lord of life and death to whom the letter is addressed is coming.

"I have but to place this in his hands," she murmurs, and runs to the entrance of the path.

But the Cuban girl is in front of her imploring: "Your sister! Your sister!"

"I shall not resist," moans Blanche frantically. Then remembering the awful agony of Laura Morales when she thought the man of her heart was to be butchered, she cries: "I—I shall destroy my sister if if I don't scatter temptation to the heavens—THUS!" And a generous hysteria flying into her soul, with quick motion of her fingers, she tears the little missive that will, in Villalonga's presence be temptation irresistible, into a hundred pieces and tosses them to the winds of Heaven.

Then the revulsion comes!

She gazes at them horrified, and murmurs brokenly: "That was Howard Temple's *certain* safety! His life was his, not mine to juggle with! What horrid thing have I done?"

But the colonel is speaking to her now, as he steps from the clump of ferns and cacti at the entrance of the path.

"You deigned to call me, Señorita Blanche?" murmurs this military Don Quixote as he comes, placidly smoking a cigarette, upon his face his happiest smile, to greet the American beauty, who, he thinks, has made almost a rendezvous with him in this romantic spot, far from the prying eyes of others; for Ortiz has whispered in his ear: "She awaits you in the little cove of palms beneath the cliff."

But Don Pablo's expression is not so radiant as he sees the second maiden.

To him Miss Grayson says : "Colonel Villalonga, let me present you to Señorita Maria Vidal."

"A young lady I have met before," remarks the martinet glumly, but bowing with military grace.

"And treated with a courtesy she will not forget," sighs the Cuban girl.

Here Villalonga raises his eyebrows slightly, and chancing to catch sight of the fragments of paper, says suspiciously : "Aha ! you have been destroying a letter ? "

"Yes," replies Blanche, forcing herself to unnatural calmness. "One Miss Vidal presented to me."

"Indeed !"

"Luis Vidal, the Señorita's brother, was a friend of ours in New York," mutters the girl, her eyes filling with tears, her fluttering hand dropping a handkerchief with which she is trying to wipe them away.

"Ah, permit me." And the Spanish colonel, sinking on one knee, picks up the kerchief and restores it with military grace to this suffering beauty who has pallid cheeks with little hectic flushes on them, and whose agitated yet drooping pose shows she is fighting for self-control in the presence of this man whose lips carry words of life or death.

"You—you are a perfect Bayard," stammers the American young lady.

"Oh *Dios mio*, you honor me !" mutters the cavalier.

"And could a Bayard grant, in his knightly way, a lady's request, and make her very happy?"

"What is it that you ask ? " mutters the colonel, casting suspicious eyes upon Maria, whose hands are clasped in unconscious appeal.

"The life of—of the man whose sentence of—of execution you signed this afternoon," gasps Blanche.

Here, catching an involuntary agonized petition in

the Cuban girl's gesture, the colonel remarks : "Ah, I believe I understand."

"At least a respite for him for a little time ? " begs Blanche, desperately.

"Did Señorita Vidal ask you to do this ? " questions Villalonga suspiciously.

"I have asked her nothing," cries Maria.

"A boon in—in honor of my visit here," Blanche's eyes are speaking stronger than her voice. "A day or two is—is not much."

"Do you make this request seriously, Señorita Blanche ? " asks Don Pablo, sternly.

"And if I—did ? "

"Then, *Dios mio*," replies the Spanish *comandante*, " I should be compelled to shoot number 93 to-night."

"O my God ! "

"*Madre dolorosa !* "

These are two sighs from tortured hearts.

"For fear," remarks Villalonga gallantly, "that your entreaties this evening would make me forget my duty as a Spanish soldier to-morrow morning."

These awful words petrify the girls, as the colonel, growing indignant at this attempt upon what he considers his military honor, says harshly : "Señorita Vidal, I have warned you to leave this post, over which the flag of Spain flies. I do not war upon women, but should you again appear within those fortifications, much as I should regret it, I shall be compelled to order your arrest immediately."

Then, turning to the beautiful *Americana*, his tone grows more suave, though there is also warning in it, as he continues : " My dear Señorita Blanche, let me suggest to you in the voice of a friend, not to meddle with the political or military affairs of this war-distracted country, which do not, I am happy to say, concern you, who live in a pleasanter and more peaceful land. Re-

member that any request you may make to me, outside
of my military duty, will be a command to your devoted
caballero, Don Pablo Guiterez de Villalonga, but please
give me no further suggestion as to my military duty
or military honor; do not again strike my heart by
compelling what must always be a refusal. Ladies, I
take my leave."

So bowing to both in courtly fashion, Villalonga
turns his back and sadly walks up the little rocky path,
wounded at this attempt from the lips of beauty and
the smiles of loveliness, on what he considers his
duty as a soldier, leaving the two girls gazing in mute
horror at each other.

Suddenly Maria speaks : "No hope from him !"

And Blanche breaking forth, lashes herself with im-
potent regret : "If I had not destroyed that letter I should
have used it, and Howard Temple would have lived.
Now if he dies, I, who should have saved him, who
had his life within my very hands, am his assassin !"

But Maria is whispering anxiously : "Restrain
yourself ; a negro is watching."

For issuing cautiously from the dense undergrowth
is a pathetic figure. The relics of Sixth Avenue fashion
are floating in tatters in the breeze about Pomp's bare
limbs and briar-scratched naked feet. His hands,
whose ebony had once been covered with delicate kid,
are waving about in filthy fervidness, pleading for
recognition.

Suddenly Blanche turns on him, saying sharply :
"You are not wanted here. Go back ! Leave us !
I presume you are Villalonga's servant, follow your
master !"

But the negro falling at her feet, moans : "O laws-
a-massey, she don't know me. O Miss Blanche, I'se
poor Massa Temple's boy. You sees Pomp—Mr.
Pompey Smith, ob New York city !"

Recognizing him, Blanche gives a gasp of astonishment: "Pomp, poor fellow!" then holding out a sympathetic hand, mutters sadly: "And you have suffered with your master?"

"I'se suffered worse!" cries the negro savagely. "Dat dam Mendoza make me slabe ag'in! I'se gone back to fust principles."

But Maria breaking in, cries: "We have so little time. You surely have some plan to save Señor Temple?"

"Do you think I would have destroyed that letter if I had not, *almost a certain one.* To-night the guard have been bribed. A boat from the yacht will be off this cove."

"Cannot my brother aid you?" eagerly suggests the Cuban girl.

"You say he is within reach with a band of armed Cubans? He can! Get word to him to be in this rocky cove outside the fort on Cayo Toro, at twelve o'clock to-night as Howard Temple leaves the Spanish lines?"

"Here?" asks Maria, her eyes blazing with sudden hope.

"Here! With his band Luis can protect him from pursuit," whispers the American girl, but gets no further in her speech.

For Maria is crying: "Tado! Tado! To me quick! *Aqui, presto,* Tado!" And the boy slinging a land-crab around his head and whirling it into the water, runs to her.

To his ear she whispers the errand she wishes him to do, and impresses on him that speed is vital. As he darts up the little tropic path, she calls to him: "By twelve o'clock to-night, you understand?"

"Ay! Ay! missie, Tado's on time!" comes echoing down the cliff, and the boy disappears in the jungle of the forest, where no step is more certain, no trail more sure.

"Your message is sent, Miss Grayson," says the girl coming to her.

"Thank you," The voice is sad, but cold. "And now, Señorita Vidal, we part."

"Howard was my friend," says Maria pathetically. "Will you not be one also?" and lays hand upon the white arm of the American.

But she is shaken off as if she were a loathsome thing, and Blanche, her eyes blazing with the jealousy that makes her heart sore, sneers: "Howard; your friend? *Your lover!*"

"Stop! You shall hear me *now!*"

"And why?"

"Because I love him!"

"And you dare to tell me this!" The blond beauty of the temperate zone confronts the dark-eyed loveliness of the tropics, and two gentle women glare at each other because they love the same man.

"Because I adore him," cries Maria whose eyes are noble in their truth. "Not as you do, with the love of this world, but as a sacred idol; a saint who saved my brother's life. But Howard was true to you, and gave me only friendship in return."

"And this ring—*my* ring—the proof of my love?" cries Blanche, holding up the dazzling circlet to Maria's eyes, who starts astounded at the sight of the glittering bauble. "Ah, you recognize it too! Oh, why did I not let them kill him as he kills my heart!"

But even as she moans this out, astonishment seizes Blanche for Maria, still gazing at the circle held flashing before her eyes, cries suddenly: "The ring Ortiz *stole* from him!"

And the black, who has been rolling his eyes

at this scene of woman's passion, mutters savagely between his set teeth : "Damn Ortiz!"

On him Blanche turns first, crying : "Sacrilege! You are cursing the man who to-night will save Howard Temple's life," then pauses horrified at the effect of her own words.

For Maria Vidal has uttered a little gasping scream, her face has grown ashen as the negro's, and she has muttered : "*Santissima!* If you have told Ortiz you have *murdered* Howard Temple!"

"No, no!" cries Blanche. "Ortiz is Howard's old friend in New York, my *true* friend."

"Ah, that is why he betrayed him. Howard Temple stood between Ortiz and your love."

"Impossible, you are lying to me!"

"Listen and believe the lie!" whispers the Cuban girl, for their voices have grown low, harsh and discordant. "To save my brother, Howard Temple gave him his passport. Who advised this? Ortiz!"

"But that was to give your brother life."

But Maria, goes on with words that strike sledge-hammer blows upon the heart of the American. "Howard Temple was arrested as Luis Vidal. Who gave him that name? Ortiz!"

"Oh, my soul!"

"Howard Temple innocently carried despatches to the insurgent leaders. Who had given them to him in a letter from New York? Ortiz!"

"O God, that letter! I remember it now. I saw him give it into Howard's own hands. I begin to understand!" screams the American girl.

"That ring—the pledge of your love! Who stole it from Howard Temple when chained and helpless? Ortiz!"

But this is interrupted by a shuddering shriek from Blanche. "Yes! He had the ring upon his finger!"

"And as despair gathered about him, who told him that he sacrificed Howard Temple because you loved him? ORTIZ!" cries Maria in savage truth. "And who, Howard Temple dead, swore to marry you? ORTIZ!"

At this, the American girl bursts out, jeering herself in horrid mutterings : "Ortiz will bribe the guard? ha —ha—ha! Ortiz will save Howard Temple's life! ho —ho—ho! And Howard loves me *still!*" For one moment, there is ecstacy in the tone, the next comes greater horror. "*And I have killed him!* Stolen his life, and scattered it to the four winds of Heaven."

As if half blind she commences to grope for the little pieces of paper that held the life she loved, but now has sacrificed. A few she clutches ; others, blown by the soft wind over bush and flower and beach and rippling wave, take the red tints of the setting sun as they elude her frantic hands.

A weird horror is in her eyes. "They are turning to drops of blood. My love's heart's blood," she shudders. "I spilled them but I can't gather them!" Then clutching her heart which seems to be trying to tear itself from her white bosom, she screams like one possessed : "Murdered because he loved *me!* Murdered because I loved *him!* KILLED BY THESE HANDS THAT SHOULD HAVE SAVED!" And, with the low cry of a breaking heart, Blanche reels crashing down senseless as the coral strand on which her lovely body falls.

CHAPTER XIV.

"THE VOICES OF THOSE MUSKETS TELL HIS FATE!"

THIS has all been done in a few short seconds. The
Cuban girl and the negro, who have gazed horrified
upon Blanche's despairing agony, run to the stricken
one, lift her up and try to revive her; though Senorita
Vidal's face is almost as white as the sufferer's she is
assisting.

They have already thrown water from the cascade
over the unconscious girl.

As they work Maria is sighing: "There is now no
one to save Howard's life but me!"

"And me also!" mutters the negro.

"Ah, true, he was good to you as—to everybody,"
assents the girl. After a moment's intense thought she
moans wringing her hands: "I know the Spanish
methods. They will accept the bribe; they will apparently let him escape; then as Howard Temple flies,
they will shoot him down! It is a common trick in
this awful war."

"Yo' sure of dat?" asks the black eagerly.

"Yes, I can guess Ortiz' methods. He will wish
his victim to think he risked his life to save the man
she loved in hopes to gain her gratitude."

"I heard him say somet'ing like dat to dat cuss
Mendoza, who's made me slabe, but didn't make out
jist what he was drivin' at. But I'll spile his game!"
mutters the negro savagely.

"How?"

"By warnin' Massa Temple of him."

"Impossible !" jeers the girl in hopeless tone.
"The prisoner is *incomunicado*."

Then suddenly she whispers : "Ortiz' victim is re-
viving." For Blanche has started up, a wild delirium
in her eyes, and uttered a piercing, shuddering
scream.

"Oh laws-a-massey, she's done gone crazy !" cries
the black as Blanche, starting from them, utters another
shriek.

But now to them comes a voice from up the cliff that
makes them both tremble. It is Mendoza shouting :
"Here, you *Americano* nigger! I hear you down
there. *Diablo*, trying to escape again !"

In a moment, Maria and Pomp disappear into the
thick undergrowth of the tropical jungle, for, though
the voice of the Spanish spy brings terror to his escaped
slave, it brings a greater fear as well as shuddering loath-
ing into the heart of Maria Vidal, who remembers his
words of passion and desire, his eyes of lust, amid the
flames of her burning plantation. Far away from aid
or friends, she knows she must avoid this man, whose
touch is worse than death.

But even as they leave the beach, a boat driven by a
couple of negro oarsmen, comes rapidly into the little
cove, George Dennison in its bow, crying : "Whose
shriek is that? What's the trouble here?"

Then he springs ashore, and mutters : "Good God,
Miss Grayson !"

But Blanche only answers him with a demented,
shivering laugh, and falls half fainting into his arms.

In an instant George has lifted her into the boat and
called to the oarsmen : "Quick, back to the yacht !
And row for your lives and five dollars ! This is a case
of sunstroke !"

A moment after, as they speed along over the clear
waters of the bay, which are now dull in the gloom of

evening, for in the tropics there is no twilight, and darkness comes with the setting sun, Dennison remarks : "It was lucky, Sanchez, you told me the best red-snapper fishing on the island was off that point!"

But the negro boatmen do not regard it as so fortunate. They fear the young lady tossing on the stern sheets is in the first delirium of yellow fever ; they have forgotten the promised five dollars, and are crossing themselves and uttering feebly some Latin prayers.

"Hang you! Lay to your work!" shouts George savagely, and some half hour afterwards is alongside the *Hermes*.

Hearing the splash of oars, Alfred Grayson puts his head over the taffrail of his vessel, crying : "Is that you, Mr. Dennison? I have something of great importance to speak to you about immediately!" And his face is a very anxious one.

But it grows more troubled as George answers : "First help me to get your daughter on deck!" and climbs the side ladder of the *Hermes* bearing the fainting form of Blanche, to put her in her father's arms.

"My God, what is it?" shudders the banker.

"Sunstroke, I fear! We must get a doctor quick!" And Dennison cries to the men in the boat : "Pull for your lives to town!"

"A surgeon! Quick!" shouts Grayson, giving the men a twenty-dollar gold piece. "As much more when you bring a doctor back!" Then he gasps anxiously : "It—it can't be snake bite?"

"That is practically an impossibility on this island, thank God!" answers the newspaper man confidently. "If it had been Martinique or Saint Lucia, I should have had the gravest fears."

A minute after the two men carry the girl down the

companionway into the cabin, where George leaves
the father and Miss Morales, who, with a cry of sympathy and alarm, has come hurriedly from her stateroom,
doing the best they can for the sufferer in the way of
ice upon the head, and stimulants administered through
the pale lips.

Some time later, Grayson, relinquishing his daughter
to Laura's charge, comes on deck, wrings Dennison by
the hand and murmurs : Thank you—but I fear—! "

" Fear what ? "

" Some damned tropical disease.   Good God, Blanche
is raving now ! "

" Ah ! "

" Crazy as a March hare."

" What does she say ? "

" Oh, the most idiotic nonsense.   She sobs : ' Killed
by these hands that should have saved !   Murdered
because he loved *me!*   Murdered because *I* loved
him !' and other rigmarole too absurd to utter."   Then
the American, putting his hand to his brow in perturbed consideration, astonishes the journalist by these
curious words : " Hang me, if I don't think my poor
child must have gone crazy *before she got to the cove,*
where you, by God's mercy, picked her up.   While in
the fort, Blanche told Laura a most incredible tale."

" What tale ? "

" The one I was going to consult you about when
the sight of my fainting daughter knocked thought of
all else out of my head."

" Can you tell me now ? "

" I must !   Blanche said that Howard Temple, my
junior partner, had been arrested on the Vidal plantation, and was—my Heaven !—to be shot at Cayo Toro
to-morrow morning."

" She told Laura that ? " askes the newspaper man,
astonishment in his voice, concern on his face.

"Yes, my poor Blanche asserted that Temple had been arrested by mistake for Luis Vidal on the Vidal plantation."

"Why, that's where I left him!" cries Dennison. Then, after a little consideration, he remarks: "Stranger things have happened on this island."

"You don't mean to say a man like Howard Temple could be cut off—condemned to death—and not permitted to communicate with his friends?"

"Why not? Other prisoners have been kept *incomunicado* not only for days, but for weeks. This is a retired spot, far away from the centers of commerce and communication. It's just a chance; but may not the first have been a fact which has produced the present delirium of your daughter!" Then George says hesitatingly: "May I venture to ask, is Miss Blanche particularly interested in Mr. Temple?"

"She is his affianced wife!" answers Grayson, sorrowfully. To this he suddenly adds: "By the Lord, you may be right! Ortiz came on board with Laura, and they seemed to think it true; in fact, appealed to me for money, and I have given my draft for ten thousand dollars on New York, so that Ortiz may bribe the officer of the guard to permit Temple's escape. Ortiz and Laura appeared to think it is his only chance. But I was only awaiting your advice to act for myself."

"Do you mind my asking Miss Morales a few questions?" queries the journalist.

"Of course not!" says Grayson quickly, and hastily calls Laura on deck.

Coming up the companion ladder, Miss Morales, in answer to her father's anxious look, remarks with a sigh: "There is no change in Blanche. Her maid is watching her. We can do nothing more till the doctor comes."

"Thank you, my dear," returns Grayson; then he

suggests : "Laura, Mr. Dennison, who found Blanche delirious in that little cove where you left her, would like to ask you a few questions as to what happened when she was at the fort, and what evidence you have that Howard Temple is the prisoner who is to be shot to-morrow morning. Of course you did not see him?"

"No," replies the girl, "but my sister declared she did! The first I knew of it was Blanche staggering along the path from the prison pen and whispering to me half dementedly that Howard Temple was to die to-morrow morning. After a little she told me how it came about. By some accident she had seen a girl, Señorita Maria Vidal, the sister of Captain Luis Vidal, of the insurgent army, my—my affianced husband," falters Miss Morales, George notes the heightened color on the girl's cheeks by the light of the binnacle lamp, "imploring Colonel Villalonga, the Spanish _comandante_, to permit her to see a prisoner. Almost immediately afterwards, Blanche said she learned the prisoner was condemned to be shot to-morrow. With that she jumped to the conclusion that it must be Señorita Vidal's brother, Luis Vidal, who was to die. To save me the anguish she knew would come upon me, Blanche felt she must be sure before she acted, and in her generous way, my sister bribed one of the guard with all the money in her possession, and obtained two minutes' sight and word in that vile cell with prisone Number 93, and found him—to her horror and despair—not Luis Vidal, the man I love, but Howard Temple, the man she loves, in misery, in filth and in chains, the doom of death upon him! She said he told her he had been arrested by a mistake on the Vidal plantation for Luis Vidal, and was to be shot at sunrise to-morrow morning!"

"Good God! do you think it's true?" shudders Grayson.

"It may be," says the newspaper man contemplatively. "And then?" This question is to Laura.

"And then," returns Miss Morales, "for Blanche was half crazy, and I almost the same, I ran to the watergate to come to the yacht and tell you, Mr. Grayson, but by the fortune of heaven met Señor Ortiz, Howard's old friend in New York, a Spaniard, who knows the Spanish officers, and he, as I before told you, promised at the risk of his own life to bribe the guard so that Temple could escape to-night if the boat is off that cove to pick him up."

"You are certain Ignacio can bribe the Spanish officer?" asks her stepfather anxiously.

"Ortiz said so. He declared it was already arranged. Even to the amount of money. You remember, ten thousand dollars."

"You believe that can be done?" mutters Grayson to Dennison.

"I have no doubt of it!" answers the newspaper man. "Most Spanish officers come to Cuba to make money."

"You think Colonel Villalonga will accept American gold for his duty? I doubt it," says the business man, contemplatively.

"I know he won't," answers George shortly, "but Ortiz knew that as well, and surely did not apply to him."

"No, no!" cries Laura. "Señor Ortiz warned us if Villalonga knew he attempted to bribe the guard, he would die by the side of Temple. It is a lieutenant. Manuel Gonzales I think his name is. You should know; Don Ignacio mentioned the man to you," she adds to Grayson.

"Yes, that was the name," says the banker. "Ortiz explained to me how it was the only way that Temple could be saved, there being no telegraphic communication, except via boat to Santiago that would be too late, and stating that Villalonga will undoubtedly execute the man, as the sentence has been approved by the Captain-General."

"Has the sentence been made upon Luis Vidal by name?" queries the newspaper man.

"Of that I am not sure," says Grayson. "All I know is that Ortiz told me it was his only chance."

"And persuaded you to sign the draft?"

"Certainly! What do I care for ten thousand dollars, or one hundred thousand dollars either, to save my partner's life! Anyway, if it gives safety to some poor devil of a Cuban patriot I don't think I regret the money!" cries the Yankee banker. "But still I don't like these Spanish intrigues. I would sooner be open and above board and use the method of the American!"

"What do you think of doing?"

"This! But I want your advice. You know Cuba better than I; you have run about the world more than I, who have simply stayed in New York and made money."

"What course do you intend to take?" asks Dennison.

"Go up to the Cayo Toro fort; demand to see the prisoner; threaten the colonel, if he shoots an American, with the vengeance of my country; declare that I will have Villalonga held responsible by my influence with the American Government if he injures a hair of Howard Temple's head!" says Grayson, determination in his tones.

"That would probably have succeeded six months ago, but now I doubt it!" remarks the newspaper man.

"Why six months ago, and not to-day?"

"Because since then they murdered in Santiago— you must have seen the place—by order of General

Burriel, commanding, nigh onto a hundred American citizens, whose blood is still unatoned for. Now that the matter has been arranged without the only adequate reparation, the execution of Burriel and those who assisted in that assassination, Spain no longer fears, she despises the State Department of the United States, which in that matter proved itself either cowardly or worse!"

"Still I shall make the demand! I believe in American methods!" cries the banker.

"Then I will go with you!" replies the newspaper man, enthusiastically.

But this action is delayed. There is a sound of oars on the still waters of the bay; a boat comes from Caimanera bearing a physician.

"They do not shoot Temple till to-morrow morning. It is now my daughter's life for an hour or two!" whispers Grayson, and hurries, trembling, into the cabin after the man of science.

To the general relief of everybody on board the yacht, this gentleman, who is an expert in the disease, declares almost immediately it is not yellow fever from which his beautiful patient is suffering. Neither does he think it sunstroke, but of that he cannot be sure. He, however, fears that Blanche will probably have brain fever in its severest form, and counsels, with rare self-denial in an impecunious physician, that this patient, who can pay him great fees, should be immediately taken from the scene of her trouble, and if possible, to a northern climate.

"That settles it!" mutters Grayson. We leave at midnight!"

"You will send that boat," queries Dennison, "to that cove as you promised?"

"Of course!" answers the yachtsman, and tells Captain Pinnock to go himself with four men and his own gig, the fastest that he has, giving nis skipper very careful directions, and ordering him to use every exertion to pick up any one at the cove.

The boat getting off on its errand, Grayson says to Dennison : "When she returns, we hoist anchor. Now come with me to interview the damned Spanish colonel! It is already eleven o'clock; we have not much time to lose!" for the physician has taken some time over his examination and diagnosis, and in pre-scriptions and directions as to what is to be done to alleviate the sufferings of the fair girl who is now deliriously screaming in her stateroom.

"Good Lord! Let me get away from my darling's shrieks!" shudders the banker. "They drive me dis-tracted."

But these also make him hurry on his errand, for he catches Blanche's ravings : "Killed because I loved him! Murdered by these hands which should have saved!"

Taking the physician with them in their steam launch, they leave him at Caimanera.

Upon the wharf, however, the doctor, leading Den-nison to one side, whispers cautiously to him : "I didn't dare tell the father, but I greatly fear his beauti-ful daughter has lost her mind permanently."

"Good Heavens! Your—your reasons for this?" says George, very seriously.

"Miss Grayson's illusions are so absurd, yet so defi-nite, and she is so determined in them," answers the physician, in a low voice. "She asserts she has mur-dered the man she loves. She cries out he was killed because he loved her, and assassinated because she loved him. You know as well as I that my beautiful patient is not a criminal. Therefore, though I have little doubt of her living, as her constitution is strong, still I fear it will only be to live insane. At your opportunity, caution her father about this with as much tact as possible. Tell him to keep an eye on her during the voyage, that she does not commit suicide."

"Thank you for the suggestion," says the newspaper man, and, wringing the doctor's hand, goes back to the father, who is anxiously calling to him : "Hurry, Dennison, we must get to the fort at once ! The moon is up, and that old church bell will be sounding before long."

"Yes, they have midnight services pretty often about here, during Lent," remarks the journalist.

So re-embarking, George crosses the estuary with Grayson, and they both make landing at the fort on Cayo Toro, where they are immediately challenged by a vigilant sentry, and the sergeant of the guard being summoned, they are taken to the guardhouse to await the *comandante's* orders.

"You don't mean to tell me any one can escape from here under this strict military routine ? " whispers Grayson, as they hear the sentry patrolling outside the place in which they are temporarily confined.

"Yes, if his purse is heavy enough," returns Dennison, grimly.

They have arrived at the fort by half-past eleven. It is something like twenty minutes before they receive word from Villalonga, who has been aroused from his bed, and apparently is not greatly pleased at his slumbers being broken.

It is five minutes to twelve when they are ushered into the *comandante's* room, where he receives them in somewhat hasty toilet for that punctilious officer.

"This late visit, Señor Grayson," remarks the colonel, stiffly, "though unexpected, is, of course, welcome. I have no doubt your charming daughter arrived safely on your yacht, though she did not permit me the pleasure of escorting her back or bidding

her *bon voyage*. May I ask the reason of the honor
you have accorded me?"

"Certainly!" says the banker, and proceeds with
business directness to answer the question. "You
have a prisoner, Number 93, I believe, who is to be
shot to-morrow morning, I have reason to think under
a mistake."

"Mistake! What mistake?" mutters the Spanish
colonel.

"An awful mistake!" answers Grayson. "I am in-
formed that Number 93 is my junior partner, Mr.
Howard Temple, of New York, who came to visit
Cuba in my step-daughter, Miss Morales' interests,
some three months ago. I have received no word from
him for over six weeks!"

"Your reasons for this astounding statement,
Señor?"

"My daughter, Miss Blanche Grayson, says she saw
him, she spoke to him in this very fort!"

"That is impossible! The prisoner has been and is
incomunicado!"

"I must speak to him to verify my daughter's information!"

"That's equally impossible! The prisoner is *incomunicado!*"

"And do you mean to tell me," says the American,
losing his temper, "that you will shoot a man and not
permit him word with those who might save him?"

"No one can save him except the Captain-General!"

"You—you don't—entirely comprehend, Colonel
Villalonga," remarks the newspaper man, breaking
into this conversation in which he sees Grayson's
anger is having the worst effect upon the Spanish
colonel. "We simply claim that under the circumstances we have a right to verify the identity of the
prisoner who is to be shot, I understand, on charges

preferred against one Luis Vidal, captain in the insurgent army."

"That was all settled by court-martial!" answers Villalonga promptly. "It cannot be re-opened again without the approval of the Captain-General. Get that for me before sunrise to-morrow morning—no, this morning." For now to them comes faintly in the night air the sound of distant church bells, "and the prisoner will be reprieved." The Spanish military gentleman's tone is suave but cold as ice and impregnable as chilled steel.

"My Heaven, do you mean to say you will shoot my junior partner under my eyes?" cries Grayson breaking forth. "Have you no fear of the government of which he is a citizen?"

"I have no fear of anything save the condemnation of my superior officers as I stand under the flag of Spain!" replies the Spanish martinet.

"By Heaven, I will see him," cries Grayson.

"You forget you are speaking to the commander of this fort," returns Villalonga, and sounds a bell to indicate the interview is ended.

"Beware the vengeance of the United States!" shouts Grayson.

"*Diantre!*" smiles the military disciplinarian. "We discovered how much that was to be feared during the *Virginius* affair. Good-evening, señor, I am sorry you have lost your temper over a matter that does not concern you. Present my compliments to Señorita Blanche, and wish her *bon voyage.*"

But here Villalonga suddenly cries: "*Diablo!* An attack upon my outposts?" For the sound of some half-dozen rifle shots comes to them faintly borne upon the breeze.

A second after a captain enters hurriedly and, saluting, reports to him : "A prisoner has escaped!"

"What prisoner?"

"Number 93, they say!"

"Who is the officer in command of the guard?" asks Villalonga shortly.

"Lieutenant Manuel Gonzales, who has gone in pursuit of the prisoner. Doubtless, he will bring him back alive or dead!"

"Humph!" mutters the colonel. "When Gonzales returns, order him to report here forthwith!" And there is an ugly gleam in the Spanish disciplinarian's eyes.

A moment later he remarks: "Gentlemen, you must see that my duty compels me to bid you adieu. *Adios!*"

"And you will not permit me to see the prisoner?' breaks in Grayson.

"That would do you no good. The voices of those muskets told his fate," remarks the *comandante*, shrugging his shoulders.

"Then, if Howard Temple is dead, I shall see my government holds you to account!" cries the American, indignant fury in his voice.

"At your pleasure. I am always at the commands of my own government, and no other!—Now," he sounds a bell and says to his orderly: "show these gentlemen from the fort, and see that they leave it! *Buenos noches*, señors!" and goes hurriedly out.

For there is a sound of more firing towards the little cove at the east, and a cry has come: "The insurgents are making an attack!"

So, being compelled, Grayson and Dennison are ushered out of the water-gate of the fort on Cayo Toro, a great fear in the banker's heart, to which is added a certain anguish when they reach the *Hermes*.

The gig is there before them, and Pinnock whispers hoarsely: "That Dago is the only one I got. They were fighting like devils out there. Bullets whizzed all about the boat, as that foreigner's clothes will show!" and points to Ortiz, who, with dripping garments, is pacing the white deck of the *Hermes*.

To them, this gentleman hurriedly comes and says: "Señor Grayson, I did the best I could to save him, but he was shot down by the guard, whose bullets you can see scathed my clothes," exhibiting the marks of rifle balls, one of which has gone through his hat and the other tearing the sleeve of his coat has slightly wounded his arm.

"Then the prisoner Number 93 was Howard Temple?" shudders his friend and partner.

"Surely," answers the Spaniard. "I clasped his hand upon the beach as they fired upon us and struck him down. Señor Temple is dead beyond a doubt. I would have brought his body to you, but had to swim to save my own life."

"Then, by Heaven!" mutters Grayson, "the poor fellow sacrificed his life to save my step-daughter's sugar! I should never have sent him on this infernal errand!" and paces the deck with tears in his eyes, and a very white, agitated and horrified face.

But Blanche's ravings coming to him from her cabin. Ortiz suddenly cries: "*Dios mio!* What do *they* mean?"

"My daughter has had a sunstroke. She is delirious," whispers the banker; then shouts to his captain: "Get up sail! Take her away from this place! Steer straight for the first port in the United States, where I can get a physician to go with us to New York!"

To Miss Morales, who has come anxiously on deck and hearing the fate of her sister's lover, has tears on her fair cheeks, the newspaper man whispers as the sails are being hoisted: "You have perfect confidence in Señor Ortiz?"

"Entire! Think how nobly he risked his life to save poor Howard Temple!" replies the girl, enthusi-astic fervor in her tone. "See, there are tears in his eyes now as he listens to my poor delirious sister."

For the Spaniard, chancing to hear some of the words of the maniac below, is wringing his hands and sobbing to himself: "*Mi querida! Santissima!* Have I murdered the woman I love? Ah, *maldito*, unhappy Ortiz!"

CHAPTER XV.

"THE FIRST KISS, THE LAST KISS."

Two minutes after Dennison's boat leaves the cove with the fainting Miss Grayson, Mendoza comes brisk-ly and angrily down the little path and searches among the palm trees and cacti for his escaped slave.

In this he is assisted by three armed soldiers from the fort, whom, apparently, he has induced to accompany him upon this expedition. But at first they don't make very good work of this. The place is growing dark, in the evening shadows cast from the high cliffs. The Spanish-bayonets with their sharp thorns repel the Spanish soldiers.

"*Caramba!* It is curious I can't find the scoundrel. I surely heard his voice down here." Hunt for him Gil, Rincon, Pepé! "Catch my runaway slave and you'll get a silver peso!" cries Mendoza, pausing to light a cigarette.

Thus inspired, the Spanish soldiers who are ap-parently expert at this business, though the thickets are tangled and darkness comes on rapidly, aided by some huge cocuyos who fly like electric lights through the undergrowth, soon gain their dollar.

They drag out despite some resistance, the despairing Mr. Smith from a clump of chaparral into the presence of his master, who scowls at him: "*Diablo!* Trying to escape again, my *Americano* citizen, and rebellious?" for Pomp is glaring at him, and muttering. "But you'll catch it at my quarters! Not yet tired of Spanish raw-hide, eh?"

Then Domingo orders: "Take him away; tie him up in my hut!" And the men using butt-end of musket upon the unfortunate black, begin to hurry him up the path.

Having found Pomp, the Spanish spy and his satellites of course search no more, and this takes a great danger from the Cuban girl who lies panting like a hunted doe in a near-by thicket.

Mendoza has turned and is walking towards the path when Ortiz, coming hastily down the hill with Lieutenant Gonzales, stops him. Ignacio says: "Let the men go on! We have followed you here. This place will do better for our conversation than nearer the fort."

"I am at your service Ortiz, *mi amigo!*" laughs Mendoza. "His advice generally means money, does it not, Gonzales? Is it about my friend, prisoner Number 93, who is to be shot to-morrow morning?"

But a look from Ignacio warns him to keep his tongue within his teeth until the soldiers have passed out of hearing. To insure this Gonzales steps up the path some little distance, then returns and says sharply: "All is safe. No one will overhear us. Now, Ortiz, give me your plan, but remember unless your gold weighs very heavy, I shall not consider it!"

"Would one thousand dollars be sufficient?"

"*Diablo!* No! Not for what you ask. If Colonel Villalonga guessed——"

"Two thousand?"

"The same answer!" says the lieutenant.

"Besides *I* must be considered!" interjects Mendoza eagerly.

"Then five thousand?"

"And we divide!" cries Domingo savagely.

"No, I take the whole of it!" jeers the Spanish lieutenant.

But after some haggling it is arranged. Gonzales *does* take the five thousand, and Mendoza receives fifteen hundred more for his services; and that the money is to be paid in advance.

"I have a draft," remarks Ortiz, "which can be cashed at any merchant's or banker's in Caimanera."

"Then we will go over for the *onzas* this evening before we do the business; for the money must be paid over first!" remarks the officer.

"Then, *hasta muerto*," adds the spy.

To this ultimatum of his confreres Ortiz assents. He knows they will not do such business with him or anybody else *on credit.*

"Now get to the details of the affair!" says the lieutenant hurriedly. "I must be back for the change of guard, as I am its officer to-night."

"Yes, that is the reason you get the five thousand dollars!" remarks Ignacio laughingly. "Would you kindly give me a light, Señor Mendoza?"

And the three illuminating cigarettes, as they puff the clouds about them, discuss quite unconcernedly Ortiz' devilish proposition.

"You must arrange, Gonzales, that prisoner Number 93's irons are taken off and the door of his cell is open without letting him think there is treachery intended."

"That is easy," remarks Mendoza. "We'll let his ex-Americano slave think he is helping his old master Number 93 to escape. *Diablo!* After he has passed through my hands in an hour from now, Señor Don

Pomposo Smith will be ready to go to the fire to get away from me !"

"But," interposes the lieutenant, "it is understood Number 93 is not *really* to escape. That would be my ruin with my commanding officer."

"Certainly ! We shoot him here !" returns Ortiz. "It is arranged Number 93 meets the boat at this point. To do that he must come down this path. Mendoza can take a few of your men and conceal them behind those rocks. The path will bring the escaping prisoner within twenty paces of their rifles, and in the moonlight, which will be strong at twelve o'clock to-night, they can't miss him."

"No, he is certainly a dead man !" mutters Gonzales.

"Did you think I would let Number 93 escape when Maria loves him ; when I will have his heart's blood?" growls the Spanish spy.

"But after you have proved his death, I must have Number 93's body," says Ortiz eagerly, "to drag it to the boat to show I risked my life to save him."

"*Cierto !* And I will shoot a hole through your hat to indicate how much you dared in the matter," grins Mendoza.

"Then the affair is arranged !" mutters the lieutenant hurriedly.

"Yes, all but this detail," remarks Ignacio impressively. "To make absolutely sure of no mistake, Gonzales, Number 93 must not escape until the bells in Caimanera church strike twelve. Then you must instruct your soldiers, Mendoza, to shoot the *first* man down the path *after* midnight. That will insure even in the gloom our making no mistake."

"I understand ! The *first* man who comes down that path after the bells strike twelve o'clock."

"Be sure of that, Mendoza ! " whispers Gonzales ; then chuckles : "*Caspita !* You might even hurt our

dear friend here who will be on the beach at that time,
if you do not take good care of this." Next cries
eagerly : " Now, to get that money ! "

"Certainly ! " says Ignacio briskly and happily.
" You and Mendoza receive the gold, and besides
you also have the credit of shooting an escaping
prisoner, Gonzales."

"And you—what do you gain, generous Ortiz?"
sneers the lieutenant.

" I ? I get the removal of an obstacle—and the
gratitude of the beautiful *Americana !* " returns Ignacio,
suavely.

They are already scrambling up the path, for now
both Gonzales and Mendoza seem anxious to put their
hands upon the money.

"And Number 93—what does he get ? " guffaws the
spy. " Number 93 he get the bullets ! Ha ! ha ! ha !
Ho ! ho ! ho ! That do Mendoza's heart good ! "

His hideous merriment is the last that comes to
Maria Vidal's alert but shuddering ears, of that infernal
conclave.

Two minutes after, the last rolling stone displaced
by their footsteps comes tumbling down the rocks, the
last waving fern of the path has grown quiet.   Then
the girl, who has been lying panting in the gloom of
the deep undergrowth where this triumvirate have held
their counsel of blood, glides stealthily into the glade,
an unnatural brightness in her dark eyes.

She places her hand to her breast and gasps : "As I
suspected.   There is but one thing now that can save
the man of my heart !   My brother and his band *must*
get here in time !   At the best that will be hours from
now !   O heaven, the agony of suspense !—But yet I
can do nothing but wait here and tell Luis how he
shall aid the man that, God help me, I love ! "

With a sigh, Maria throws herself down upon a little

bank of wild jasmine and heliotrope, though she notes not their perfume, and lies waiting beside the splashing cascade, the wind blowing towards her at times from the distant town the faint sound of church bells which reaches her ears to tell the passing hours.

Then the terror of the darkness and the night, and of the lonely tropic forest comes upon her brave but yet womanly soul; for the first time in her young life she is alone and unprotected. The grand solitude, the inky darkness, might crush her spirit were it not for the thousand cocuyos that light, with varying tints and darting rays, the shrubbery, and make it like a fairy land illuminated by magic gems that shine only at night.

So the girl waits, listening for some sound that will say to her that her brother's band is coming. "Even though the paths are steep, Tado will lead them here in time," she thinks confidently, and once or twice starts up, made eager by the noise of some wandering wild dog, aguti or iguana, for the Cuban woods contain no large wild animals.

Then suddenly over the darkness rises the great tropic Cuban moon, round as a shield of fire, but shedding softest light, and making fantastic beauties of the waving palms, feathery bamboos and trailing vines and creepers. The vivid green of each leaf grows more vivid, the bright hues of each flower become more delicate. The land breeze plays upon her soft as from a lady's fan.

It is a tropic paradise, and within it a woman with a breaking heart who thinks: "I will save him! Then he will bless me. But O *Dios de mi madre*, I have seen her beauty! He will be for her arms, not for mine! He will sail away, and those cruel waves forever will roll between my love and me." Then her face grows grand in its generous fire; she cries: "He will be free and happy,—that will be enough for the little Cuban

girl who gave him her first, her only love." Yet the
agony of her passion coming on her, she sobs : "And
I—in all my life—shall know he is another's. In her
arms he will forget me, but still I will save him !
Even for her who scorned me, because he risked his
life for my brother—no, no ! because I love him, shall
ever love him ! Howard, my joy, my despair,
Howard ! *Estrella de mi alma!*"

Suddenly beside her glides a silent footstep, and into
her ear is whispered : " Ay, ay, Tado's found yer ! "

"God be praised ! " screams the girl springing up.
" My brother is here ! "

"*Dentro de poco!*"

" And you dare to say to me 'not yet' ! " she shudders ; then asks, anxiously : "But you found him
and gave him my message ? "

"Yes, but Don Luis had moved his camp. It took
me longer. He'll be har in half an hour."

"Half an hour ! *O misericordia!* He will be too
late. Tado ! " she gasps, wringing her hands, "Look,
at the moon ! Tell me how near it is to midnight ! "

The boy inspects the shadows thrown by the trees
and says contemplatively : "Reckon de bells in dat
old church at Caimanera will be t'umping soon ! "

"O-o-oh ! " This is a shuddering cry. "Quick !
To the top of the cliff ! From there, perhaps we can
see Luis in the moonlight and signal him to greater
speed ! "

Guided by the boy she flies up another little trail to
the opposite cliff, and reaching the summit, gazes
with all her eyes over the valley that lies below her
towards the northeast, Tado pointing out to her the
path by which the Cubans must advance.

The soft moon makes green, with unnatural bril-
liancy, some patches of growing sugar-cane, and gives
weird effects of light to swampy undergrowth, and at

a hill scarce a mile away, as it breaks rugged yet tropical from the lower land, she sees the gleam of what she thinks must be a gigantic fire-beetle. But it dies out, and another takes its place, and so on, regularly, till she counts twenty.

To her Tado mutters : "See dar guns gleam ! Dat's your brother's band ! "

"In time ! *In time !*" she whispers joyously ; then suddenly pauses, her limbs trembling, her voice stilled ; for there is noise of moving men along the little path leading to the cove below. She sees Mendoza in the moonlight placing behind the rocks his six assassins ; their barrels gleam, enfilading the path along which Temple must reach the boat.

"*Dios de mi madre !* Tado, fly and hurry my brother's coming ! Tell him——" She pauses with a rattling gasp in her fair throat, for the bells are sounding sadly their midnight chimes from Caimanera. She knows they are tolling the funeral march for her love ! She knows Luis cannot come in time !

Horror breaks forth within her soul. The wind brings to her on the soft air of night the sound of crunching leaves and breaking branches far up the trail that leads down from the fort ; she shudders : "He is coming ! My brother won't be here ! Howard will die !" then cries : "He shall not die ! But *mi madre*, how to turn those bullets from him ? They shoot the *first* man coming down that path !" Her eyes raised to Heaven for inspiration glow brighter than the fireflies about her, her soul is in prayer ; she mutters : "Holy Virgin by whose sacred name I'm called, teach a poor girl to save the man she loves.— The first man down that path !—The *first*—Oh *Dios mio !*" This is a shivering gasp, her eyes grow frightened as to her mind comes quick divinement— cold as the touch of death.

Suddenly she cries hoarsely: "Tado, into that thicket and take off your clothes!"

"*Santos!*" howls the boy. "Dese pants wid silber buttons? De red sash I swiped from de Spanish officer? Dis big sombrero I cotched from de *pacifico?*"

"Take them off!" she orders desperately. "You can fly faster through the undergrowth nude, as is your wont! Take them off! It is the—the last command of thy mistress whom you love!"

"Well, if yer think I ken go faster, but, O *Diablo!* dat blood-red sash!" And Tado, wailing his plaint, obeys her, in a thicket of heliotrope and limes and flowering jasmines.

"Tell my brother to speed, and he will be in—in time!" Her voice is strained like an Eolian harp in its intensity, she cries savagely: "Now *go!*"

Nude as a black statue the boy flies from her, to hurry aid that she knows cannot be in time.

The girl looks upon the tropic vale below her. In the moonlight, the water of the cove gleams like rippling silver. The perfume of its flowers comes sweet to her nostrils. Its waving palms are sighing to her. She moans: "The earth is beautiful, but what have I to live for now!"

Then, as she sees the gleam of muskets raised to murder the man of her soul, and hears his coming footsteps, her beatitude comes on her, her face lights up with sacrificial fire, she murmurs: "He will never know how much I loved him. *Adios* Howard! I will never kiss you, but good-by—forever!"

Scarce a minute after Mendoza whispers to his men: "*Caramba.* He's coming!"

For down the rocky trail that leads in terraces covered with the ferns and flowers from the Cayo Toro fort, the path that prisoner Number 93 must take to reach the boat, glides a boy, beautiful as an angel.

The shades of the ferns and the long shadows cast by the palm trees make the form indistinct to his assassins, but there is moonlight enough to shoot him down.

He is coming slowly, hesitatingly, at times tremblingly. He is crossing himself and praying with all his soul : " Holy Virgin receive my spirit. God, take me to your heart."

He is near the gleaming barrels.

" FIRE ! "

And to the sharp rattling volley of rifles at twenty paces, the boy with a shrill gasping cry staggers and crashes headlong down the path to the white beach, which his blood makes red as the moon that shines above him.

"You need not load again, men ! That settles Number 93 ! " chuckles Mendoza. " Now five dollars a piece for each of you *mis amigos !* Gonzales who posted you here has a rare eye for escaping prisoners ! " But here he mutters astoundedly : " *Santos y demonios !* There is another one ! "

For coming down the path, by the moonlight, they can see a man crouching and stumbling, but going rapidly all the time. A second more with a faint cry of joy he has sprung upon the beach, and is waving his hand as if summoning a boat.

But beside him is now another figure screaming : " Mendoza, a mistake ! Number 93 is here ! Quick, seize him ! "

And before Temple, weakened by his imprisonment, can fly or resist, half a dozen stalwart hands are upon him. He is seized and bound, and Domingo who has run down the path kicking out of his way the body, cries : " *Maldito !* We've shot some boy by mistake ! But that makes little matter. Quick, form a firing party ! "

"You are going to shoot me here?" mutters Temple faintly, for he is half reeling from destroyed hope, and the weakness of a Spanish prison,

"Precisely," jeers Ortiz. "You see that boat? Blanche is in it. I shall take your body through the surf to her. She will think with my own life I tried to save you."

"My God! You are not demon enough for that!"

"Time's up!" cries Mendoza shortly; for the men have loaded.

"No, no! Not in her sight!" moans Howard as they force him to stand against a palm-tree. "If you have no mercy on me, have mercy on her!" he whispers to Ortiz.

"I have had mercy on her!"

"Ah!"

"I have made her despise you *before* I killed you."

"Dog, you lie!"

"For I have proved to her you were untrue to her. The little Cuban girl on the Vidal plantation, eh?" And Ignacio turns and walks away, so that his soft heart may not be wounded by the sight of blood.

"You have too tender a spirit, Ortiz!" laughs Mendoza. "Quick, Sergeant Lope! *Los muertos no hablan.*"

The men drawn up in line are some ten feet from Temple, their muskets gleaming in the moonlight.

"Give me time to pray!"

"Pray in the other world."

"Make ready!" cries the sergeant hoarsely.

The soldiers handle their arms.

Suddenly the valley rings with a rifle shot, and the sergeant as he gives the order falls dead in front of his men.

Then comes like lightning a crashing volley, and before the Spanish soldiers know who attacks them some are shot down and others butchered by the machete as over rock and fern and tree-top and the arch above the waterfall, appear the gaunt soldiers of *Cuba libre*, always hungry for Spanish blood.

At the first shot Ortiz, with a shuddering scream, has fled into the surf. But in the waves just to his head he turns, and moans as he sees Temple cut loose by Luis Vidal, who is wringing his hand, and crying: "Thank God, Howard, my saviour, in time!"

"You would not have been," answers Temple, "but some one came down the path before me, and was shot in my place. This poor boy." He picks up the dying form, and is bringing it from the shade of the trees on to the beach.

"*Jesus!* Poor Tado!" mutters Luis.

"No, I'se safe!" cries the urchin, stepping forth, naked as the ace of spades. "But oh good Lordy! See de blood on my fandango pantaloons!"

Then the moonlight falls upon the dying face, and Luis screams: "God of my life! It is my sister!"

"Maria!" shudders the American.

At the voice she adores, sentiency for one moment comes to the girl. She opens her glorious eyes, and beams on the man for whom she has given her young life.

And he, some intuition flying through his mind, whispers: "Good God, you died——"

"That you might live!" she gasps; then falters: I—I couldn't help loving you, my knight who stole my soul from me. No, no! I don't reproach!" for he is whispering words of anathema on himself. Then she pleads piteously: "Kiss me, Howard, before I die. She who—who has your heart will not begrudge."

Her soft arms are clinging to him as if he were the Rock of Ages.

Bending down, he lifts up the fair face that has even

now the dew of death upon it, and, with reverence and gratitude—ay, and even love, kisses the sweet lips that once were warm and glowing, but now are growing cold as ice, even under his caresses.

"The *first* kiss, Howard," she murmurs, ecstacy making her glorious eyes like stars, then sighs, struggling for breath : " The—the—*last* kiss."

At the words, the lovely arms relax their grasp about his neck, the beautiful form stiffens in his clasp, the love-light dies in the exquisite orbs, and the soul of Maria Vidal has gone to where earth's passions can no more break her gentle heart.

Suddenly from out the jungle comes a pistol shot, and Temple, muttering : "She died for me in vain l" falls over the body of the girl, who has given her life for his.

Running towards him, knife in hand, is a wild-eyed wretch, screaming : "I have killed her that I love. *Carajo!* Thy blood for hers, *Americano!*";

But, even as Mendoza springs, the form of a negro, crazy with his wrongs, leaps from the rock above the waterfall, and with a club beats down the Spanish spy, and tramples on his body. Again the club crashes down upon the cracking skull, and Pompey, rising up, shakes himself like a water-dog and guffaws, grimly : "By Hell! Now I feel like a 'Merican cit'zen ag'in !" But here the savage fire leaves his eyes, the soft faithfulness of the poor African comes into his face, he falls to sobbing : "Poor Massa Howard, has dey knocked yo' out at last !"

"If there's life in him, we must carry him away !" cries the Cuban leader, hoarsely and hurriedly.

"Dat ain't hard!" mutters Pomp. "He ain't no more dan a bag ob bones." And he lifts Temple in his arms and follows the Cubans up the rocks, as Luis hastily orders his men to retreat ; for there are sounds of sortie arms from the fort above, the Spanish drums are beating the assembly, bullets from an advance party already splash the waters of the cove.

"And Maria never thought of me," mutters the Partisan chief, sadly. He feels the girl's cold, pulseless wrist, and sighing: "The last of my race," takes his sister's body tenderly in his arms, and climbs up the cliff, his men shooting from rock and tree, protecting his escape.

So they pass away into the shadows of the night, that patriot band, leaving behind them many drops of blood, but none so precious as those tender drops from the heart of that brave girl, who shed them for love—pure, unselfish, and undying—the noblest gift Eve ever gives to Adam.

BOOK V.

THE FAIR HAND OF JUSTICE.

CHAPTER XVI.

THE RETURNED FILIBUSTERO.

THE *Hermes* drives straight for the Bahamas. The wind being fair, she makes Nassau in a little over two days. The balmiest breezes play through the open port-holes of the sufferer's stateroom ; but Blanche seems in about the same miserable state as when they brought her delirious on board.

Of her ravings, neither Ortiz nor the journalist hear a great deal. They both have taken staterooms well forward, the later from the fear that he may embarrass the family in the care of the invalid, the former because the screams, outcries, and plaints of the woman he loves are too distressing to his soft Spanish heart, and at times frighten him too greatly as to the outcome of his passion.

At Nassau, Dennison, who, with the instinct of a gentleman, guesses he is *de trop* under the circumstances, disembarks, remarking he thinks he can write a letter or two from these islands that will be of interest in New York.

Here, fortunately, Mr. Grayson succeeds in inducing Dr. Charles Acker Lawson, a well-known New York physician, who has been taking a needed vacation in

217

these summer islands, to return with them to New York.

But, before George leaves the yacht, taking proper opportunity, he tells Dr. Lawson what the Cuban physician has hinted to him on the night Blanche had received the shock that caused her malady. Hearing this, the New York doctor looks very grave, but devotes himself with even greater assiduity to his beautiful patient.

On the voyage Dr. Lawson, having heard her father's and her sister's versions of the affair that has apparently shattered Blanche's mind and nervous system, takes the first convenient opportunity to question Ortiz most carefully as to the occurrences that have made Miss Grayson at least temporarily insane—they all acknowledge that now—as he thinks the *ami de la maison*, being the least interested of any of the party, can tell him most accurately what occurred.

For this gentleman all through the voyage has proved himself a most useful friend, companion and assistant to the New Yorker and his family. He has taken with Spanish tact every little detail of the yacht's provisioning and supplies at Nassau from the suffering father's shoulders, who has only one thought now : his daughter, delirious in her stateroom. He has ingratiated himself with the crew by his delicate attention to their owner, until Pinnock, who had called him a Dago the night the yacht left Guantanamo, now speaks of him with reverence as "the Don."

"I have already the newspaper man's account, clear and succinct as one of his own articles, but unfortunately Mr. Dennison personally knew nothing of the causes of the shock, only the effects upon the poor girl he picked up at the little palm-tree cove that awful day," the physician says to Ignacio. "Now will you kindly give me all you know, Señor Ortiz?"

"With my whole soul!" cries the Spaniard; and does so.

Listening to this, Lawson discovers to his astonishment that Ignacio is probably deeply interested in the young lady's health from a romantic standpoint.

"Permit me to thank you, Señor Ortiz," remarks the physician, "for the delicate consideration you have shown the suffering family, your beautiful flowers that you brought from Bermuda for the young ladies." The doctor bites his lips here, for Blanche in one of her moments of frenzy has thrown the beautiful flowers out of the stateroom window. "Miss Morales, Mr. Grayson and myself as Miss Grayson s physician, all thank you for the burden you have taken off her father's mind in his daughter's extremity."

"You—you think the case is so serious?" falters Ignacio growing pale, between puffs of his cigarette.

"It would be useless to disguise the fact," replies the medical man. "The young lady's condition is extremely precarious. It is more a malady of the mind than of the body."

To this he adds musingly: "It was really Mr. Howard Temple who was a prisoner in that Spanish fort?"

"It was. *Cierto!* God help us, it was!"

"Then Miss Blanche has no hallucination as to the fact of Mr. Temple's death."

"No, no! *Dios mi!* Poor Howard is surely dead! I saw him shot down. Mendoza, the spy, killed him over the body of a boy on the beach. There is no doubt of that," answers the Spaniard, a satisfaction in his assertion that the physician deems is rather curious, though thinking this over he presumes it only reflects Ortiz' pleasure at knowing the patient so far at least has no mental aberration on that point.

"Then Temple being dead," goes on the doctor,

"how about these other curious assertions the girl
makes and still continues making : 'Killed by these
hands that should have saved! Murdered because he
loved me! Murdered because I loved him!'"

"Ah! That I cannot answer you. Would that I
could," cries Ortiz, who is very curious about these assertions himself. "This blow has been as great a one
to me as to any man upon this earth," and tears come
in the great dark glittering eyes.

"Indeed? You—you astonish me!"

"Yes. I—oh Señor Medico—pardon me, but I——"
And Ignacio's face is so agonized that the physician
mutters : "I believe I understand you," and does not
tell him that Blanche has also raved : "Ortiz will bribe
the guard! Ortiz will save Howard Temple's life!"
and jeered with miserable maniac laugh, each suggestion that aid would come from this Spanish gentleman
as if that was a possibility beyond her brain.

For now the doctor guesses what Laura already
knows : that Ignacio has loved Blanche for many a day.

An idea that makes Miss Morales very sympathetic
with the fellow. She believes his risking his life to save
Temple was the height of disinterested nobility, and
begins to regard and treat this gentleman as a particular and personal friend, and sometimes to think perhaps
in the future, if Blanche regains her health and her
mind, no reward would be too great for such a gallant
spirit.

So each morning as Ortiz comes upon the white deck
of the *Hermes* as it speeds to northern latitudes and
reaches cooler breezes, Laura clasps Ignacio's hand, as
he falters : "And our—our patient?"

"The same; always the same," answers the girl in
a broken-hearted voice ; then sighs : "God help us all!"

"Ah, you include me. *Gracias*, Señorita Laura."

"Certainly! We can never forget your kindness.

You in all this misery have become one of us," answers
Miss Morales with grateful eyes.

To this, on the day they arrive in New York, Grayson
adds his mead.

They are passing the Narrows when the banker
comes to the Spaniard and wrings his hand. "You,
Don Ignacio, are one of the few pleasant recollections
I shall have of this miserable voyage," he says. "I
cannot tell you how much I thank you for all you have
done for me in my trial."

"Ah, let us not speak of that," answers Ortiz. "Your
trial has been my trial. Let us only think of what
happiness may be in store for us when you reach some
specialist upon the maladies of the mind."

"Yes," whispers Grayson, "Dr. Lawson, who has
done everything possible, has demanded an immediate
consultation with the first expert in New York city!"
on—My God, how can I say it!—on insanity!" moans
the father.

"Insanity—*Maldito!*" the Don wails, and going
away puts his fevered head in his hand and glances
over the bright waters towards Fort Wadsworth.
Scalding tears roll down his cheeks as he moans to
himself: "*Niña de mi alma!* Have I, O miserable
Ortiz, brought destruction on my love in order to win
your smiles, your kisses? Have I destroyed the mind
that made your passion dear to me?" And he wrings
his hands in his Punic way and curses himself.

For this gentleman has not only adored the exquisite
body but has worshiped the beautiful spirit that illuminated it, and caused, in his peculiar romantic yet
sensuous way the thought of making that vivacious
mind his own, of dominating and possessing not only
the body but the soul of Blanche Grayson, a glorious
joy, a heart-entrancing rapture.

In New York during the next few days, greater

misery comes upon Grayson and Miss Morales.   They
consult not only one expert but several, upon mental
and nervous diseases, and these scientists all agree that
the girl will most probably live, but when they hear of
her peculiar and absolutely unreasonable hallucina-
tions, have such grave doubts as to her mental recovery that they drive her father to distraction.

Still the patient recovers slowly.   Blanche has been
delirious, she has been insensible ; yet, her bodily
strength returns little by little.   Her mental strength
both father and sister fear is gone, but even this in
time wears away ; and when the spring is well ad-
vanced hope comes again to Mr. Grayson's heart, his
daughter says no more about her dead lover.

With this also joy comes to Ortiz.   That gentleman
has resumed his old life in New York with even more
glory than before, for great honor has come upon the
returned *filibustero*, from Cuban patriots.   His form is
conspicuous at the little cigar store on Fifth Avenue
below Twenty-third Street.   He has even been admitted to the inner council of the Cuban revolutionary
committee.   Has he not again risked his life for the
"Ever Faithful Isle?"   Has he not once more braved
Spanish bayonets and bullets for the cause?

This permits him to forward some important evidence to the Spanish Government, and an expedition
that has just sailed for the island, by some unfortunate
fate, is prevented landing, and on its return comes to
an untoward end at the hands of United States revenue
officers.

In addition fortune smiles on Don Ignacio Ortiz.   The
balance of the money he received in Cuba from Grayson
to save Temple's life gives him some funds available.
Getting a deft hint on Spanish bonds which are recu-
perating after the *Virginius* excitement in the markets
of Paris and London, he comes with this to Grayson's

down-town office, and that gentleman, who in all his family sorrow sticks like an American business man to trade and keeps careful watch of the market, as Miss Morales has some capital invested in these securities, by means of Ortiz' advice and assistance makes considerable money, not only for his step-daughter but for the Spanish adventurer, who has brought him the information.

During this business the banker discovers that Ignacio has not only a wily head for the cabals and conspiracies of Wall Street, in which, like any other stock market, trickery, deceit and misrepresentation must be its chief weapons, but also that rare tact of manner which enables a man to gain the confidence of associates and take advantage of it.

In fact Ortiz' tact of manner is so great that Grayson himself doesn't guess the Spanish adventurer is creeping into his heart by that most insidious of all flatteries, apparent admiration for his horse-sense and unlimited expressions of wonder at his financial genius.

During these interviews, of course, some conversation passes about what is upon Grayson's mind more than his money—the state of his daughter's health. He has hardly need to tell Ignacio his hopes and fears, for his face and manner always indicate the varying symptoms of the patient. These have grown gradually brighter, with this the banker's step has become more elastic, and his eye happier.

So it comes to pass in Grayson's down-town office one day, for the doctors have requested that all unnecessary persons or things that may remind her of the death of the man she loves be kept away from Blanche, and Ortiz has therefore not visited her father's Fifth Avenue mansion, the banker slaps his Spanish visitor on the shoulder and cries joyously : " We will soon be able to invite you up again to dinner, Ortiz."

P

"*Dios mio!*" This is a cry of such rapture that the father says: "That makes you happy as well as me! My dear Señor Ortiz, I have a little surprise for you."

"What's that?" The Spaniard's eyes gleam hungrily, for long absence has made his appetite very great for a sight of the beauties from which his senses have been divorced.

"You have taken a great deal off my shoulders in the last two months, Don Ignacio, ever since that awful night. You have not only assisted me as a friend, but as a business man. I need in the place of poor Temple, an assistant in my affairs. The trouble of these few weeks has told upon me. Can I offer you a position in my office? I only hesitated about it because I feared the sight of your face would be too unhappy a recollection for my poor child, but thank God, that is all past! She now asks to see you."

"*Santissima! Asks* to see me?" There is rapture in the Spaniard's voice.

"Yes! Will you to-morrow afternoon visit my house again?"

"*Gracias à Dios!* I accept both your propositions," cries Ortiz. "How happy you make me, Señor Grayson. To-morrow afternoon you say?"

"Certainly! I have a proposal to make then in regard to my business that I think will be satisfactory to you," says the banker. "I want a friend in my office as well as a financial man, one who has tact for great affairs, and you have proved this to me in the last few weeks."

"Then at three o'clock," purrs Ortiz, happy as a cat at sight of mice. His face blazes with southern passion as he murmurs: "Señorita Blanche has asked for me!"

"Yes, many times. At first I did not dare to mention it to you, but now, as it would seem to please my daughter, I am delighted to invite you to become once more the friend of my household."

"Ah, you do not know what you say. It is the breath of life!" cries the Spaniard with such ineffable delight in his face and voice, that as he goes away, Grayson looks after him and mutters: "As Laura suspects. Risking his life to save my daughter's affianced when he is himself in love with her. By George, my friend Ortiz is indeed a noble fellow!"

As for Ignacio. Driving out that afternoon, for this gentleman has, with increased financial status, added to his establishment a fast team of horses and a dashing equipage, the spring looks as bright to him as if Central Park were the Garden of Eden.

As he passes up Fifth Avenue he gazes at the house where his adored has fought with disease and conquered it, and kissing his hand to it in his Latin way, murmurs: "*Mi querida, mi alma, carissima Blanchita !* Ah, God has been good to me! She will be the Blanche of old. I shall see her beautiful face inspired by her exquisite spirit; her eyes will look in mine and say they love me. She shall worship and adore me. I shall have her to be my own forever and a day."

And the sun in Central Park, as he drives through its leafy avenues, seems more brilliant to Don Ignacio Pasquale Ortiz than it ever shone on Cuban plantation when he destroyed the only thing he thinks stood between him and her love.

CHAPTER XVII.

THE DELIRIUM OF TRUTH.

THE next day, about the hour arranged for Ortiz' visit, George Dennison, just returned from the tropics rings the bell at Mr. Grayson's Fifth Avenue residence, and sends his card to Miss Laura Morales.

He wishes to ask about the health of the young lady whose ravings still ring in his ears as he left the yacht at Bermuda. In addition, he has to disclose a little further news that he has obtained in Cuba. For during his stay at Nassau the journalist had been ordered by letter from his paper to again visit that island to report if there was any chance of an armistice between the insurgents and the Captain-General, rumors of that floating about New York at the time.

The appearance of the banker's house as Dennison enters gives him hope that all is well with the beautiful daughter of the mansion. The servants look bright and cheerful. The great windows are thrown open to get the soft breezes of a bright May day.

A moment after Miss Morales comes pleasantly to meet him, with good news on her radiant face, for her bright eyes have lost the look of anxiety that was in them when he last saw them, and the young lady is dressed in the prettiest of light summer tissues to greet the warm spring weather.

Her voice is cheerful and cordial as she gives him her hand and says : "Welcome, Mr. Dennison," then adds : "Thank heaven, Blanche is once more well enough for us to receive our friends."

"She has recovered entirely?" asks the newspaper man, delighted.

" If not recovered, very near to it," answers the girl. "So near to it that Señor Ortiz for the first time visits us since our return to New York. The doctors feared that the sight of that noble gentleman might revive the memories of that awful night when poor Temple——" The girl's voice trembles here ; she passes her hand over her eyes.

" Don't refer to that matter if it agitates you," interjects George hastily.

"Your note to me last night indicated you had returned to Cuba. Have you any more information?" suggests the lady, waving him hospitably to a chair.

" Only a little," replies the journalist, " though I called at Guantanamo to obtain the very latest news."

" Yes, the exact truth !" smiles Miss Morales.

"Synonymous terms !" replies the newspaper man briskly in support of his profession ; then taking a seat indicated to him by the gracious hand of his hostess, goes on rapidly : "All I could learn was that a prisoner had been shot in attempting to escape, and that Lieutenant Gonzales, the officer of the guard, was being court-martialed for the affair. I tried to interview Colonel Villalonga, but that austere warrior hinted that in Cuba journalists often received bullets instead of bulletins. Still I know several Spanish soldiers were killed, so Temple must have had assistance."

"Of course ! The gallant Ortiz !" cries Laura enthusiastically. " You remember when he came on board he himself was slightly wounded and his clothes riddled with bullets."

" Miss Blanche must be very grateful to him," remarks George sympathetically.

"To this day she does not know it," answers the

girl. "We have never dared to mention to Blanche the details of Ortiz' gallant conduct."

"Of course," mutters the newspaper man, "the brain fever?"

"Yes, even after we came to New York the doctors said if Blanche lived it would be only to live insane. Then how her poor father prayed to God to save his darling's life and his darling's mind."

"But she is convalescent?"

"So much so that two days ago we took her to the theatre to see Mr. Lester Wallack play in 'Ours,' still I fear the noise of the guns in the Crimean scene reminded her. But Blanche has grown very brave now, though we are told if that terrible hallucination ever returns to her she will become incurable; the more certainly, because now she has thrown it out of her mind entirely. She no more talks of having scattered Temple's life to the four winds of Heaven. She even asks to see a man who in her awful delirium she accused of murder——" The girl checks herself suddenly here.

"Who?" asks the newspaper man eagerly.

"A true friend whom it would wound most cruelly, a gallant gentleman whose name I must never mention." Miss Morales's manner indicates she will answer no questions on this subject.

"I beg your pardon," remarks George, biting his lip. "The instinct of a journalist is to question."

But at this moment the banker comes in, apparently in the highest spirits, and cries cheerily to him : "Ah, Dennison, my boy!" and shaking his hand, continues : "I am delighted to see you. I wish to thank you for keeping this unhappy affair out of the newspapers."

"A difficult matter," says George.

"Indeed?" cries Miss Morales.

"Yes; tearing a sensational article from an average

reporter is pretty much like pulling a meaty bone out of the jaws of a bull-dog." Then the instinct of new journalism coming to him, the young man goes on enthusiastically : " I had it embellished by all the romantic details imagination could throw about it. I had written the letter from Bermuda to the New York 'Graphic.'"

"*You ?*" cry Laura and her father together, a tone of horror in their voices.

"Of course!" replies George earnestly. "You don't suppose I would give such a sensational item to any one *else* to publish? Great heavens, what kind of a newspaper man do you think me?" This is in a rather indignant tone, which grows sad as he continues : "Ah, I had sketches of Ortiz, the hero. But I succeeded, I conquered myself, I threw that letter into my waste-paper basket. You need never fear your daughter's seeing a newspaper."

"Thank you!" cries the banker warmly. "I appreciate your self-control," then asks eagerly : "You have no further information from Cuba?"

"Only what I told Miss Morales a few moments since which is unimportant. But a Bermuda steamer arrived about two hours ago. They sometimes bring both passengers and mails which have crossed from the insurgent lines. But I must be going," and he rises.

But both the banker and his daughter insist upon his remaining. "You must wait and see Blanche," remarks Laura warmly.

" But will not my presence make her remember?" suggests the newspaper man.

"We have outgrown the fear of that," replies Grayson, "otherwise do you suppose I would have invited Señor Ortiz here this afternoon. I wish my daughter *to remember*, but only to remember *the truth*. If you will excuse me, I will bring Blanche to you."

For a sweet voice is calling to him down the great stairway: "Papa dear! Is not that Mr. Dennison I hear in the hall. Don't let him go; I want to see him for a few minutes."

George notes Blanche's tone is the same as the girl's had been when first he met her, only now there is a strange determination in it, a firmness that astonishes him, considering the severity of the mental attack from which she has just recovered.

But this is swept out of his mind very rapidly, for, as Grayson runs up the stairway, Miss Morales says suddenly to Dennison: "What is that commotion among the servants down-stairs?" And listening, the journalist hears shrill feminine screams and excited negro guffaws and ejaculations.

"Good gracious!" cries Laura. "Our awful cook must be drunk again!" and runs down-stairs hurriedly, followed by the journalist. But in the kitchen the girl gives a horrified, startled scream: "Pomp!"

For in the center of the room stands a negro, clothed most exquisitely in Sixth Avenue fashion, who is fanning a pretty abigail quite gallantly and tenderly with a frying-pan, and jabbering: "Laws-a-massey! Dey all t'inks I'se a ghost!"

This is the undoubted truth, as the cook, a great burly negress, has fainted dead by the kitchen fire; the housemaid is in hysterics in a chair; and from the appearance of Mr. Dodson, the butler, it is evident he is in terror of the supernatural.

"Hit come in on us sudden-like, miss—and hit uttered such 'ideous laughs; blow me—hi'm—hi'm nearly gone!" shudders the flunky.

"Pomp!" again ejaculates Laura, astonishment in her voice.

"Yas, all dat's left ob me, back from Cuba! Praise de Lord! Home ag'in!" cries the negro, with rolling

eyes. "Don't go travelin' no more. Reckon Newport
is far enough fo' de next trip."

With this, Miss Morales mutters hastily to George :
"Mr. Temple's old servant, whom he took with him
to the island."

"Yes, I know," says the newspaper man. "You
came by the Bermuda steamer ? "

"Yas."

"Poor fellow," breaks in Laura, "you have returned, but your master——" and tears come into her
eyes.

"I'se got somet'ing from 'im," says the negro hurriedly, and produces a letter.

"His—his handwriting ! " gasps Laura, seizing it.

"Yas ; de last words he spoke was gibe dis to Miss
Blanche," says the negro solemnly.

"His *last* words ? " cries the newspaper man.

"His *last* words ? " falters Laura.

"His *bery* last words," mutters Pomp. "Say, let
me take dis to Miss Blanche," and Mr. Smith turns to
the door.

But Laura has hold of him, and is crying : "She
must neither see you nor this letter—not for the
present."

"I don't understand."

"You will remind her too much of the past," cries
the newspaper man.

"Remain down-stairs ! " says Laura excitedly, putting the epistle in her pocket, for light steps from the
upper stairway come to them, and they hear the rustle
of laces and *frou frou* of summer garments on the floor
above.

A moment later, with excitement in both their faces,
they are in a drawing-room, the one in which Temple
had parted from Blanche but six months before.
Glancing about, the journalist finds it is bright with

beautiful flowers, the great conservatory behind it being opened, the perfume of its orchids and flowers
mingled with the sight of its graceful palms, reminds
him of the tropics. "Miss Blanche is not here?" he
remarks.

"No, she is not very strong yet," says her sister,
"though she pretends to be. The journey from her
room will take some little time." Then the girl suddenly cries: "Ah, Señor Ortiz, welcome!" and gives
the Spanish gentleman an eager hand, as Ignacio is
shown into the room.

To the servant she says: "From now on we are at
home to nobody until further instructions," then turns
to this gentleman, who is arrayed in afternoon dress
de rigeur, light trousers and Prince Albert coat embellished with the prettiest of white *boutonnières*, a smile
upon his face, an eager look in his dark eyes. In his
hand he bears a magnificent basket of cut roses, and
murmurs: "I would trust no florist to bring these.
They are for the fair invalid," and places them on one
of the marquetry tables of the room.

"Invalid no more!" cries Laura cheerfully. "But
this is only another obligation for which Blanche has to
thank you. You remember Mr. Dennison?" And the
two gentlemen bow, though Ortiz is not very well
pleased at seeing the newspaper man, having hoped
this would be a special interview for himself.

"Your father said he wished me to come to-day,"
he suggests, looking at George to give point to this
hint.

But Laura breaks in: "Yes; day after day ever
since her recovery, Blanche has asked: 'When shall I
be permitted to see Señor Ortiz?'"

"How kind! *Dios mio*, how kind!" cries Ignacio,
his voice as happy as his face.

"I think she wishes to thank you for trying to save

poor Temple's life, though Blanche does not know how bravely you risked your own to do it."

"You do me too much honor."

And the Spaniard bows to the earth as the girl goes on : "But we have all another duty to perform, and that is to make my sister forget the memory of that unhappy gentleman. Her life is too young to be destroyed by one cruel remembrance."

"You are wise ; Temple is surely dead," asserts the adventurer.

"Yes, we have just had the news again confirmed," remarks the journalist, and turning away, interests himself in a painting, noting that Miss Morales has a word for the private ear of Señor Ortiz.

For that young lady is speaking in low tones to the hero of the afternoon, whispering : "Mr. Grayson, who has relied on you for so many things, hopes you will aid us in our plan to make her forget Mr. Temple."

"With my whole heart," whispers Ignacio gallantly. "Trust Ortiz !" Then his voice grows suavely tender. "Perhaps when time has dimmed her memory," he looks into Laura's sympathetic face, and murmurs, " I may ask your aid myself ? "

" I have always understood your feeling for Blanche," replies her sister. "And that makes your conduct to her lover so much the more noble. When the time comes, trust the friendship of Laura Morales !" Her eyes answer his and she offers him her hand. "Now come with me into the conservatory," says the girl lightly. "Blanche will be here in a moment and I will prepare her gradually to see you, and to thank you."

Then the day does indeed seem beautiful and the hour most benign to Ignacio Ortiz as Laura, her bright eyes looking in friendship and admiration upon him, leads him into the semi-seclusion made by the tropic plants and brilliant flowers, and he murmurs to him-

self : "At last I stand upon the threshold ot success ! "
then in a sort of trembling rapture adds : "She is
coming ! " as his face lights up, for though Ortiz loves
gold, Blanche Grayson is now his only thought.

To him Miss Morales whispers : "Remain here a
moment. Blanche is in the next room," and trips
away.

And Ortiz, hearing soft rustle of laces and gauzes,
steals a look through the palm trees and sees a vision
that makes his heart beat and his tropic nature become
torrid as a furnace. He thinks he sees his future wife
—given to him by the basest treachery, by practically
a moral murder—but still his own.

And Blanche looks like a bride, for she is dressed in
purest white. There is just enough suspicion of *neg-
ligé* about the semi-invalid robe that outlines her
graceful figure to make it suggest the easy abandon of
delicious honeymoon interviews between a lady and
her lord. Above all she is more beautiful than ever,
for suffering has made the girl ethereal, her form
though somewhat slighter, is as exquisitely rounded as
before her sickness, and the white arms gleaming under
the laces of her summer toilet are as graceful in their
gestures as when the young lady was the light-hearted
belle of the early winter.

As she sinks into a chair, her father is bending over
her, and whispering : " This journey from up-stairs has
not fatigued you too much, my darling ? "

Then the voice that comes to Ortiz makes him start.
It has such a curious ring mingled with its liquid
pathos. "No," says the invalid, "I feel strong enough
to do my work—stronger and better to-day than at
any time since——"

Ignacio can see the girl's hand go to her white throat
as if a clutch were on it. Her eyes become agonized.

But her sister, who has run from the conservatory,

completes her sentence by : " You were here before,"
then adds hastily : " You know Mr. Dennison ? " for
George has risen as Blanche has come into the apartment.

"Yes, I remember him," murmurs the invalid, and
holds out her hand politely, but even as the gentleman takes it she suddenly breaks out : " He came
to us on the yacht that day—*the day !* Ah, Laura, this
is the room in which Howard parted from me ! Here
it was we uttered the vows that bound us until death
do us—*join !* "

" My child," mutters the father nervously, " you
must live for the living, not for the dead. You have a
long life before you. You have a duty to all of us to
perform ! "

But if Grayson is afraid of further outbreak, his
daughter's answer destroys the fear.

Blanche says slowly, a peculiar strident quality in her
tone : " I have *one* duty to perform, and shall do it ! "

"And that is," cries Laura, " to become our light-
hearted Blanche of old ! "

"And you have many kind friends to make that
duty a pleasant one," adds her father cheerily.

"These flowers," suggests Miss Morales lightly,
anxious to introduce the name of the gentleman waiting in the conservatory, " are a present from one of
your best friends," and she holds the cut roses towards
her sister who has sunk into a reclining chair and
passed her hand rather wearily over her brow.

" They are very beautiful," answers Blanche, and
picking a bud from the basket, smells it languidly.
"Am I to thank you, Mr. Dennison ? " she smiles at
the journalist.

" They are from the gentleman you have asked so
often to see, Señor Ortiz, who is in the conservatory."

"Ortiz ! " Blanche's delicate finger and thumb flip

the rosebud from her; invalid weakness seems to leave her; she starts erect and, raising her voice, gives them all a shock by crying these astounding words: "Thief Ortiz, come here and give me my engagement ring that you stole!"

But this is answered by the Spanish gentleman, who, allured by the charms that he has hoped to make his own, has left the conservatory and gradually drawn near to her. He mutters in a dazed and feeble way: "She does not know what she says! *Dios de mi madre*, she does not know what she says!"

"Too well I know. Alas, too well!"

"Thank God! Then you must know me for a friend!" And Ignacio holds out his hand to her pleadingly.

Then pandemonium seems to break forth in the girl. She cries hoarsely in horrible jeer: "Friend? Murderer! Assassin!"

And her father, whose face has grown pale and anguished, groans: "I should never have permitted this. The delusion again possesses her!"

"Murderer? Assassin?" gasps Ortiz with a start of anguish, for now he fears she knows; then trying to put indignant astonishment into his trembling voice, adds: "Of whom?"

"Of the man you betrayed in Cuba! Of the man you promised with your life to save! The man whom you killed because I loved him!" And the girl stands like a statue of justice with uplifted hand, but with no blinded eyes, for these are glaring with contempt and fury into the face of the Spaniard, who cannot meet her glance.

"My sister, be calm!" cries Miss Morales.

"Would you be calm standing face to face with the murderer of the man you loved?"

"Oh, horrible!" shudders Laura.

"Then this man is horrible to me!" says Blanche in awful monotone; and seems astonished.

For her sister is whispering to her father: "The madness of the fever has come back to her!"

And Grayson is raising his hands to Heaven and moaning: "God pity me, my poor little girl!"

So she, standing in the middle of the room with before her the villain who has ruined her life, looks upon the faces of her relatives and cries with a shudder: "You all look at me as if I were insane!"

To this her father answers: "Blanche, Ortiz risked his life to save the man you say he murdered!"

And that shrewd scoundrel adds: "I pardon her. She does not know what she says; how she wounds me!" the tears of despair dimming his expressive eyes.

"Generous Ortiz, forgive my poor sister," whispers Laura, stepping to him with outstretched hand.

But Blanche is between them, and her voice comes sternly: "Laura, I command you not to touch that villain!"

And, driven to it despite himself, Ortiz mutters: "She is surely insane!"

On him the girl turns pale as a statue, and sneers mockingly: "Ah, you would deprive me of reason as you did of happiness!" then goes on, a forced calmness in her terrible invective: "But my mind, thank Heaven, is now clear, and its whole force shall be used to bring the truth home to you! I will drive you out of society! I will brand you as the hypocrite, criminal and traitor that you are!"

Unable to withstand her eyes, the man she denounces turns from her, and, shrugging his shoulders in his Latin way, falters to her father: "Mr. Grayson!"

To him, that unhappy gentleman pleads: "Señor, I apologize to you for my poor demented child."

"Father, you shall not apologize to that man,"

cries Blanche, "till you know the truth!" then breaks forth into a rhapsody of woe: "Who gave Howard Temple the letter—in this very room—you remember it? *Ortiz!* That letter was his death warrant! Who denounced him as Luis Vidal? ORTIZ! Who tore the badge of my love from his manacled hands? You saw the ring upon the yacht, Laura! ORTIZ!"

And Blanche, holding up the glittering circlet, her sister cries: "Yes, I remember the ring!"

Her father adds: "Part is truth!"

And Dennison mutters: "By the Lord, she speaks as if she believed."

But now the girl's voice becomes pathetic, her eyes are filled with the same agony that was in her that day in Cuba, as she flies on: "But who, when she had Howard Temple's life in her very hands, tore it in pieces and flung it to the four winds of Heaven? Ah, that was I who loved him so well!"

At the announcement of this monstrous fact, Grayson gives a groan, Laura shudders, and even Dennison looks unbelieving.

"This would be absurd," gasps Ignacio, "were it not so painful." And for one moment he himself thinks the girl crazy; for this statement is as wildly improbable to him as it is to the others.

He has little time to think. Blanche is before him shuddering: "But who stole Howard Temple's last chance on earth from him? Who is his real assassin? That man standing there! The man I denounce! ORTIZ!"

"Mr. Grayson, this is madness!" falters the scoundrel, who is growing desperate in his agony, under the invective of the lips he loves, the scorn and hate of the face he adores.

"No, no, father; only the truth!" Then she breaks out again: " Must I once more go through the agony

of that awful day to make you believe? Must I tell
how from Maria Vidal's hands I seized the letter that was
Howard Temple's life, and I—for the love of you, my
sister—tore it up, and tossed it to the winds of Heaven.
For had I delivered it to the Spanish, your heart, Laura,
would have been breaking now, not mine—not mine!
How when I discovered that Howard's only chance
had been taken from him by this ineffable monster,
who I thought was true as steel, but now I know is
false as Satan, he who swore to me he had bribed the
guard, I tried to gather up the pieces of that letter; and
the wind blew them from me; and the sun turned
them to drops of blood, even as I clutched them in my
frantic hands!"

But these frenzied statements are so absolutely incredible to them all, that Laura whispers: "The very ravings of her delirium."

And Grayson mutters: "You shall not be troubled
more, Señor Ortiz." Then turning to his daughter,
who is standing like a priestess of revenge, with hair
that has become unbound and disheveled, and eyes
glaring upon Ignacio, he falters in broken voice:

"Come with your father, my poor child."

On this, Miss Morales, taking her sister tenderly in
her arms, whispers: "Blanche, dear one, they shall
not part us."

But Blanche, breaking from her, goes on in higher
key, her voice singing like strings played on by the
wind: "I tell you all the living truth, and you all
think I am insane, mad, a maniac!"

She looks upon the faces of those she loves, and
reads the despairing answer in their sorrowing eyes.
She shudders: "I cannot prove to my dear father and
my dear sister the facts I know!" Then shocks them
all, for she cries: "But last night I proved in a letter
to the Cuban General Committee that Señor Ignacio

Q

Pasquale Ortiz was a Spanish spy, and that to his information they owed the loss of two expeditions to the island with many men! Ah, that struck you!" jeers the girl.   "And now, Señor Infernal Villain, the door!" So, stepping to the entrance of the apartment, she opens it.

At this Ortiz screams, his limbs palsied, his face growing pale with the fear of death : "Told the Cuban Junta! *Dios mio*, she has murdered me!"

And Grayson mutters in horror : "Good Heavens! Dennison, for God's sake, fly to the Cuban Committee! Tell them that letter was from an insane girl! Laura, you should have kept watch upon her! She does not know what she is doing!"

George is moving to the door, and her father and sister are stepping to seize Blanche in their arms, for they fear she may in her frenzy run out into the street —when she tortures them again.

There is a little commotion in the hall outside, and the girl, looking along its vista, her face, of a sudden, grows radiant as the sun, the love-light plays about her glorious eyes, she whispers : " Howard," and beckons with her white arms.   The next instant each feature gleams white in unnatural pallor.   Her eyes have in them that misunderstanding, doubting, maniac look.   She mutters : "O God, the dream of my fever!" staggers back, and shivers : "You—you are right! *When dead men walk before my senses, I am mad!"*

And suddenly she lifts her head, on which the waving tresses are floating about in varying beauties, and shrieks : "I hear his steps! The dead to life—my love!" makes towards the door, but trembles and pauses as if she feared to test her senses.

As Dodson enters, and falters with putty face and trembling limbs : "Mr. T—T—Temple!"

And a figure still wan with misery, and gaunt with

privation, with a face still bronzed by tropic sun, flies in, and cries in joyous voice: "Blanche!"

"Howard!" With a scream the girl has fallen into his arms, her hands are clutching his bosom, and she is sobbing: "I feel his heart beat! I know he lives!" then the room reels to her, and she goes to sleep in the spectre's arms.

"My God, he is alive!" screams Ortiz, and falls, stricken and writhing, in a chair.

"Then the others all crowd about him, and cry: "Temple!" Though for a moment they scarce know him, for besides the lines suffering, famine and prison have put upon his face, his arm hangs disabled by his side.

But he, not heeding them, is whispering to the girl upon his heart: "I had you to live for, and could not die! Blanche!" then cries: "She is fainting! You should have prepared her. Where is that scoundrel Pomp?"

"I gib de lettah, sah!" mutters the darky, who, with two or three of the servants, is looking in cautiously.

"But I feared to show it!" ejaculates Laura. "You said they were his *last* words!"

"Dey was his *last* words *den;* dey ain't his last words *now!*" says Mr. Smith; but seeing Ortiz, a low and subdued guttural of joy comes in his voice, and chokes further speech, though his eyes flame as they did that night upon the beach when he cracked Mendoza's skull, and cried: "By Hell, I'se a 'Merican cit'zen agin!"

But Grayson, breaking in, says, tears coming into his eyes: "My poor boy, I have very sad news for you. My daughter's mind is, we fear, gone!"

"Gone! Her reason!" "What I most loved, her soul—gone! Gone from me forever! And to-day I thought I would be happy. Have I come back for this?" moans the man as he fondles the girl, who is still swooning on his breast.

"Yes," answers her father. "She accused Señor Ortiz——"

"Ortiz!" cries Temple half hysterically, and seeing his prey, drops his sweetheart into her sister's arms, strides to Ignacio, and mutters: "At last! God be praised! AT LAST!" and there is the look of the hunter in his eyes, who has sought his game for many a long day.

"This—this is a family party," stammers the Spaniard rising, though his limbs are trembling. "I—I will not intrude."

He would step to the door, but Temple is before him muttering: "And you think to escape me, and have left me in this world only vengeance. With that pale face rising in judgment to tell me you have destroyed her mind!"

And with a single arm he would seize the man of his hate.

But, Ortiz gasps: "She is sane—her ravings I think told only the truth."

"Sane! The truth!" and Temple reels.

"Then by Heaven, Ortiz, you're the meanest villain unhung!" cries George.

"One I will spend my life and my fortune to convict!" screams the banker.

"Bah! I am above your revenge!" snarls Ignacio; but here is stricken for the moment dumb.

Blanche, who has gradually under Laura's efforts regained her senses, suddenly glides between them, and cries in savage triumph: "But not above *mine!* This is a fitting place for your punishment, Señor Ortiz! In this room your crime began with the letter you hoped would consign the man I love—" her arms go around Temple—"unto death."

Then to Ortiz she begins to look not the Juliet for

whose caresses he had longed, but the Medea whom wrong has made the embodiment of vengeance implacable.

For she is commanding : "Give me the ring upon your finger, villain, that you received in exchange for the one stolen from my darling's hand, that I wear now— the one by which you made me think he was untrue to me !"

"I—I always comply with the request of ladies," murmurs Ignacio. "Permit me," and drawing from his finger, the bauble, would place it in Blanche's hand, but she shudders, draws back, and orders harshly : "Put it on that table !"

"I am equally complacent to the requests of beauty." Though there are blinding tears in his eyes, Ortiz does her bidding.

"Now go !"

"My God, you are not going to let that scoundrel sneak away unpunished?" screams her father.

"Pooh !" says the girl, airly. "I leave that to the Cuban Junta."

"You have not told *them! Santa Maria!* That cannot be true?" screams Ortiz, clasping his hands in an agony of terror.

"True as that you are a traitor to their cause. Think how long you will be able to live here when every Cuban in this city knows you are a spy of Spain."

"*Maldito!*"

"By Heaven ! you have condemned him to death," whispers Temple.

"Certainly !"

"*Caramba!*"

"Do you suppose that you, from now on, even if you wander the world over, will not shudder at your own shadow, thinking it the vengeance of the Cuban ? Go ! I leave your punishment to them ! I meet the methods

of the Borgias by the same stiletto-in-the-back subtility!" laughs the girl; and as Ortiz staggers from the
room gives him another pang, for her arms are round
the man she loves.

A moment after she questions eagerly: "Who really
rescued you?" Then her eyes blaze, her lips whimper,
her voice trembles: "Was it I, or was it the other
girl?"

Looking on her, Temple knows Blanche must hear
the truth and all of it.

Then and there he tells them all his wondrous story,
his voice trembling as he whispers how she, who is
now an angel, gave her life for him; how wounded
nigh unto death by Mendoza's pistol, he had been carried in the faithful arms of Pomp over miles and miles
of swampy jungle and tropic mountain trail to the
Cuban haunt; that whenever Vidal's band, pursued by
Spanish troops, had to flee, the devoted African had
borne his fever-racked and helpless frame; how Tado
had caught paroquets to make broth for the convalesc-
ing invalid till strength had returned to him, and he had
the vigor to make his way to the coast and, escaping Spanish gunboats, to sail in a small sloop to Bermuda, where he had caught the passing steamer which
had brought him to her arms.

While he speaks Blanche, lying on a sofa by his side,
is holding his hand as if she feared even now to lose
him.

At its close the tears are swimming in the beautiful
eyes of his betrothed, and she falters: "I—I believe
that saint, whose life-blood flowed for you, loved you
the best."

To this Temple does not answer. He sees Maria
Vidal as she murmured: "The first kiss, the last kiss,"
and the love-light in her sweet face, died as he held her
in his arms on that coral strand in Cuba.

But here comes a fortunate interruption. Grayson cries suddenly : "By Jove, I always suspected that Ortiz was an infernal scoundrel !" though that astute financier says nothing of that transaction in Spanish bonds, and of having thought to have made Ignacio his junior partner. A moment after he suggests to the journalist : "Dennison, not a word of this must get into print ! "

" My Lord ! You ask for greater self-abnegation than newspaper flesh and blood can bear. Temple gives me the "*beat*" of the year, and yet you forbid me to publish it," returns George despairingly ; but fights down the instinct of new journalism.

Consequently, there only appear some vague rumors in regard to Señor Ortiz, the Cuban patriot, in the morning journals a few days after. All they know is that Ortiz has mysteriously disappeared.

Mr. Smith, however, is the great danger as to publicity. That African citizen of the United States talks about hiring a lawyer and presenting through the State Department a claim for enormous damages against Spain.

Discussing this matter with his fiancée, Howard announces triumphantly : " But I've squelched Mr. Smith."

" How ? " asks Blanche.

"By buying his claim ! "

" I hope you paid the noble fellow well for it ! " cries the girl.

" I gave him a good deal more than I imagine he would have ever got for it out of Spain, who seldom pays debts of this kind," returns her lover ; then adds grimly : "Since his arrival at fortune, my clothes have suffered woefully at Pomp's hands."

" Yes, Señor Smith is simply awful," laughs Blanche.

"Tremendous ! " jeers Temple ; then asks, his heart

coming into his voice : "But what am I going to say
or do to a faithful fellow who carried my fainting body
over one hundred miles in the Cuban mountains?"

"Do to him?" cries Blanche. "Give him everything on earth!"

"Oh, he has that now—six new suits of clothes, and
gewgaws to match, for our wedding tour," laughs
Howard.

"You're—you're always bringing up that subject,"
whispers Miss Blanche, getting red as wild fire, "I—I
presume by such remarks, you—you wish our wedding
to take place soon."

"Immediately!" answers her sweetheart, "and so
does your father."

For Grayson has held forth in this manner : "The
sooner Blanche settles down to married life, the sooner
she will forget the cruel incidents that have led up to
it. Even now, though she admires, though she loves
the memory of that noble girl who gave her life for
you, hang me—my boy—if I don't think she is jealous
of her. Some people never think the bargain is complete till the stocks are delivered."

So it comes to pass one day in early June, Grace
Church is decorated for festival and wedding march.

Coming out from the ceremony in the crowd that
blocks Broadway, Miss Alicia Gushee whispers to her
friend, Miss Lucia Orthodax : "See, he is putting
Blanche into the carriage. Great goodness, how
romantic the groom looks!"

"Yes, if by romance you mean sun-tan, an arm in a
sling and the suggestion of famine in his eyes," laughs
her intimate.

"Pshaw!" cries Miss Gushee, "haven't you heard
the extraordinary story?"

"What's that?"

"Why, Blanche went to Cuba and nursed Temple

through an attack of yellow fever ; took it herself ; was insane for two months, and•tried to murder him."

" *What* ? "

" Yes, shot him through the arm. That's the reason he carries it in a sling. I wonder how he *dares* to marry her ? "

" Papa gave Blanche a million dollars," answers Miss Orthodox simply. "She is nearly as rich as her half-sister. There she is now, Laura Morales ; the one with the dark eyes, and the far-away look in them ; the one who cried half through the ceremony. I wonder what that means ? "

"Laws, haven't you heard ! " cries Miss Gushee. "You're not up to snuff. Laura had a lover, Don Ignacio Pasquale Ortiz, the rich Spaniard who committed suicide in the East River. She threw him over for a Cuban who has gone away to fight—a chap named Vidal. She'll have another fellow before the Newport season is over. I went to school with Laura and *know* her ! "

But Señorita Morales, though she has many suitors, takes no other fellow.

So it happens some years later, one bright spring afternoon, a few minutes after the arrival of the New York train, Temple comes out upon the portico of his little country place at Irvington on the Hudson, and looking at the croquette grounds, in which Miss Morales and two or three other young ladies are knocking the balls about, shouts : Where's Blanche ? "

"Drivin' wid her father, and dat little angel Maria," cries Mr. Pompey Smith, who has been acting in a languid way as the returner of lost balls, and general suggester of delicate points of play to the young ladies.

But not answering this, Howard, with a very curious look on his face, cries to Miss Morales : "Laura, come in as soon as you can. I've brought a gentleman to see you."

"All right; as soon as I croquette Georgie Dawson to the other end of the world," laughs the girl.

This she does vivaciously and viciously, murmuring to herself: "I suppose it's that inevitable Charlie Masten, who won't take a hint," then sighs: "Come up to spend Sunday, I suppose. I'll have to give him a stronger suggestion some day."

As Laura is performing with her mallet, Howard noting the young lady taking her time, chatting frivolities to her friends and remarking: "I'll be back in a minute," chuckles grimly.

Then the beautiful girl turning to the house, her superb figure, exquisite face, and bright eyes which have sometimes an expectant look in them, impress him; he thinks: "How poor Charlie Masten would envy that fellow inside."

But as Miss Morales steps upon the veranda looking like an animated French fashion plate in her *chic* spring toilet, which is a mass of floating muslins, Temple's mien changes; his face becomes serious; he steps hurriedly to Laura who has her croquette mallet in her hand, and says: "I'll take your place down there."

"No you won't; I'm winning!"

"Still I had better—" He pauses abruptly: for from the lawn come excited negro exclamations in Mr. Smith's strident tones; "O glory hallelujah! by gumbo! Tado!" Then Pomp screams: "Oh, good Lordy! If dat imp ain't up to his old tricks ag'in. He sportin' my new black swallow-tail suit in which I dances de cotelon! I gibs yo' five dollars if yo' takes dem off at once!"

"Done! Right heah?" shrieks the voice of the negro Puck.

And screams come from the damsels on the lawn, as Tado, in the freedom of the tropics would proceed deliberately and effectively to disrobe.

"Not in de presence of de ladies, you barbarous, indelicate, Cuban ruffian!" shrieks Pomp.

But at the word 'Cuban,' Laura, who has glanced upon the scene, merriment yet surprise in her face, for she has never before seen the Spanish plantation imp, suddenly begins to tremble; tears spring into the beautiful eyes.

"Don't go in for a moment," whispers Temple. "I want to tell you about the gentleman I brought to see you."

"O God!" For an instant she looks into his face, then the mallet drops from her hands. "Howard, you mean—" Her hand goes to her heart as if trying to stop its beating.

"Just take it quietly. There's no rush. You've waited for three years." And Temple would lay detaining hand upon her, but she shakes it off, springs past him, through the open French window, and the next instant with a muttered shriek would fall fainting.

But mountain campaigning has made a bronzed, machete-scarred gentleman extremely active, and Temple glancing in sees Laura Morales caught to the heart of Colonel Vidal of the insurgent army.

He whistles meditatively a moment; then hearing the sound of horses' hoofs, steps quietly but quickly to the *porte cochère* of the house, where a lady's phaeton drawn by a couple of smart cobs is just drawing up.

In it sits Blanche, looking as girlish as to figure and to face as when he put his engagement ring upon her finger. Were it not for a darling little creature who sits by her side on grandpa's knee, she might be the Blanche Grayson of the opera night.

"You came up a little earlier than usual, dear," says Blanche lightly, handing the reins to the groom. "Maria, you angel, stop pulling grandpa's whiskers, and get off grandpa's lap. Papa will take you out of the carriage." For Temple is reaching eagerly for the little girl.

But suddenly Grayson calls out: "Great Scott! What makes you look so solemn? Has the market broken suddenly?"

"No," answers Howard, and places detaining hand upon Blanche, who is about to step into the house.

"What's the matter?" she falters, for his face alarms her.

"Don't go in for a little while."

"Laura?" and Blanche utters a little cry of alarm.

"Laura is *at last* happy."

"Good God! She's not *dead?*" screams Grayson, jumping from the carriage.

"No; happy. That means life. A fellow back from Cuba has her in his arms and is kissing her."

"You—you mean Luis?"

"Yes."

"Thank Heaven!" cries Blanche.

"Not if he is going back to Cuba to fight again!" mutters Grayson savagely.

"No; Colonel Vidal says that Spain has given Cuba autonomy. But it will never be put in practical operation, he thinks."

"No, I rather imagine Cuba's only chance is Spain's stinging Uncle Sam till he gets fighting mad. With an eye for such an outcome, I've gradually been getting all Laura's property that I could out of Cuba," remarks the old financier.

"Well if that war comes in my generation," says Temple savagely, "I'm going down there to fight. I want to see the star-spangled banner hoisted over that old fort at Cayo Toro, where they made me *incomuni-cado*, and refused to let me see the American Consul."

"Holy Moses ! Stop that kind of talk ! " cries Grayson wildly. "Look at your wife. Drive that fiend away ! "

For a black-haired, dark-eyed, brown-skinned Cuban Mephisto has come out on the veranda and cried : "Ay ! Ay ! Say, you got dem tassels on dose boots yit ? "

And Blanche is murmuring : "the awful boy of that awful day—that day, Howard, when I thought you lost to me in Cuba."

FINIS.

F. M. EVANS AND CO., LIMITED, PRINTERS,
CRYSTAL PALACE, S.E.

PRICE 2s. each.

ROUTLEDGE'S RAILWAY LIBRARY.

Bound in Fancy Boards.

Collins, Wilkie.—

Basil
Antonina
Hide and Seek

Daudet, Alphonse.—

With Illustrations.

Tartarin of Tarascon
Kings in Exile
Thirty Years of Paris
Recollections of a Literary
    Man
Artists' Wives
Robert Helmont

Grant, James.—

The Aide-de-Camp
The Scottish Cavalier
Jane Seton ; or, The Queen's
    Advocate
Philip Rollo
Mary of Lorraine
Oliver Ellis ; or, The
    Fusiliers
Lucy Arden ; or, Holly-
    wood Hall
Frank Hilton
Harry Ogilvie; or, The Black
    Dragoons

Grant, James—*continued.*

Cavaliers of Fortune
Second to None
The Constable of France
Phantom Regiment
The White Cockade
First Love and Last Love
Under the Red Dragon
The Queen's Cadet
Shall I Win Her ?
Morley Ashton
Did She Love Him ?
The Ross-shire Buffs
Six Years Ago
Vere of Ours
The Lord Hermitage
The Royal Regiment
Duke of Albany's Higl
    landers
The Dead Tryst
The Scots Brigade
Violet Jermyn ; or, Tend
    and True
Jack Chaloner
Miss Cheyne of Essilmont
The Royal Highlanders
Colville of the Guards
Dulcie Carlyon
Derval Hampton
Scottish Soldiers of Fortur

BROADWAY HOUSE,
LUDGATE HILL, E.C.
September, 1898.

GEORGE ROUTLEDGE & SONS'
List of Novels.

"Novels form the principal staple of the world's literature."—DAILY TELEGRAPH, *May* 11, 1898.

*** *The largest collection of Popular Fiction in the world, ranging in price from threepence to six shillings. The very best works of the very best authors.*

ROUTLEDGE'S NEW SIX SHILLING NOVELS.

A Woman in Grey. By Mrs. C. N. WILLIAMSON, Author of "The Barn Stormers."

"If the author of 'The Woman in White' is able to gratify in the shades a taste for current fiction, he must recognise some strokes not unworthy of himself in 'A Woman in Grey.'"—*Illustrated London News.*

The Peril of a Lie. By Mrs. ALICE M. DALE.

Others in preparation.

ROUTLEDGE'S NEW THREE AND SIXPENNY NOVELS.

Captain Stormalong : the Bushranger. By JOHN SHAW.
Traitors Twain. By "OAKSHAW."

Others in preparation.

PRICE 5s. each.

LIBRARY EDITIONS.

Ainsworth's Novels.—

The Original Illustrated Edition.

With 433 *Plates, Steel Engravings, and Woodcuts by* GEORGE CRUIKSHANK, SIR JOHN GILBERT, H. K. BROWNE, *and* FREDERICK GILBERT. 16 *vols.,* 8*vo.*

Auriol
Boscobel ; or, The Royal Oak

Ainsworth's Novels—*continued.*

Crichton
The Flitch of Bacon
Guy Fawkes
Jack Sheppard
The Lancashire Witches
Mervyn Clitheroe
The Miser's Daughter
Old St. Paul's

I

LIBRARY EDITIONS—*continued.*

Ainsworth's Novels—*continued.*

Ovingdean Grange
Rookwood
The Spendthrift
The Star Chamber
The Tower of London
Windsor Castle

Fielding's Novels.—

8vo., printed from new type, with full-page Illustrations.

Joseph Andrews
Tom Jones.   *Vol.* 1
Tom Jones.   *Vol.* 2
The History of Amelia
Mr. Jonathan Wild the Great, and A Journey from this World to the Next.

Smollett's Novels.—

8vo., printed from new type, with Plates by HABLOT K. BROWNE.

Roderick Random
Peregrine Pickle.   *Vol.* 1
Peregrine Pickle.   *Vol.* 2
Ferdinand, Count Fathom
Sir Launcelot Greaves, etc.
Humphry Clinker

Lytton's (Lord) Novels

The Caxton Edition, demy 8vo

My Novel ; or, Varietie: English Life.   *Vol.* 1

My Novel ; or, Varietie: English Life.   *Vol.* 2

Night and Morning

Kenelm Chillingly : His ventures and Opinions

A Strange Story, and Haunted and the Haun

The Coming Race, Falkl; Zicci, and Pausanias

Ernest Maltravers and A

Devereux and Godolphi

The Last of the Barons

The Parisians

Pelham and The Disow

The Last Days of Pom and Lucretia

What will He do with *Vol.* 1

What will He do with *Vol.* 2

Paul Clifford

Leila and The Pilgrim: the Rhine

PRICE 3s. 6d. each.

THE NEW KNEBWORTH EDITION OF

THE NOVELS AND ROMANCES OF EDWARD LORD LYTTON.

In 29 Volumes, crown 8vo., cloth.   With Bibliography and Introduction.

List of the Series.

Pelham

Falkland and Zicci

Devereux

The Disowned

Paul Clifford

Eugene Aram

Godolphin

The Last Days of Pompeii

Rienzi

The Last of the Barons. *Vol.* 1

The Last of the Barons. *Vol.* 2

Leila, Calderon and Pausanias

Harold

A Strange Story

Zanoni

The Pilgrims of the Rhin and The Haunted an Haunters

Ernest Maltravers

Alice

Lucretia

Night and Morning

Kenelm Chillingly

The Parisians. *Vol.* 1

The Parisians. *Vol.* 2. Th Coming Race

The Caxtons

My Novel. *Vol.* 1

My Novel. *Vol.* 2

My Novel. *Vol.* 3

What will He do with It? *Vol*

What will He do with It *Vol.* 2

" In the highest qualities acquired in the delineation of the secret feelings th dwell in the recesses of the heart, Bulwer Lytton stands pre-eminent, and entitle to a place beside Scott himself, at the very head of the prose-writers of works imagination in our country."—*From Alison's " History of Europe."*

The "King's Own" Edition of
Captain Marryat's Novels.

In 19 Volumes, Crown 8vo., cloth, price £3 6s. 6d. ; or in separate Volun price 3s. 6d. each, with original Illustrations drawn specially for this Edition W. H. Overend, Frederick Barnard, E. J. Wheeler, and F. W. Hay A.R.C.A., reproduced in the highest style of Photogravure by Lemercier, of Pa With Introductions to each Volume by W. L. Courtney, LL.D.

List of the Series.

The King's Own	The Dog Fiend
Frank Mildmay ; or, The Naval Officer	Rattlin the Reefer. Edited Captain Marryat
Newton Forster	The Phantom Ship
Peter Simple	Olla Podrida
Jacob Faithful	Poor Jack
The Pacha of Many Tales	The Poacher
Japhet in Search of a Father	Percival Keene
Mr. Midshipman Easy	Monsieur Violet
The Pirate ; and The Three Cutters	The Privateersman
	Valerie ; An Autobiography

A Large Paper Edition of these Novels, limited to 125 Numbered Copies, is ready, price £9 19s. 6d. the Set, net.

"Captain Marryat stands second in merit to no novelist but Miss Edgewo His strong sense and utter superiority to affectation of all sorts command respe and in his quiet effectiveness of circumstantial narrative he sometimes approac Defoe."—J. G. Lockhart.

THE NOTRE-DAME EDITION OF

VICTOR HUGO'S NOVELS.

PRINTED FROM NEW PLATES.

In 14 *Volumes, crown 8vo., cloth, price* £2 9s. ; *or in separate Volumes, price* 3s. 6d. *each.*

List of the Series.

Notre-Dame de Paris
In Two Volumes

The Toilers of the Sea
In Two Volumes

Les Misérables
In Five Volumes

Ninety-Three
In One Volume

The Man who Laughs
In Two Volumes

Hans of Iceland
In One Volume

The Last Days of a Condemned ; Bug Jargal ; and Claude Grieux
In One Volume

The volumes included in this series are the greatest works of this great writer.

THE D'ARTAGNAN EDITION OF

ALEXANDRE DUMAS' NOVELS.

PRINTED FROM NEW PLATES.

In 9 *Volumes, crown 8vo., cloth, price* £1 11s. 6d. ; *or in separate Volumes, price* 3s. 6d. *each.*

List of the Series.

The Three Musketeers
In Two Volumes

Twenty Years After
In Two Volumes

Vicomte de Bragelonne
In Five Volumes

" Dumas is neither so witty as Dickens nor so ingenious as Defoe or Swift, nor so elegant as Thackeray, but he bears them all down before the incomparable flow of his personality. Probably that is the reason why the passion for Dumas is as strong as ever."—*Daily Chronicle.*

PRICE 3s. 6d. each.

THE NEW EDITION OF

FIELDING'S AND SMOLLETT'S NOVELS.

Reset from New Type.

List of the Series.

Fielding.—

Tom Jones
Joseph Andrews
Amelia

"The prose Homer of human nature."
—BYRON.

Smollett.—

Roderick Random
Humphry Clinker
Peregrine Pickle

"A perpetual fount of sparklin
laughter."—THACKERAY.

SCOTT'S (SIR WALTER) NOVELS.

A New Edition, with the Author's Notes, and the original Steel Plates by GEORG
CRUIKSHANK, J. M. W. TURNER, *and others, red cloth.*

Waverley
Guy Mannering
Old Mortality
Heart of Midlothian
Rob Roy
The Antiquary
Bride of Lammermoor
Ivanhoe
The Monastery
The Abbot
The Pirate
Fortunes of Nigel

Peveril of the Peak
Quentin Durward
St. Ronan's Well
Redgauntlet
Betrothed, and Highlan
  Widow
The Talisman, and Tw
Woodstock [Drove
Fair Maid of Perth
Anne of Geierstein
Count Robert of Paris
Surgeon s Daughter

Smedley, Frank E.—

Frank Fairlegh

Harry Coverdale's Courtship

Sue, Eugene.—The Mysteries of Paris

THE STANDARD NOVELISTS.

The Best Novels of the Best Standard Novelists. Printed from new type, with full-page Illustrations, crown 8vo., cloth, gilt top, **3s. 6d.** *each.*

Smollett.—
  Peregrine Pickle

Fielding.—
  Tom Jones

Dumas.—
  Monte Cristo

Scott.—
  Ivanhoe

Hugo.—
  Notre Dame

Dickens.—
  David Copperfield

Cooper.—
  The Last of the Mohicans

Lytton.—
  The Last Days of Pompeii

Ainsworth.—
  The Tower of London

Lover.—
  Handy Andy

Marryat.—
  The King's Own

Thackeray.—
  Vanity Fair

Cockton.—
  Valentine Vox

UNABRIDGED NOVELS.

Les Misérables. By VICTOR HUGO. Complete Edition. With Illustrations. 1,500 pages. Reset from New Type.

Notre Dame. By VICTOR HUGO. Complete Edition. With Illustrations.

The Three Musketeers. By ALEXANDRE DUMAS. Complete Edition. With Illustrations by M. LELOIR.

Uncle Remus and Nights with Uncle Remus. Complete Edition. With many Illustrations.

Twenty Years After. By ALEXANDRE DUMAS.

Toilers of the Sea. By VICTOR HUGO.

The Tower of London. By W. HARRISON AINSWORTH. With 20 Plates by GEORGE CRUIKSHANK.

STANDARD NOVELS.

With full-page Illustrations, crown 8vo., cloth, price **3s. 6d.** *each.*

Ainsworth's Novels.—

St. James's. With Steel Plates by CRUIKSHANK.

Crichton. Plates by H. K. BROWNE.

Mervyn Clitheroe. Plates by H. K. BROWNE.

Boscobel. Plates by H. K. BROWNE.

Ovingdean Grange. Plates by H. K. BROWNE.

The Miser's Daughter. With Steel Plates by CRUIKSHANK.

The Flitch of Bacon. With Illustrations by Sir JOHN GILBERT.

Preston Fight. Illustrated by FREDERICK GILBERT.

The Leaguer of Lathom. Illustrated by FREDERICK GILBERT.

Auriol. Illustrated by H. K. BROWNE.

Stanley Brereton. Illustrated by F. GILBERT.

Cooper's Novels.—

The Deerslayer
Last of the Mohicans
The Pathfinder
The Pioneers
The Prairie

} *The Leather-stocking Tales in the Order of the Sequels.*

The Red Rover

The Pilot

The Two Admirals

The Waterwitch

The Sea Lions

The Spy

Miles Wallingford. (Sequel to "Afloat and Ashore.")

Lionel Lincoln

The Headsman

Homeward Bound

The Crater; or, Vulcan's Peak. (Mark's Reef.)

Wing and Wing

Jack Tier

Satanstoe. *Littlepage* MS. *Vol.* 1

The Chainbearer „ MS. *Vol.* 2

The Red Skins „ MS. *Vol.* 3

The Heidenmauer

Precaution

The Monikins

The Ways of the Hour

Mercedes of Castille

Wyandotte

Afloat and Ashore

Home as Found; or, Eve Effingham (Sequel to "Homeward Bound.")

The Oak Openings

STANDARD NOVELS—*continued.*

Dumas' Novels.—

Count of Monte Cristo
  Complete.
The Three Musketeers
Twenty Years After [*Vol.* 1
The Vicomte de Bragelonne
         ,,   *Vol.* 2
The Forty-five Guardsmen
The Regent's Daughter
Memoirs of a Physician
The Queen's Necklace
The Taking of the Bastile
The Countess de Charny
The Chevalier de Maison
  Rouge

Hugo's (Victor) Novels.—

Uniform English Edition.

Illustrations by LUKE FILDES *and other Artists.*

By Order of the King

Toilers of the Sea

Notre Dame

Ninety-three

The History of a Crime

Things Seen

PRICE 2s. 6d. each.

LORD LYTTON'S NOVELS.

Crown 8vo., red cloth.

Lytton's (Lord) Novels.—

A Strange Story
Night and Morning
Paul Clifford
Kenelm Chillingly
Lucretia
Disowned
Harold
What will He do with It?
  Vol. 1

Lytton's (Lord) Novels—*continued.*

What will He do with It
  Vol. 2
Ernest Maltravers
Alice (sequel to Ernest Ma
  travers)
Caxtons
Godolphin
My Novel.   *Vol.* 1

LORD LYTTON'S NOVELS—*continued.*

Lytton's (Lord) Novels—*cont.*

My Novel. *Vol.* 2

Pelham

Devereux

Zanoni

Pausanias the Spartan

Falkland, and Zicci

Lytton's (Lord) Novels—*cont.*

The Coming Race

The Parisians. *Vol.* 1

The Parisians. *Vol.* 2

Leila, and the Pilgrims (
the Rhine

Rienzi

MEDIUM 8VO. NOVELS.

Cloth, *price* **2s. 6d.** *each.*

Dumas' Monte Cristo, The Three Musketeers, and Twenty Yea
After.   In One Volume.

Sue's Mysteries of Paris, and The Wandering Jew.   In One Volum

Lytton's The Caxtons, My Novel, and What will He do with It
In One Volume.

HALF A CROWN NOVELS

*Of the most popular authors. Well printed on good paper, and neatly boun
in cloth.*

Balzac, Honore De.—

The Two Brothers

The Alkahest

Modeste Mignon

The Magic Skin

Bureaucracy

Daudet, Alphonse.—

Tartarin of Tarascon

Kings in Exile

Thirty Years of Paris

Daudet, Alphonse—*continued.*

Recollections of a Litera
Man

Robert Helmont

Artists' Wives

Gould, Nat.—

The Double Event

Running it Off

Jockey Jack

Banker and Broker

HALF A CROWN NOVELS—*continued.*

Gould, Nat—*continued.*

Harry Dale's Jockey
Thrown Away
Stuck Up
Only a Commoner
On and Off the Turf in
  Australia
The Miners' Cup
The Doctor's Double
The Magpie Jacket
Who Did It?
Horse or Blacksmith?
Not So Bad, After All
Seeing Him Through
A Lad of Mettle
A Gentleman Rider

Gunter, A. C.—

Mr. Potter of Texas
That Frenchman!
Miss Nobody of Nowhere
Miss Dividends
Baron Montez of Panama
  and Paris
A Princess of Paris
The King's Stockbroker
How I Escaped
  Edited by A. C. GUNTER
The First of the English
The Ladies' Juggernaut
The Love Adventures of
  Al-Mansur
  Edited by A. C. GUNTER
Her Senator
Don Balasco of Key West
Bob Covington

Gunter, A. C.—*continued.*

Susan Turnbull
Ballyho Bey
Billy Hamilton

Loti, Pierre.—

Madame Chrysanthème
  With 199 Illustrations

Savage, R. H.—

My Official Wife
The Little Lady of Lagunitas
Prince Schamyl's Wooing
The Masked Venus
Delilah of Harlem
For Life and Love
The Anarchist
The Princess of Alaska
The Passing Show
The Flying Halcyon
A Daughter of Judas
In the Old Chateau
Miss Devereux of the Mari-
  quita
His Cuban Sweetheart. By
  Col. SAVAGE and Mrs. A. C.
  GUNTER
For Her Life: a Romance
  of St. Petersburg
Checked Through
Her Foreign Conquest
Lost Countess Falka
An Exile from London
A Modern Corsair
A Fascinating Traitor
In the Shadow of the Pyra-
  mids

PRICE 2s. each.
ROUTLEDGE'S RAILWAY LIBRARY.

Bound in Fancy Boards.

Collins, Wilkie.—

Basil
Antonina
Hide and Seek

Daudet, Alphonse.—

With Illustrations.

Tartarin of Tarascon
Kings in Exile
Thirty Years of Paris
Recollections of a Literary
   Man
Artists' Wives
Robert Helmont

Grant, James.—

The Aide-de-Camp
The Scottish Cavalier
Jane Seton; or, The Queen's
   Advocate
Philip Rollo
Mary of Lorraine
Oliver Ellis; or, The
   Fusiliers
Lucy Arden; or, Holly-
   wood Hall
Frank Hilton
Harry Ogilvie; or, The Black
   Dragoon

Grant, James—*continued.*

Cavaliers of Fortune
Second to None
The Constable of France
Phantom Regiment
The White Cockade
First Love and Last Love
Under the Red Dragon
The Queen's Cadet
Shall I Win Her?
Morley Ashton
Did She Love Him?
The Ross-shire Buffs
Six Years Ago
Vere of Ours
The Lord Hermitage
The Royal Regiment
Duke of Albany's High-
   landers
The Dead Tryst
The Scots Brigade
Violet Jermyn; or, Tender
   and True
Jack Chaloner
Miss Cheyne of Essilmont
The Royal Highlanders
Colville of the Guards
Dulcie Carlyon
Derval Hampton
Scottish Soldiers of Fortune

ROUTLEDGE'S RAILWAY LIBRARY—*continued.*

Gunter, Archibald C.—

Mr. Potter of Texas
That Frenchman
Miss Nobody of Nowhere
Miss Dividends
Baron Montez of Panama and Paris
A Princess of Paris
The King's Stockbroker
How I Escaped. Edited by A. C. GUNTER.
The First of the English
The Ladies' Juggernaut
The Love Adventures of Al-Mansur. Edited by A. C. GUNTER
Her Senator
Don Balasco of Key West
Bob Covington
Susan Turnbull
Ballyho Bey
Billy Hamilton

Loti, Pierre.—

Madame Chrysanthème. With Illustrations

Rives, Amelie.—

The Quick or the Dead?
Virginia of Virginia
A Brother to Dragons

Savage, Colonel.—

My Official Wife
The Little Lady of Lagunitas

Savage, Colonel—*continued.*

Prince Schamyl's Wooing
The Masked Venus : A Story of Many Lands
Delilah of Harlem : A Story of New York
For Life and Love ; A Story of the Rio Grande
The Anarchist : A Story of To-day
The Princess of Alaska
The Passing Show
The Flying Halcyon
A Daughter of Judas
In the Old Chateau
Miss Devereux of the Mariquita
His Cuban Sweetheart. By Col. SAVAGE and Mrs. A. C. GUNTER
For Her Life : A Romance of St. Petersburg
Checked Through
Her Foreign Conquest
Lost Countess Falka
An Exile from London
A Modern Corsair
A Fascinating Traitor
In the Shadow of the Pyramids

Smedley, Frank.—

Frank Fairlegh
Lewis Arundel
Harry Coverdale's Courtship

ROUTLEDGE'S RAILWAY LIBRARY—*continued.*

Various Authors.—

Whom to Marry.
With Cruikshank's Plates
MAYHEW

The Greatest Plague of Life
MAYHEW

False Colours.
ANNIE THOMAS

Through the Mist
Mrs. ADAMS-ACTON

Unspotted from the World
Bridget
M. BETHAM-EDWARDS

Jane Eyre
CHARLOTTE BRONTÉ

Can Such Things Be ?
KEITH FLEMING

John Dorrien
JULIA KAVANAGH

The Prodigal Daughter
MARK HOPE

A Century's Sensations
W. SAPTE, Junr.

Loyal

Old London Bridge
G. H. RODWELL

A Complication in Hearts
EDMUND PENDLETON

Something Occurred
B. L. FARJEON

The Queen of Ecuador
R. M. MANLEY

The Mystery of Stephen
Claverton and Co.
H. KNIGHT

Various Authors—*continued.*

A Hasty Marriage
Sir RANDAL H. ROBERTS,
Bart.

A Son of Esau
MINNIE GILMORE

Poppæa
JULIEN GORDON

Rough Mischance
BRADNOCK HALL

Ladies First
Mrs. DOMINIQUE FRAN-
ÇOIS VERDENAL

A Sawdust Doll
Mrs. REGINALD DE KOVEN

Two Women and a Fool
H. C. CHATFIELD-TAYLOR

The Woman who Stood
Between
MINNIE GILMORE

Crowned with Fennel
L. M. PROCTER

The Postmaster of Market
Deignton
E. PHILLIPS OPPENHEIM

That Girl from Bogota
CLARICE IRENE CLINGHAM

Tales of the Old Régime
PRICE WARUNG

A Frisky Matron
PERCY LYSLE

Since First I Saw Your Face
Mrs. KER-SEYMER

SPORTING NOVELS.

Crown 8vo., boards, **2s.** *each.*

Gould, Nat.—

Jockey Jack

Running it Off

The Double Event: A Tale of the Melbourne Cup

Banker and Broker

Harry Dale's Jockey

Thrown Away

Stuck Up

Only a Commoner

On and Off the Turf in Australia

The Miners' Cup

The Doctor's Double

The Magpie Jacket

Who Did It?

Horse or Blacksmith?

Not So Bad After All

Seeing Him Through

A Lad of Mettle

A Gentleman Rider

Various Authors.—

Beaten on the Post
J. P. WHEELDON

The Tale of a Horse
BLINKHOOLIE

Jorrocks' Jaunts and Jollities

The Tommiebeg Shootings; or, A Moor in Scotland. Illustrations by P. SKELTON.
THOMAS JEANS

Nimrod's Northern Tour

Frank Maitland's Luck
F. MASON

Horses and Hounds
SCRUTATOR

Reminiscences of a 19th Century Gladiator
J. L. SULLIVAN

The Young Squire
"BORDERER"

Soapey Sponge's Sporting Tour
By the Author of "Jorrocks' Jaunts"

Very Long Odds
J. CAMPBELL RAE-BROWN

There is always a brisk demand for sporting novels, and Nat Gould's are among the best specimens of this class. Jorrocks, too, needs no recommendation.

STANDARD NOVELS.

Strongly bound in Cloth, price **2s.** *each.*

Ainsworth, W. H.—

The Windsor Edition, in 21 *vols.*

Miser's Daughter
St. James's
Flitch of Bacon
Guy Fawkes
Crichton
Spendthrift
Boscobel
Ovingdean Grange
Mervyn Clitheroe
Auriol
Preston Fight
Stanley Brereton
Beau Nash
Jack Sheppard
The Lancashire Witches
The Manchester Rebels
Old St. Paul's
Rookwood
The Star Chamber
Windsor Castle
The Tower of London

Austen, Jane.—

Pride and Prejudice
Sense and Sensibility
Mansfield Park
Emma

Bronte, Charlotte, Emily and Jane.—

Jane Eyre
Shirley
Wuthering Heights
Villette

Carleton, William.—

Willy Reilly

Cockton, Henry.—

Sylvester Sound
Stanley Thorn

Collins, Wilkie.—

Antonina

Cooper, Fenimore.—

The Deerslayer
The Pathfinder
The Last of the Mohicans
The Pioneers
The Prairie
The Red Rover
The Pilot
The Two Admirals
The Waterwitch
The Spy
The Sea Lions
Miles Wallingford

STANDARD NOVELS—*continued.*

Cooper, Fenimore—*continued.*

Lionel Lincoln
The Headsman
Homeward Bound
The Crater ; or, Vulcan's
  Peak
Wing and Wing
Jack Tier
Satanstoe
The Red Skins
The Heidenmauer
Precaution
The Monikins
The Ways of the Hour
Mercedes
Afloat and Ashore
Home as Found
  (Sequel to " Homeward Bound ")
Oak Openings

Cooper, Thomas.—

The Family Feud

Crowe, Mrs.—

The Nightside of Nature

Croly, Dr.—

Salathiel

Dickens, Charles.—

Barnaby Rudge
Old Curiosity Shop
Dombey and Son

Dickens, Charles—*continued.*

Grimaldi the Clown
  With Cruikshank's illustrations
Martin Chuzzlewit
Pickwick Papers
Pictures from Italy and
  American Notes
Bleak House

Du Boisgobey, Fortune.—

The Bride of a Day
The Half-Sister's Secret
Married for Love

Dumas, Alexandre.—

*The Fleur-de-lis Edition, in
  15 vols.*

The Three Musketeers
Monte Cristo
Forty-five Guardsmen
Taking the Bastile
The Queen's Necklace
The Conspirators
The Regent's Daughter
Memoirs of a Physician
The Countess de Charny
The Vicomte de Brage-
  lonne. *Vol.* 1
The Vicomte de Brage-
  lonne. *Vol.* 2
Chevalier de Maison Rouge
Chicot the Jester
Marguerite de Valois
Twenty Years After

2

STANDARD NOVELS—*continued.*

Ferrier, Miss.—

Marriage
The Inheritance
Destiny

Fielding, Henry.—

Tom Jones
Joseph Andrews
Amelia

Gaskell, Mrs.—

Mary Barton

Grant, James.—

The Aide-de-Camp Edition. To be completed in 56 vols.

The Aide de Camp
The Scottish Cavalier
Jane Seton
The Yellow Frigate
The Romance of War
Oliver Ellis
Mary of Lorraine
Lucy Arden
Colville of the Guards
The Constable of France
Did She Love Him?
The Duke of Albany's Highlanders
Dulcie Carlyon
First Love and Last Love
The Lord Hermitage
Philip Rollo

Haliburton, Judge.—

The Clockmaker
The Attaché

Hugo, Victor.—

History of a Crime
Ninety-Three
Toilers of the Sea
By Order of the King

Kingsley, Charles.—

Yeast
Hypatia

Lever, Charles.—

Harry Lorrequer
Jack Hinton
Arthur O'Leary
Con Cregan
Tom Burke

Lover, Samuel.—

Handy Andy

Lytton, Lord.—

The Stevenage Edition, in 28 vols.

Author's Copyright Editions, containing Prefaces to be found in no other Editions.

Pelham
Paul Clifford
Rienzi
Ernest Maltravers

STANDARD NOVELS—*continued.*

Lytton, Lord—*continued.*

Alice ; or, The Mysteries
Disowned
Devereux
Godolphin
Leila ; Pilgrims of the Rhine
Falkland ; Zicci
Zanoni
Harold
Lucretia
The Coming Race
Kenelm Chillingly
Pausanias: and The Haunted
    and the Haunters
My Novel. *Vol.* 1
    ,, *Vol.* 2
What will He do with It ?
           Vol. 1
    ,, *Vol.* 2
The Parisians. *Vol.* 1
    ,, *Vol.* 2
The Caxtons
Eugene Aram
Last Days of Pompeii
The Last of the Barons
Night and Morning
A Strange Story

Marryat, Captain.—

Frank Mildmay
Phantom Ship
Peter Simple
The King's Own
Newton Forster
Jacob Faithful

Marryat, Captain—*continued.*

Dog Fiend
The Poacher
Percival Keene
Rattlin, the Reefer.
    Edited by CAPTAIN MARRYAT.
Valerie
Olla Podrida

Maxwell, W. H.—

The Bivouac

Mayhew, The Brothers.—

The Greatest Plague of Life

Miller, Thomas.—

Gideon Giles

Mounteney-Jephson, R.—

Tom Bullkley
The Roll of the Drum
The Red Rag

Poe, Edgar Allan.—

The Gold-Bug, and other
    Tales
Landor's Cottage, and other
    Tales

Porter, Jane.—

The Pastor's Fireside
Thaddeus of Warsaw

STANDARD NOVELS—*continued.*

Radcliffe, Mrs.—

The Mysteries of Udolpho
The Romance of the Forest

Reade, Charles.—

Peg Woffington and Christie
Johnstone

Reid, Captain Mayne.—

*The War Trail Edition.   To be
completed in 38 vols.*

The War Trail
The Quadroon
The Headless Horseman
The Tiger Hunter
The Guerilla Chief
Lost Lenore
The White Chief
The Hunter's Feast
Gaspar the Gaucho
The Lost Mountain
The Wild Huntress
The Wood Rangers
The Lone Ranche

Richardson, Samuel.—

Clarissa Harlowe
Pamela
Sir Charles Grandison

Roche, R. M.—

The Children of the Abbey

Rodwell, G. H.—

Old London Bridge

Scott, Michael.—

Tom Cringle's Log

Scott, Sir Walter.—

*The Kenilworth Edition.   To be
completed in 25 vols.*

Waverley
Guy Mannering
Old Mortality
Rob Roy
Ivanhoe
The Antiquary
The Bride of Lammermoor
The Monastery
The Abbot
The Pirate
The Fortunes of Nigel
Peveril of the Peak
Quentin Durward
St. Ronan's Well
Redgauntlet
Betrothed   and   Highland
Widow
The   Talisman   and   Two
Drovers
Woodstock
Anne of Geierstein
Count Robert of Paris
The Surgeon's Daughter

STANDARD NOVELS—*continued.*

Smedley, Frank.—

Frank Fairlegh
Lewis Arundel
Harry Coverdale's Court-
ship

Smollett, Tobias.—

Roderick Random
Humphry Clinker
Peregrine Pickle

Sue, Eugene.—

The Mysteries of Paris

Thackeray, W. M.—

Vanity Fair
Pendennis
The Luck of Barry Lyndon

Warren, Samuel.—

The Diary of a Lat
    Physician   [Sp
Vidocq, the French Polic

PRICE 1s. each.

LORD LYTTON'S NOVELS.

The Pocket Edition.

An edition, in spite of its low price, fully worthy of this great writer.

Size 6½ by 4¾ in. Printed from new, clear type, and bound in neat cloth covers.

Pelham
Ernest Maltravers
Alice (sequel)
Night and Morning
Paul Clifford
The Disowned
Harold
The Caxtons
Devereux
Godolphin ; Calderon
The Coming Race ; Leila ;
    Zicci ; The Haunted
Eugene Aram
Lucretia
Zanoni
The Parisians. *Vol.* 1

The Parisians. *Vol.* 2
My Novel. *Vol.* 1
My Novel. *Vol.* 2
My Novel. *Vol.* 3
The Last of the Baron
                    Vol.
    „   *Vol.*
What Will He Do With It
    Vol. 1
What Will He Do With It
    Vol. 2
A Strange Story
Falkland ; The Pilgrims c
    the Rhine, etc.
Kenelm Chillingley

To be completed in 28 Volumes.

1s. Novels—continued.

HARRISON AINSWORTH'S NOVELS.

The Pocket Volume Edition.   Cloth, cut edges.

The Tower of London
Windsor Castle
Old St. Paul's
Rookwood, with Memoir of
    Mr. Ainsworth, by LAMAN
    BLANCHARD
Guy Fawkes

Jack Sheppard
Miser's Daughter
Star Chamber
Crichton
Flitch of Bacon
Spendthrift
Auriol

The 12 volumes, cloth, gilt tops, in cloth box, **21s.**

MARRYAT'S NOVELS.

The Pocket Volume Edition.   Cloth, cut edges.

The King's Own
Frank Mildmay
Newton Forster
The Dog Fiend
Jacob Faithful
Peter Simple
Pacha of Many Tales
Japhet in Search of a
    Father

Mr. Midshipman Easy
Rattlin the Reefer.
    Edited by CAPT. MARRYAT.
The Phantom Ship
The Pirate and the Three
    Cutters
Olla Podrida
The Poacher
Percival Keene

To be followed by other Volumes.

RAILWAY LIBRARY.

Paper covers price, 1s. each.

Amelia B. Edwards.—

    Half a Million of Money
    My Brother's Wife

Frederick Gerstaecker.—

    The Haunted House

Mark Twain.—

    Roughing it
    The Innocents Abroad
    The New Pilgrim's Progress
    A Curious Dream
    Information Wanted

Various Authors.—

Nadine : The Study of a
Woman, by Mrs. CAMP-
BELL PRAED

The Year of Miracle, by
FERGUS HUME.

The Log of the "Water-
Lily" during Three Cruises

Uncle Remus, Illustrated
J. C. HARRIS

Adventures of a Mounted
Trooper in the Aus-
tralian Constabulary

Helen's Babies
JOHN HABBERTON

Jennie of "The Prince's"
Mrs. BUXTON

Various Authors—*continued.*

Won
Mrs. BUXTON

Nights with Uncle Remus
J. C. HARRIS

The Luck of Roaring Camp
BRET HARTE

An Episode of Fiddletown
BRET HARTE

The Story of a Mine
BRET HARTE

Out of the Hurly Burly
MAX ADELER

Elbow Room
MAX ADELER

Artemus Ward : His Book
and His Travels

LARGE-SIZE SHILLING NOVELS.

Medium 8vo., paper covers.

Dickens, Charles.—

The Pickwick Papers
Nicholas Nickleby
David Copperfield

Dumas, Alexandre.—

Monte Christo
The Three Musketeers, and
Twenty Years After. 1 *Vol.*
Vicomte de Bragelonne

Du Boisgobey.—

The Condemned Door
Cash on Delivery

Hugo, Victor.—

Les Misérables
Notre Dame

Lever, Charles.—

The Knight of Gwynne
Harry Lorrequer and
Charles O'Malley. 1 *Vol.*

Lytton, Lord.—

Ernest Maltravers, and Alice
(the Sequel). 1 *Vol.*
My Novel
What will He do with It ?
The Parisians

LARGE-SIZE SHILLING NOVELS—*continued.*

Sue, Eugene.—

The Wandering Jew
The Mysteries of Paris

Smedley, Frank E.—

Lewis Arundel

Verne, Jules.—

Twenty Thousand Leagues Under the Sea
The Fur Country
From the Earth to the Moon, and Round the Moon. 1 *Vol.*

Various Authors.—

Tom Jones
FIELDING

Tristram Shandy, and Sentimental Journey
STERNE

Old London Bridge
RODWELL

The Headless Horseman
CAPTAIN MAYNE REID

Torlogh O'Brien
LE FANU

The Wolfe of Badenoch
SIR T. DICK LAUDER

PRICE 6d. each.
THE CAXTON NOVELS.
AUTHORS' UNABRIDGED EDITIONS.

This Series, which includes more than 300 volumes, embraces the masterpieces of English fiction : the best works of the best authors, romantic, humorous, pathetic, from Daniel Defoe to the present day. Many of the novels are copyright, and each is complete and unabridged, the author having been allowed to tell his story in his own words, free from the mutilation too common in cheap reprints. Each volume is printed in clear type, on paper of good quality, the cover bearing an illustration by some well-known artist.

In medium 8vo., Printed in clear Type, Picture Covers.

Ainsworth, W. H.—

Rookwood
Mervyn Clitheroe
The Spendthrift
James II.
The Tower of London
Jack Sheppard
Old St. Paul's

Ainsworth, W. H.—*continued.*

Windsor Castle
The Miser's Daughter
The Star Chamber
Lancashire Witches
The Flitch of Bacon
Crichton
St. James's

THE CAXTON NOVELS—*continued.*

Austen, Jane.—

Pride and Prejudice
Sense and Sensibility

Bronte, Charlotte.—

Jane Eyre
Shirley
Villette

Bronte, Emily and Anne.

Wuthering Heights, and Agnes Grey

Carleton, W.—

Ned M'Keown, and other Stories
Phil Purcell, and other Stories
The Poor Scholar, and other Tales
Phelim O'Toole's Courtship, and other Tales
Willy Reilly.

Chamier, Captain.—

Ben Brace

Cockton, Henry.—

Valentine Vox, the Ventriloquist
Sylvester Sound, the Somnambulist

Collins, Wilkie.—

Antonina

Cooper, J. F.—

The Headsman
The Deerslayer
The Heidenmauer
Satanstoe
The Prairie
The Last of the Mohicans
The Waterwitch
The Pathfinder
The Pioneers
The Oak Openings
The Spy
The Pilot
Eve Effingham
The Two Admirals
Miles Wallingford
Afloat and Ashore
Wyandotte
Lionel Lincoln
The Bravo
The Sea Lions
Precaution
Mark's Reef
Ned Myers
The Borderers
Jack Tier
Mercedes

THE CAXTON NOVELS—*continued.*

Dickens, Charles.—

Martin Chuzzlewit
Oliver Twist
The Pickwick Papers
Grimaldi, the Clown
Nicholas Nickleby.   *Vol.* 1
          „   *Vol.* 2
The Old Curiosity Shop
Barnaby Rudge
A Christmas Carol, with Illustrations
The Cricket on the Hearth
American Notes
Sunday under Three Heads
The Chimes
Hard Times
Bleak House
Sketches by " Boz "

Dumas, Alexandre.—

Twenty Years After
Marguerite de Valois
Monte Christo.   *Vol.* 1
          „   *Vol.* 2
The Three Musketeers
The Queen's Necklace
The Forty-five Guardsmen
Chicot the Jester
Ten Years Later.   *Vol.* 1
          „   *Vol.* 2
Memoirs of a Physician. *Vol.* 1

Dumas, Alexandre—*continued.*

Memoirs of a Physician. *Vol.* 2
The Vicomte de Bragelonne. *Vol.* 1
The Vicomte de Bragelonne. *Vol.* 2

Fielding, Henry.—

Joseph Andrews
Tom Jones.   *Vol.* 1
          „   *Vol.* 2
Amelia

Gaboriau, Emile.—

Marie de Brinvilliers
The Widow Lerouge
The Clique of Gold
Mons. Lecoq.   *Vol.* 1
          „   *Vol.* 2

Gaskell, Mrs.—

Mary Barton

Grant, James.—

The Scottish Cavalier
The Aide-de-Camp
The Romance of War
Philip Rollo
Bothwell

THE CAXTON NOVELS—*continued.*

Green, Anna K.—

The Leavenworth Case
Seven to Twelve
The Mill Mystery

Holmes, Oliver Wendell.

The Autocrat of the Breakfast Table
The Professor at the Breakfast Table
The Poet at the Breakfast Table

Hugo, Victor.—

Les Misérables.   *Vol.* 1
  „   *Vol.* 2
Notre Dame
The Laughing Man (L'Homme Qui Rit)
Ninety-three
Toilers of the Sea

James, G. P. R.—

The Smuggler
The Convict
The Brigand
Morley Ernstein
The Forgery

Kingsley, Charles.—

Alton Locke
Yeast : A Problem
Hypatia

Lever, Charles.—

Tom Burke of " Ours "
The O'Donoghue
Charles O'Malley
Harry Lorrequer
Arthur O'Leary
The Knight of Gwynne. *Vol.* 1
The Knight of Gwynne. *Vol.* 2
Jack Hinton

Lover, Samuel.—

Handy Andy

Lytton, Lord.—

[Author's Copyright Revised Edition.]

Kenelm Chillingly
A Strange Story
My Novel.   *Vol.* 1
My Novel.   *Vol.* 2
The Caxtons
What Will He Do With It ? *Vol.* 1
What Will He Do With It ? *Vol.* 2
The Coming Race; Pausanias the Spartan, etc.
The Parisians. *Vol.* 1
  „   *Vol.* 2
Godolphin
Rienzi

THE CAXTON NOVELS—*continued.*

Lytton, Lord—*continued.*

Alice
Ernest Maltravers
The Last Days of Pompeii
The Last of the Barons
Eugene Aram
Night and Morning
Zanoni
Leila, Calder on the Courtier, and The Pilgrims of the Rhine
Paul Clifford
The Disowned
Harold
Pelham
Devereux
Lucretia
Falkland

Marryat, Captain.—

The Little Savage
Mr. Midshipman Easy
Peter Simple
The Pirate, and The Three Cutters
The King's Own
Jacob Faithful
The Pacha of Many Tales
The Phantom Ship
Percival Keene
Rattlin the Reefer.
    Edited by CAPTAIN MARRYAT
Children of the New Forest

Marryat, Captain—*continued.*

Frank Mildmay
Newton Forster
Valerie
The Mission

Maxwell, W. H.—

Stories of Waterloo
Hector O'Halloran
Wild Sports of the West
Captain Blake

Pinkerton, Frank.—

Cornered at Last
The Great Adams Express Robbery
The Crime of the Midnight Express

Reade, Charles.—

Peg Woffington and Christie Johnstone
It is Never too Late to Mend

Reid, Captain Mayne.—

The Scalp Hunters
The Headless Horseman.
    Vol.
The Headless Horseman.
    Vol.

THE CAXTON NOVELS—*continued.*

Scott, Michael.—

Tom Cringle's Log
The Cruise of the *Midge*

Scott, Sir Walter.—

Guy Mannering
Kenilworth
Ivanhoe
St. Ronan's Well
The Bride of Lammermoor
Waverley
The Heart of Midlothian
The Antiquary
The Pirate
Old Mortality
Quentin Durward
The Black Dwarf
Anne of Geierstein
Woodstock
The Betrothed
The Fair Maid of Perth
The Surgeon's Daughter
Count Robert of Paris
Redgauntlet

Smedley, Frank E.—

Frank Fairlegh
Lewis Arundel. *Vol.* 1
　　　„　　　*Vol.* 2
Harry Coverdale's Court-
　ship
The Colville Family

Smith, Albert.—

Mr. Ledbury
The Scattergood Family
The Pottleton Legacy
The Marchioness of Brin-
　villiers

Smollett, Tobias.—

Humphry Clinker
Roderick Random
Peregrine Pickle. *Vol.* 1
　　　„　　　*Vol.* 2

Thackeray, W. M.—

The Luck of Barry Lyndon
Pendennis. *Vol.* 1
　　　„　　　*Vol.* 2
Vanity Fair. *Vol.* 1
　　　„　　　*Vol.* 2
The History of Henry Es-
　mond
The Yellow Plush Papers
A Shabby Genteel Story

Twain, Mark.—

The Innocents Abroad
The New Pilgrim's Progress
The Celebrated Jumping
　Frog

THE CAXTON NOVELS—*continued.*

Verne, Jules.—

A Journey to the Centre of the Earth

Twenty Thousand Leagues under the Sea. *Vol.* 1

Twenty Thousand Leagues under the Sea. *Vol.* 2

Three Englishmen and Three Russians

Five Weeks in a Balloon

Warren, Samuel.—

Ten Thousand a Year. *Vol.* 1

   „   „   *Vol.* 2

Various Authors.—

The Arabian Nights' Entertainments

Uncle Tom's Cabin

The Last Essays of Elia
CHARLES LAMB

Robinson Crusoe

The Quick or the Dead?
AMÉLIE RIVES

The Vicar of Wakefield

Mr. Barnes of New York

Æsop's Fables
With fifty Illustrations by HARRISON WEIR

Poe's Tales of Mystery and Imagination

A Sentimental Journey
STERNE

Various Authors—*continued.*

Mrs. Caudle's Curtain Lectures
DOUGLAS JERROLD

The Scarlet Letter
NATHANIEL HAWTHORNE

The Colleen Bawn
GERALD GRIFFIN

Whitefriars

The Green Hand
GEORGE CUPPLES

Monte Cristo and His Wife

Tristram Shandy
LAURENCE STERNE

The Sketch Book
WASHINGTON IRVING

Peck's Bad Boy and His Pa

The Swiss Family Robinson

Gulliver's Travels

The Luck of Roaring Camp

The Scottish Chiefs

The Trials of Margaret Lyndsay

Frankenstein
Mrs. SHELLEY

Susan Hopley
Mrs. CROWE

The Clockmaker
JUDGE HALLIBURTON

The Whiteboy
Mrs. HALL

Buffalo Bill

Old London Bridge. *Vol.* 1

   „   „   *Vol.* 2

A Friend's Victim

St. Clair of the Isles

THE CAXTON NOVELS—*continued.*

Various Authors—*continued.*

The Crystal Button
    CHAUNCEY THOMAS
Condensed Novels
    BRET HARTE
Shadowed by Three
Good Luck
    WERNER
The Stolen Bonds
    GAY PARKER
The Rokewood Tragedy
    MYRON PINKERTON

Various Authors—*continued.*

The Nightside of Nature
    Mrs. CROWE
Two Years before the Mast
    DANA
Story of a Feather
    DOUGLAS JERROLD
A Good Boy's Diary
Diary of a Naughty Girl
Peter Wilkins
The Wild Irish Girl
The English Opium Eater

THE HANDY NOVELS.

"Books that you may carry to the fire and hold readily in your hand are the most useful after all."—DR. JOHNSON.

[This Series exactly answers the above description.]

Crown 8vo., picture covers, 6d. each.

The Double Event
    By NAT GOULD
Hide and Seek
    WILKIE COLLINS
The Fatal Cord
    By Captain MAYNE REID

Mr. Barnes of New York
    By A. C. GUNTER
One of the Six Hundred
    By JAMES GRANT
Free Joe
    By the Author of " Uncle Remus "

Eothen. By A. W. KINGLAKE

ROUTLEDGE'S THREEPENNY NOVELS.

AUTHORS' COMPLETE COPYRIGHT EDITIONS.

The Cheapest Novels ever issued. 192 pages in each Book. Size of page 8½ by 5½ inches. Good Printing. Excellent Paper. Picture Covers.

Lord Lytton's A Strange Story.   (Copyright.)

Dickens's Hard Times.

Grant's Scottish Cavalier.

Victor Hugo's Notre Dame.

Charles Lever's Jack Hinton.

Samuel Lover's Handy Andy.

Ainsworth's Old St. Paul's.

Captain Marryat's Peter Simple.

Anna K. Green's The Mill Mystery.   (Copyright.)

Frank Pinkerton's The Great Adams Express Robbery.

Lawrence P. Lynch's Shadowed by Three.

Gay Parker's The Stolen Bonds.

Anna K. Green's The Leavenworth Case.

Myron Pinkerton's The Rokewood Tragedy.

Emile Gaboriau's The Widow Lerouge.

Frank Pinkerton's Cornered at Last.

Maxwell's Captain Blake.

Dana's Two Years Before the Mast.

Mrs. Crowe's Night-side of Nature.

Professor Wilson's The Trials of Margaret Lindsay.

LONDON:

GEORGE ROUTLEDGE AND SONS, LIMITED,

BROADWAY HOUSE, LUDGATE HILL, E.C.

www.ingramcontent.com/pod-product-compliance
Lightning Source LLC
Chambersburg PA
CBHW030618030726
47497CB00006B/1546